THE

FOUR COURTS

MURDER

THE
FOUR COURTS
MURDER

ANDREW NUGENT

THOMAS DUNNE BOOKS
ST. MARTIN'S MINOTAUR
NEW YORK

THOMAS DUNNE BOOKS.
An imprint of St. Martin's Press.

ISBN 0-312-32758-7
EAN 978-0312-32758-3

First Edition: May 2005

10 9 8 7 6 5 4 3 2 1

FOR PATRICK AND SIBYLLE
WITH ALL MY LOVE

ACKNOWLEDGMENTS

Fervent thanks to Tom Dunne, Ruth Cavin,
and a host of good friends
without whom . . .
. . . believe me!

Special thanks to Bobby Barr for allowing me to tell his parrot story. He is, I must point out, a *much* nicer person than Albert Singer.

THE

FOUR COURTS

MURDER

TUESDAY, JULY 14

As CHAUFFEUR AND CRIER FOR THE HONORABLE MR. Justice Sidney Piggott, judge of the High Court, Ned Frost was no stranger to *taedium vitae*. It went with the job. Each morning he drove his judge from Baldoyle to the Four Courts in Dublin. Each evening he drove him back again from the Four Courts to Baldoyle. At 11:00 A.M. precisely, and again at 2:00 P.M., wearing a modest black gown and equipped with his master's tipped staff of office, he led Piggott down the splendid sweep of stone steps from judges' chambers, across the elegant expanse of Round Hall, and into courtroom number 2, declaiming as he crossed the threshold, "Silence in court. Stand up."

That was about it. Occasionally he might have to run for a volume of the Law Reports, or even to place a judicial, if injudicious, bet on a classic horse race. Otherwise, for the rest of the day, Frost sat in court, silent and immobile, like a vampire in his coffin, awaiting the evening. His attention was not required. A Walkman or a newspaper would nonetheless be out of the question. Like lackeys in all times and seasons, Frost was paid to emulate the furniture.

It was a day in mid-July, glorious out of doors, hot and airless in Courtroom 2. Legal proceedings, at the best of times, are fairly unexciting, except for those who may gain or lose money or go to jail for protracted periods. On this day, as if to exacerbate the soporific effect of the weather, some gremlin had insinuated into Piggott's court list a chancery suit of mind-boggling dreariness that showed every sign of outlasting any Irish heat wave.

Counsels' benches were occupied by unfamiliar practitioners from the Elysian Fields of Equity, strange lantern-jawed gentlemen speaking an exotic dialect of Elizabethan English, Latin, and medieval French. The sultry air was heavy with matters *uberrimae fidei, estoppels,* and *cy-pres* applications. When someone mentioned an *extinct tail-male,* Frost thought briefly that he had understood something. He was wrong.

Before lunch an instructress with purple hair shooed a herd of bewildered children into the emphatically empty benches for citizenry at the back of the courtroom. One little girl, blessing herself, sketched a genuflection toward Piggott. Frost enjoyed that. The puce-headed pedagogue hissed meanwhile at her charges to be quiet, which they already were, to stop fidgeting, which they had not yet begun, and to pay attention, which no reasonable person possibly could.

The court rose at 1:00 P.M. Piggott ate lunch in Mr. Justice Bradshaw's chambers. Colleagues since student days, they often lunched together.

The afternoon was worse. Mercilessly hot. The court registrar was blatantly asleep; the elderly garda at the door, less obviously so, slept standing up like a horse. Counsel droned on remorselessly about *contingent remainders* and the great importance of *squashing* or *quashing* something or somebody.

Frost tried to avoid looking at the clock on the wall facing the bench. When he did eventually steal a glance, he was astonished to see a face in the public gallery above the clock. He had never seen anyone there before. These galleries were almost never used, there being sufficient accommodation for the public down-stairs. Besides, Frost remembered hearing that they were gener-ally kept locked for security reasons.

The face he now saw was that of a handsome, fair-haired young man, perhaps in his early twenties. Even more surprising, the lad seemed totally absorbed in the turgid court proceedings, leaning forward in his seat as if to catch each word and gesture. When Frost looked up again shortly before the court rose at 4:00 P.M., the young man had vanished.

Back in his chambers, Piggott dismissed his crier with instruc-tions to bring the car round at 6:00 P.M. He was presumably go-ing to spend time looking up law or writing reserved judgments, a routine chore toward the end of term. Frost, who was currently building a caravan in his back garden, escaped gladly to browse around do-it-yourself shops in Capel Street. He was back in good time, agreeably laden with gadgets, brochures, and plenty of new ideas, and Piggott's blue Mercedes was duly parked in Chancery Place four minutes before the hour.

When Piggott had not appeared by 6:35, Frost headed upstairs to inquire discreetly. The judge's room was on the first floor, third in a row of five along one side of a spacious corridor. Opposite each door was a large casement window overlooking the judges' car park. Piggott's door was slightly ajar. Frost, as was his prac-tice, knocked lightly and went in.

His Lordship was sitting squarely in his plushly upholstered desk armchair, side face to the door. His head was thrown back as if in hearty laughter, but his eyes wore that mildly vexed look of one who has forgotten something quite important, or even everything. Understandably so, because Sidney Piggott was dead.

WEDNESDAY, JULY 15

"MOLLY, HAVE YOU EVER DONE AN ABSOLUTELY CLASSIC murder case?"

"I don't know. What is an absolutely classic murder case?"

"You know: The duke of wherever found dead in the library, by his faithful footman, of course, Oriental dagger peeping out between the shoulder blades, so on."

Sergeant Molly Power gazed disapprovingly at Inspector Denis Lennon. "Denis, have you been reading comics again?"

"No comic, Molly, just fact stranger than fiction. Not a duke, a High Court judge. Not in the library, in His Lordship's chambers. And not the butler. His Lordship was found by his crier."

"His what?"

"His crier, tipstaff, man Friday. And it was not a knife in the back. That, too, was poetic license. He was strangled."

"Denis, how can you throttle a judge in the middle of the Four Courts?"

"No better place. Big thick walls, solid mahogany doors, it's designer-made for throttling judges. The president of the High Court was in his room next door. He heard nothing—that is, until Piggott's crier came crying to his doorway."

"Piggott, is that who was murdered, Judge Sidney Piggott?"

"Correct. About six o'clock last evening. The president got the police, and even managed to keep the press out of it until the body was moved, about four o'clock this morning. The chief was still here. He went down in person with the state pathologist and half the Technical Bureau. He rang me at midnight and gave us the case."

"It wasn't in the papers."

"No. but the media have it now. The chief will keep them happy. Needless to add, with his customary consideration for us underlings, he'll be promising the nation a hanging by suppertime."

"Sidney Piggott. I gave evidence before him a few times. Not a nice man, to be honest."

"Oh. Caught you out in a few white lies, did he, or was it pulling people's hair to get confessions?"

"Don't be sexist, Denis. He was a good judge, I think, but not a nice man. I always felt it."

"Intuition?"

"Well, you always know more than you can prove, don't you?"

"Perhaps, but our job is to prove what we know. Isn't that what separates the good cops from the bad ones?"

"The ones who nail their man, and the ones who don't?"

"No. The ones who get the proof, and the ones who fabricate it."

"Does that happen?"

"You must be joking."

Lennon's desk telephone rang.

"Yes, Saunders, thank you. The judge, Piggott, yes. We are on the job. Sergeant Power and I will be going down to the Four Courts shortly to meet the powder-puff boys at the scene, Tweedy and his almighty technicals. No, go out to the judge's house. The chief has the keys. Took them off the body. Tweedy will scream at that when he hears. Chat up the cook, neighbors, anyone. Give the house a once-over. I'll try to get out there by three o'clock. We can bring Tweedy out later, if it seems useful. OK? Thanks. Enjoy. Bye."

He hung up. "Right, Molly. Let's get down to the jolly old Palais de Justice. We have to meet the juju men. Before that, I want to hear the truth about His late Lordship from Ben Silverman."

"Who is Ben Silverman?"

"Ben Silverman is the Delphic oracle. I'll tell you in the car."

Denis Lennon had met Ben Silverman five years previously when they were both having the dubious pleasure of bypass surgery. They had supported each other on the long haul back to health and strength. Each found the other amusing, honest, and wise. After six months the two men and their wives had become fast friends.

Ben was a barrister with a peculiar but fairly lucrative practice, specializing in a medley of subjects: admiralty, trademarks and patents, copyright, medical negligence, and local government. He had never taken silk, preferring to operate by himself, and he usually declined to be fronted by senior counsel. Old-worldly in many respects, he was nonetheless quite aware of what went on around him. He was also well liked and respected by colleagues who willingly overlooked a faint aureole of mild eccentricities.

Lennon had had his "temporary" office in Dublin Castle lower yard for over ten years. Molly, who did the driving, turned left into Dame Street, circled Christ Church Cathedral, and headed down Wine Tavern Street into the heart of Viking Dublin—or what the neo-Vikings have left of it.

They came out onto Merchant's Quay beside the Franciscan church known to all Dubliners as Adam and Eve's, which was actually the name of a pub through which papists had to enter during times of persecution to hear clandestine mass in an ecclesiastical speakeasy to the rear.

Across the river grandiloquently styled Anna Livia Plurabelle by Joyce, the Four Courts bares its colonnaded teeth on old Inns Quay. This noble facade is appropriately topped by Moses, the lawgiver, supported by graven images of Justice, Mercy, Wisdom, and Authority. Below a massive green dome lies the great Round Hall, off which, like segments of an orange, open the original four courts of Chancery, King's Bench, Common Pleas, and Exchequer. These have long since been supplemented by dozens of courtrooms and offices for judges, masters, registrars, and quasi- and frankly nonjudicial officials of every kind and description.

Out back, nearer to the Bridewell holding prison, stands the Law Library, where, in the odd Irish way of doing things, barristers live, move, and have their being. At the entrance to this most exclusive of clubs, solicitors and others in need of counseling mill around all day calling out the names of barristers they want to consult to a functionary endowed with lungs of bronze who, seated at a high desk, bellows these names ceaselessly to every nook and backwater of the labyrinth. Counsel, it is said, are conditioned to hear only their own names above the pervasive hubbub and babble.

If a bellow produces no result, this Stentor can usually say where any of several dozen prominent counsel might be found: Supreme Court, Number 7, Church Street, Master's, or, increasingly, Tribunal. If the elusive practitioner is in fact playing truant, the conventional calls are *"Working at home today,"* which means Lansdowne Road Rugby Ground, *"Arbitration,"* code for the Curragh racetrack, and *"European Court,"* if the venue is Longchamps or Parc des Princes.

A mecca of wit, slander, and good conversation, the Law

Library is indeed an excellent club. It is also a unique reservoir of competence, erudition, and culture extending far beyond the already wide parameters of jurisprudence. By inviolable tradition, the youngest and least experienced member of the library may approach the busiest and most eminent silk for advice about a case. The senior is honor bound to drop everything and give full attention to the junior's great affair. In this way even the poorest litigant with the least experienced counsel can have free access to the best legal brains in the country.

Nobody was picking Ben Silverman's brains when his name was called that morning. Spotting the inspector at the far end of the library's main runway, he trumpeted back, "A fair cop, Inspector. I'll come quietly," causing several learned friends to raise startled heads from Law Reports or the racing page.

At the door, once apprised of their business, Ben gestured like a latter-day Raleigh casting cloaks over muck for Good Queen Bess. "To the watering hole," he decreed.

The Four Courts bar is hidden away in a basement dungeon. There Annie the Great presided, and had done for longer than anyone could remember, svelte in black spangled frock and crimson apron. A blond beehive hairdo, balanced on each side by crystal chandelier earrings, gave Annie the surreal appearance of a walking Scales of Justice. Thick layers of frescoed makeup had mummified her countenance as definitively as Tutankhamen's. Like a fine calvados, Annie was *sans âge*.

The Irish Bar conducts quite a lot of its business in Annie's bar. Years of overhearing conversations and of coping with the profession in various conditions had made of her a surefooted go-between. Balancing a tray of gin and tonics, she would trot between the plaintiff's counsel and attorneys in the tiny outer barroom and the defendant's team, including insurance moguls, in the still tinier snug behind the counter.

Silverman and his guests arrived in time to witness the closing moments of a settlement.

"Mr. Murphy, Mr. Carson says he will give you a hundred and eighty thousand, not a penny more."

"A hundred and eighty, Annie. You can't be serious! Well, you can tell Carson where he can put that."

There being no need to relay this firm rejoinder, perfectly audible to the Crusader in his crypt beneath St. Michan's Church three blocks away, Annie trots back to the rival camp and whispers, "You are getting close, Mr. Carson. Another ten should do it."

"Another ten, is it? Very well. Tell Murphy to send us in a drink. And ask him does he know that his client is a whore."

Voice off: "Wouldn't she want to be, Carson, to get money out of the likes of you? Annie, give those insurance buggers strychnine or whatever they are having."

At this point, Mr. Willoughby, the claims manager, on his first visit from London, is struggling to his feet to engage in the quintessentially English activity of taking a stand. Carson pats him on the knee reassuringly.

"There there, Mr. Willoughby, don't fret yourself at all. Murphy is actually being nice this morning."

Annie, having settled the case, acknowledged the arrival of the police by crinkling her wrinkles further, to indicate grief. She delivered her invariable encomium for all former customers.

"Ah, Inspector, poor Judge Piggott. Such a lovely man!"

"Nonsense, Annie," Silverman expostulated, "a most unsatisfactory person." He led the way into the snug, where suitable drinks were distributed.

"Well, Ben, tell us about His Lordship."

"Sure, Denis, you know all about him. You must have given

evidence in thousands of cases with, against, and before him."

"Hardly thousands, but a fair number certainly. Still, tell it your way, Ben."

"Let us see, then. Sidney Piggott, born about 1930, I should think. He was two or three years ahead of me at King's Inns, where he did no work but ate the requisite forty-eight dinners, which was all one needed in those days to get called to the bar. Well, that—and money. All changed now, of course, pink-faced youngsters spouting European law, even in the District Court. Anyhow, Sid was from Sligo, so he went on the northwestern circuit for a while. Those were hard times, postwar, little work, less money, awful hotels. A chap could spend three or four weeks in the depths of winter crawling around Sligo and Donegal, dying of cold, damp, and boiled chicken—can you imagine that, Miss Molly? They boiled it! At the end of it all, he could get back to Dublin with a net surplus of five or six guineas—if even.

"After a few years Sid settled in Dublin. He eventually built up quite a big criminal practice. There was no money in it then, of course, but as free legal aid developed he began to make a few bob. Also he took sides politically, and that brought him state work, prosecutions. That was before the invention of the director of public prosecutions, the good old days when briefs still went to party true believers. Actually, Sid's finances have always been a little bit murky. He had no money to start with, and he never earned a fortune at the bar. Most barristers don't, you know."

"Come off it, Ben. You fellows are coining."

"There are a few, yes. But don't heed the green-eyed little scribblers who write in newspapers, Denis. What sticks in their craws, actually, is not our money but our independence. Well, some people upstairs pay dear for that. There are fellows in that library who are deaf and blind, still working in their eighties because they cannot afford to retire. There are chaps up there who don't eat lunch, who—"

"Stop, Ben, I cannot bear it," Lennon cried. "Here, dry your tears. I'll buy you a drink."

He did, and Ben resumed his narrative.

"Sid's finances, I was saying, are mysterious. He went through thin times. Then he began to make some money. Even then he was often hard up. Of course, he was pretty wild in those days, what with horses, drink, and—saving your presence, young lady—lots of women. His wife left him about ten years ago, just before he went on the bench. Strangely, round about then things seemed to improve for him financially. He also quietened down. I imagine that the party of the incandescent patriots made quietening down a condition of getting on the bench. They are very moral people, you know, Denis." Ben closed one eye and pulled a death-mask face.

"The interesting thing, anyhow," he continued, "is that Sid seemed to have more money, and for no obvious reason. Nasty rumors went around at the time, and indeed since, for instance that Sidney had become too friendly with some of his gangster clients, that some of them had cut him in on the action. What about that, Denis, is it likely?"

"I wonder, Ben. Those chaps give nothing for nothing. So what was Sid doing for them in return, tearing up their parking tickets? It would take more than that."

"Perhaps he knew too much," Molly said. "He may even have been blackmailing somebody. So they took him out."

"I doubt it, Molly. Those people do not operate like that. A bullet in the head perhaps, or a friendly push off Dun Laoghaire Pier, but not the old-fashioned garotte, and certainly not in the middle of the Four Courts."

Lennon rubbed his chin reflectively. "Whoever did this job is certainly . . . unusual, the joker in the pack, I should think."

"What about Piggott's marriage?" Molly asked.

"Not happy, as I have said. Jenny must be twenty years younger, lovely girl. Sid did not deserve her. She lives out in Killiney, I think, has an arty-crafty shop somewhere on the south side, does well. They had one child, a son. There was some rumpus about him, too. Was it drugs? Hardly drugs. They didn't get fashionable until later. He ended up in Good-bye."

"Dubai?"

"Yes, one of those Arab places."

"What about the judge's crier?" Molly asked.

"Frost? A harmless man. His father tipstaffed before him. Don't worry. Ignatius Frost's son is the last man in the world to murder anyone. Upstanding Protestants. That is how Ignatius got the job."

"What do you mean?"

Silverman laughed. "Back in the 1930s, such jobs were reserved for veterans of the War of Independence. Ignatius Frost hadn't a hope. Not only had he not played his part in Ireland's heroic struggle for freedom, he was actually too busy fighting for the king in Flanders when his country needed him to fight that same king."

"So?"

"So he wrote in to whoever makes the appointments saying, 'I suppose I have no hope of being employed by the Irish state because I am not a Catholic.'"

"And?"

"Panic stations! Appointed by return of post! The young state was very sensitive to accusations of religious bigotry."

"They sure got over that one in time," Molly commented acidly.

"Yes and no, young lady, yes and no."

Annie put her head around the door. "Mr. Silverman, the chief justice has the place turned upside down looking for you. His man is here."

"I am edified," said the inspector, "if this is the last place he thought of looking."

Silverman arose, swallowing the remains of his drink hastily. "I forgot. The long vacation is upon us. I promised to divulge secrets about flies for catching fish on Lough Corrib. Ready about! I cannot waste time on the likes of you, Denis, when the very Woolsack is calling. Farewell. Keep me posted. Good-bye, Miss Molly, and catch the bad lad!"

"Or lassie," Molly amended Pavlovianly.

Silverman hurried away and was soon followed out of the bar by the officers who, according to police regulations, should not have been there in the first place.

As they left, Mr. Willoughby was having his fifth Bailey's Irish Cream, in the odd belief that this was the way for a chap not to be conspicuous in Ireland. "Mr. Carson," he enthused, not for the first time, "this is an excellent settlement, a really splendid settlement. I don't mind telling you that it has saved my company a considerable sum of money."

"I am gratified to hear you say so, Mr. Willoughby."

"Yes, really splendid. Incidentally, how much will your own fees come to? I mean approximately."

"Oh, about fifteen, I imagine."

"Fifteen hundred guineas. A very reasonable fee—even if the case was settled and you did not have to fight it. Thank you once again."

"Not at all, my dear fellow, not at all. By the way, thousand, Mr. Willoughby, fifteen *thousand* guineas. The same again, Annie. Mr. Willoughby is paying."

The judge's room was on the first floor, its generous window overlooking the quay and the river. It was a film-set judge's chambers: solid hardwood furniture, thick carpets, heavy satin curtains, massive bookcases filled with leather-bound gold-lettered tomes.

Piggott had left no personal stamp on the room, no family photographs or specially chosen pictures, no private papers, golf clubs, or even drinks cupboard. On that last point, to his own surprise and that of others, he had followed the wise practice of many judges who treat the Four Courts as a dry ship.

Des Tweedy of the Technical Bureau was there to meet them. "Come in, come in, Denis. We are almost finished."

Indeed, on their way in they had passed a man and a woman coming out, dressed in what seemed to be matching white pajamas.

"We have cleaned things up a bit, as you can imagine. But I'll be sending you photographs and drawings of how things were when we got to the beano. Body in the chair here, life and soul of the party. Chair sideways to the desk, just as you see it. So the desk was not between the assailant and his victim. Easy access, total surprise, no signs of struggle, instantaneous."

"How can strangulation be instantaneous?" Molly exclaimed.

"Who said anything about strangulation?"

"That is what the chief told us," Lennon said, weighing in on the side of his sergeant.

"Jesus Christ, these layman policemen! Wild approximations. How do we ever solve anything? Yes, the judge got it in the neck all right. But he was not strangled. His neck was broken. This is not the same thing at all. A single blow, you see, *click*, not *glug glug*, not strangled. It's like a good hangman and a bad one. Good ones break the neck, *click*, instantaneous. Bad ones are stranglers, *glug glug*. It takes time. Messy."

"Thanks, Des, thanks. We get the idea," Lennon interrupted.

"Something wrong? Are we not enjoying? That is the trouble

with you people, no intellectual curiosity. How do you ever solve anything if you don't ask the hard questions? But very well, I'll leave the rest to the pathologists. Those boys will spare you nothing, Denis. Perverts, of course, the whole lot of them, necrophiliacs. Ha! Ha!

"One thing: look at these wheel tracks in the carpet under the judge's chair. A foot, what, fourteen inches long. I think the beak was sitting down, enjoying life, expecting nothing. Then, wham! One mighty blow launches him into eternity and drives this chair back a foot or more. Strange, though. If the killer was standing, how did he get in such a strong wallop below him, so to speak, and on the right trajectory to propel the chair backward like that? A downward blow would not do it. This was a hefty rising clout. Look for a good golfer, Denis, perhaps. Ha! Ha!"

"We have taken fingerprints, some hair, fiber, the usual droppings. They won't add up to anything until you have a suspect to check them against. No easy clues this time, Denis. No Turkish cigarette ends, pawn tickets, chopsticks with tooth marks on. Sorry, chaps, you'll have to use your heads this time. Sorryo! Oh, but yes, except, I am forgetting, except for this. We missed it last night. I picked it up this morning." Tweedy produced a transparent plastic sachet containing a small circle of gilt metal. "An earring, I imagine, such as not normally worn by High Court judges."

"Where was it?"

"On the desk chair with the body, just balancing on the corner of the cushion here at the front. Freshly there. Inevitably, it would have soon slipped down the side of the cushion or onto the floor."

"Could it be off one of your chaps or the ambulance fellows?"

"Hadn't thought of that! I'll check. Not one of my lads, anyhow. They are all grown up, serious people, you know. Now if it was one of yours . . . Anyhow, my guess is you have a clue here, maybe your only one. Just look for someone with an empty ear. Ha! Ha!" Des Tweedy always laughed at his own jokes, out of sympathy, because nobody else did.

"What about theft? Drawers opened, presses ransacked, so on?"

"On the contrary. The judge's wallet was here on the desk with over a hundred euro in it. Not touched. Ditto for his watch, signet ring, even that sexy little tape recorder. Incidentally, he left two completed tapes for his typist, probably reserved judgments that he planned to deliver before the end of term. That is why he stayed back late, I suppose. There is even a third tape still in the machine. I'll get the chief registrar to check them all out. He may need them. So there you are, Denis. That's your lot. Who is the main suspect? Don't forget the president of the High Court. He lives just next door. Looks to me like a bit of a lad. Ha! Ha!"

"No suspects yet, Des, except the usual."

"The usual, Denis, who is that?"

"Everyone. Thanks, Des. You have been very helpful. Keep the faith."

"I will . . . Which one?"

Molly drove out through Phoenix Park onto the M50, which brought them to Baldoyle in less than half an hour. The judge's house stood in its own rather unkempt grounds: one story at the top of six stone steps, with a basement floor beneath, to which grass banks sloped down. A garda stood at the gate.

Sergeant Saunders was in the kitchen writing up a report. "Not much to tell," he said. "There is a cleaning woman, Mrs. Walsh. She comes in twice a week. Barely knew the judge. He left money on the hall table for her. He did his own garden—sketchy by the look of things. Shopped at a supermarket in Sutton mostly. During term he took his main meal in the Four Courts. Other times he cooked for himself, ate at the Boat Club, or telephoned out for meal delivery. Mrs. Walsh ran the two washing machines, clothes and crockery. He let the dishes pile up for three days at a time, wouldn't even steep them."

"I can imagine Mother Walsh on that subject."

"Right. He sometimes went to the local in the evening, amiable but not chatty, according to the landlord. Most of the regulars would not have known as much as his name, still less that he was a judge. Nobody knew much about him. Occasionally women around the house, but nothing to get your teeth into, if you know what I mean."

"I could not possibly imagine," Lennon remarked archly.

"'Ladies,' Mrs. Walsh called them, 'no better than they ought to be.'"

"Ah. Fury of a woman scorned!"

"Miaow!" said Molly.

"There are some personal papers in the study—insurance, bank statements, including an interesting account in Jersey with quite a tidy sum put by—but nothing *really* personal. No love letters, death threats, blackmail demands. But just look at the house. No photographs, nothing sentimental or nostalgic, is that the word? You would almost think the judge had no family."

"Sadly, you would be almost right. An estranged wife in Killiney, an alienated son in the Gulf, and some country cousins in Sligo, none of whom has shown any indecent haste about getting in touch," Lennon said.

"There was just one little something that might be significant. Perhaps if we could take a look together."

They went downstairs to the basement study, a comfortable room at the front of the house. The most lived-in area, Saunders suggested. Here were the television, video, and stereo units, a fax and telephone, and a well-stocked drinks cupboard.

Sitting down at the black steel desk, Saunders riffled through papers in a wire basket. "The more current stuff," he explained. "Here is what took my fancy, a receipt for a booking on Irish Ferries from Rosslare to Cherbourg. Sailing date, July twenty-first. That is Tuesday of next week. Two passengers and a Peugeot station wagon. This is made out to Isabelle Roundstone. It must be her car. His is a Merck, isn't it? So what have we got here? Two lovebirds heading for Euro Disney?"

"I doubt if Piggott was meant to be one of them," Molly said. "The courts will still be sitting on July twenty-first, and indeed right till the end of the month."

Lennon scratched his chin. "Who is Madame Roundstone, and why has Piggott got her receipt? See, her address is on the docket. Temple Bar. Good Lord, she is hardly living there, is she?"

"No," Saunders replied, "business. I have got her in the telephone book. Roundstone Antiques in Temple Bar. And there is also a Felix Roundstone in Donnybrook. That might be the residence."

"Right," said Molly. "I remember it now. Roundstone Antiques, Isa and Felix. She wears the trousers. They used to be in Baggott Street when my sister had her flat there. Then they moved to Temple Bar when that got fashionable."

"Well, I'm not finished yet," Saunders continued. "Here is the funny bit. The judge seems to have financed at least half a dozen trips abroad for the Roundstones over the last five years. Sometimes by air and sometimes on the ferry. Sometimes just missus. That's usually by air. When it is by sea there is always two of them and the station wagon. Mister and missus, I think, not the judge. Felix is mentioned on at least one of those receipts. Here, take a look at this."

Saunders slid open the bottom left-hand drawer of the desk

and took out a plain manila file, which he opened flat on the desk. It contained eight slim sheafs of paper, each held together by a metal paper clip. Each subfile contained a travel receipt or air-ticket counterfoil. These were usually made out to Isabelle Roundstone, sometimes to Felix. There were also receipts for hotels, meals, and incidental travel expenses. Six journeys had been made to Paris, two to London.

Each dossier was backed by an A4 sheet of paper setting out figures in respect of one particular transaction. These sheets had one-word titles, such as Vouet, Pistols, Chess, Le Nain, Figurines, Gauffier. There followed a cash account in what the investigators quickly established by comparison was the judge's handwriting. The most impressive of these was for a trip to Paris by Isa alone in April 1995. The money figures were given in pre-euro currency—pounds, whether sterling or Irish was not clear.

SISLEY

Paid	£4,500	Sold	£65,000
Dublin-Paris	£180	Expenses	£4,900
Hotel etc.	£220	Balance	£60,100
Total	£4,900	Roundstone	£6,500
		Net	£53,600

Lennon took the whole file and went to sit near the window, where he stayed for half an hour, making notes and doing sums, muttering to himself. The others, familiar with this phase in his mental operations, went off to the kitchen and stole coffee.

He came in presently, visibly pleased with himself. "Saunders, you are a bloody genius."

"Thank you, sir. I agree. But just spell it out for me. What exactly was going on?"

"Well, Sisley is a painter. I know that much. So is Vouet, I think. Piggott was trading in pictures and in antiques, figurines, old chessmen, that sort of stuff. It is perfectly obvious. The Sisley was his single biggest coup. But if you total the eight trips over the period, he made a net profit of how much?" He glanced at his notes and muttered. "Well, the older ones are in pounds, and the more recent ones in euro. But, approximately, you are looking at something in the region of a quarter million euro. Not so bad for a mere amateur, and all tax free, I don't doubt. The Roundstones obviously sold the goods for him in London or Paris. He paid them ten percent commission.

"The most incredible aspect of the whole performance is the staggering differences between what Piggott paid for his bits and pieces and what he got paid when he sold them. Look at this Sisley thing, for God's sake. Purchase price 4,500. Net profit fifty-something thousand. Now how in God's name did he do that, and so often, and so consistently? I doubt if Piggott had a flair for spotting old masters. I mean, just look around this house, for heaven's sake. It has about as much artistic feel as the local dole office."

"His wife is a bit into that line," Molly remarked.

Lennon paused. "That is a thought," he said, "but even if they were in business together—which I doubt, in view of what Ben had to say about their happy marriage—I don't think that either of them spent their time touring round the country auctions wiping the eyes of the local dealers."

"Well, where did he get them?"

"Where do you think? Stolen!"

"Denis, for God's sake. He was a bloody High Court judge. Are you actually saying that Piggott was a thief, that he stole these things?"

"Not quite, but almost. I think he was a fence. My guess is that he bought from people, or more likely from one chap who had to off-load his stock quickly for whatever he could get. That means someone who has acquired the goods illegally and who can expect a visit from the police in the very near future."

"You mean a professional thief or burglar, and one with a record?"

"Exactly. Somebody who will be routinely checked every time an art robbery job is done."

"What about the Roundstones?" Molly asked.

"They probably identified the stuff for Piggott, valued it, and knew where to dispose of it. In which case they almost certainly knew that they were handling stolen property."

"So we dash over to Temple Bar and interview the Roundstones."

Lennon thought for a few moments. Then he shook his head. "No, Molly, I don't think so. What we are seeing here will certainly interest some of our friends, the art robbery people, tax diddler brigade, so forth. But *we* are investigating a murder. Has all this any meaning for us? Is it in any way connected with Piggott's death? Let us sit tight. I should be very curious to know whether or not the Roundstones will travel to France next week. And if they do, what will they be carrying? And if they come back with money, what will they do with it—now that the vendor, their valued client, has sadly left us?"

"We could stop them at the ferry, see what they have in the boot."

"Yes, maybe. My guess is that when Isa Roundstone goes by plane she is carrying something small. When they both go by ferry, it will be a bulkier consignment, so they need the station wagon. This time, therefore, it is something big. I wonder . . ."

"Wait a moment," Molly said eagerly. "Where is that ferry docket you were waving around? The current one, I mean. I may even be able to help you."

Saunders went back to the study and retrieved the receipt. Molly took it, turned it over quickly, and caught her breath with excitement.

"Ha! I thought so. I remembered noticing something scrawled on the back of this. Well, here it is."

She flattened the paper on the kitchen table. Three heads bent forward like surgeons in pursuit of an appendix. The inscription in red biro was short and cryptic.

Notty - 10,000	Tr 124
Ex ?	???

"Well, well," said Saunders, "what is that the formula for?"

"It is in Piggott's handwriting, I think. It is a sketch account for next week's outing," Molly replied. "Just like in the balance sheets he did for all the other trips, Piggott has jotted down the expenses side of the equation. 'Tr 124.' You don't have to be a genius to crack that one. Travel, 104 euro, which is exactly the amount of the receipt overleaf. The three excited question marks on the right side mean 'Ooooh, how much lovely money am I going to end up with when all is done?'"

Lennon was nodding vigorously.

"Janey Mack," Saunders exclaimed. Then '10,000' presumably means the cash Piggott forked out for 'Notty'—whatever that is. That is by far the biggest money he ever paid for anything. On track record, given his usual margin, that probably means he was expecting, what? Over a hundred grand. By God, this is the big one!"

Lennon nodded himself to a halt.

"Yes, Saunders, yes. This is the big one, and this time Piggott gets killed. Coincidence, do you think? I really feel we should not spoil the French outing for the Roundstones."

"Denis, do you seriously think that the Roundstones murdered Piggott, so that they could sell his painting and keep the money?" queried Molly.

"Well, let's give them some rope, shall we, and see what happens."

"Who or what is Notty?" Molly asked. "It is written with a capital. Is that just because it is the first word on the page, or is it the name of an artist? I never heard of anyone called Notty, did you?"

Lennon shook his head and looked at Saunders, who grinned cheerfully.

"Me, sir? I never even heard of Picasso."

FRIDAY, JULY 17

INSPECTOR LENNON HAD TO SPEND THE NEXT DAY AND A half in Naas extricating himself from a wearisome and stalemated investigation, which he was glad to be rid of. Returning at lunchtime on Friday, he ingested the technical reports with his cheese and tomato sandwich. The hairs, fibers, and fingerprints from Piggott's room were all as Tweedy had said, there but not yet of any apparent significance. The gilt circlet was indeed an earring, one of billions on the planet, not worth ten cents and available everywhere for a euro or more.

The pathologist's report confirmed that Piggott had died instantly of a broken neck inflicted by a forceful blow from a blunt hard instrument. Given that the victim was almost certainly seated at the moment of impact, the trajectory and force of the blow, together with the detail of bruising and fracture, would suggest that the injuries were inflicted by a violent right-footed kick delivered by a sturdy boot or shoe or by an upward swinging blow with some other blunt instrument. If the assailant used a kick, he was almost certainly young and vigorous, and probably skilled in one of the more lethal martial arts.

"Needless to say," the report continued, but nonetheless went on to say it, "suicide and accident are ruled out: These injuries were deliberately and expertly inflicted by an assailant other than the deceased." Lennon mused perversely about whether a person intent on suicide might not engage the services of the local karate club to kick his head off.

Molly came in shortly after 3:00 P.M. "What will you do if I have solved the whole thing in your absence?" she asked.

"I'll kick you violently under the left ear."

She organized more coffee and sandwiches. "The judge's funeral is tomorrow."

"Ah yes, Saturday, good! I might even go there myself, to see who is not crying enough. We can visit the widow on Monday. How did you get on with your shopping list?"

"Good, bad, and so-so. The chief registrar checked the judge's papers for me. Nothing seems to be missing. It is near the end of term, so he did not have much on hand. His two reserved judgments were both on tape, ready for typing. It seems he always used a separate tape for each judgment. Actually, there was a third tape as well."

"Yes, still on the machine."

"Correct," Molly said. "That wasn't a judgment; it was some excruciating talk he was going to give somewhere about the law of libel. Imagine, two sides complete of a ninety-minute tape. Ugh!"

"So, everything neat and complete! I wonder did Piggott have a premonition."

"I doubt it. If he had, he would have cleared Notty and Mrs. Roundstone out of his larder. Besides, Judge Bradshaw, who had lunch with him a few hours before he was done in, says he was in the best of form."

"Really?"

"Yes. Moaning a bit about the heat in court and about the hideous case he had at hearing, but nothing like premonitions.

On the contrary, he was making poor Bradshaw envious about his upcoming holiday."

"Oh, and what and where was that to be—Euro Disney with Isa Roundstone?" Denis asked.

"No way. Bali, fancy free."

"Ah dear, it does make Ballybunnion in the rain with the missus sound tame, doesn't it?"

"Bradshaw said, 'How do you do it, Sid, on our salary?'"

"Well, good for Brad. And what did Sid say?"

"Just what you would like him to say: 'I have been lucky, Dick, a bit of a windfall.' No details added."

"Dear me! Counting his chickens before they came home to roost, poor man, wasn't he? If I may mingle the metaphors."

"Then I saw Ned Frost, the crier," Molly said.

"Oh yes. Did he cry much?"

"Not a drop, and I doubt that he will. When a new judge is appointed, it seems, he inherits his predecessor's man."

"Very feudal."

"Yes, and a pig in a poke for both of them, I should think. He says Piggott was OK, but they had no rapport. He used to drive the judge home in the evening, then continue home himself on the bus. Frost was never even inside the house, except once or twice to carry in luggage."

"What did he say about the day of the murder?"

"Pretty well what we already have in the statement he made that night. The judge seemed the same as any other day. No tension, no agitation or foreboding. But there was one detail Frost forgot to mention in that first statement."

Molly went on to describe the fair-haired young man who had appeared and disappeared so mysteriously in the disused gallery of courtroom two. She read from her notes. "'He just stared in front of him all the time, almost as if he were sitting in judgment on us, the judge, the registrar, possibly even myself. Age? Early to middle twenties. A good-looking boy, fair hair, leather jacket'— imagine that, Denis, a leather jacket in this heat wave? 'Height? No idea. He was sitting all the time. Probably average height. He was hunched forward, staring.' I asked if he was wearing an earring."

"Good girl."

"Frost could not say. You probably would not notice at that distance. But he told me that the boy had also been sighted in the Round Hall by the Admiral."

"And who, pray, is the Admiral?"

"Aha! I thought you knew everything about the Four Courts. Well, the admiral, for your information, is the tall, distinguished-looking commissionaire chap in fancy dress who presides in the Round Hall."

"Really? Is that what they call him? Very apt, too. I could just picture him in a tall ship sailing up the river."

"He would have trouble getting his tall ship under the Ha'penny Bridge. Anyhow, he, too, saw Goldilocks. Apparently he notices everyone and knows all the regulars. He spotted this boy because he didn't fit any of the categories. Not a witness, not a juryman— there were no juries empanneled that afternoon—not a tourist, nor a journalist. Not a solicitor's apprentice—the Admiral knows the new crop of those every academic year by Christmas. About the earring—same as Frost, he did not notice one way or the other. Height? Yes, he is clear on that, five foot nine or ten."

"Interesting. The boy is probably a red herring. Still, he does sound like the type who might wear an earring and know a little jujitsu or whatever. Also, he is sufficiently out of place in the right place, if you take my meaning, to be precisely the joker in the pack. But tell me, what was he doing in that upstairs gallery?

And a leather jacket in such an unusually tropical July. Isn't it almost as if he *wanted* to be noticed? Hardly the demeanor of somebody who, half an hour later, is going to sidle in and murder the judge."

"Perhaps he was a decoy. A smoke screen."

Lennon looked at his sergeant with interest. "Now there is a thought," he said appreciatively. "Listen, ask Tweedy to sweep the gallery. He just might find something to match his rags, bones, and bottles from the judge's room."

"He might find another earring."

Lennon chuckled. "Another would be one too many. Also, will you get O'Sullivan—you know, the chap who does the Identikits—ask him to talk to Frost and the Admiral and to do one of his doodles. For limited circulation at this stage, just the Four Courts community. If we get some better sightings we might be able to run a good Identikit in the newspapers afterward."

"Why not go for it now? The sooner the better."

"No, I don't think so. If you launch a vague Identikit, you get three thousand sightings within twenty-four hours. The boy will be seen simultaneously everywhere from Skellig Michael to the Giant's Causeway. Let's not get involved in more wild goose chases than we have to. By the way, did you ask Frost if he killed the judge himself?"

"Don't be silly, Denis. Of course not."

"Whyever not? Isn't that the first rule: Everyone is a suspect?"

"Even your Delphic oracle, Ben Silverman, says that Frost is harmless."

"Let me tell you something, Molly: Harmless people commit murders. Anyhow, let's get the Identikit and run it round the Four Courts. I wonder how one goes about that."

"Well, I can tell you how not to do it, which brings me to the last part of my report. I tried to see Albert Singer, the chairman of the Bar Council. I thought in my innocence that he might help me to appeal to the various categories of people who work in the courts for information or whatever assistance they might be able to give."

"A most reasonable request."

"Tell that to Mr. Singer. His reply was 'I do not speak to sergeants.' And he meant especially women sergeants."

"Perhaps."

"Perhaps nothing. He did. But it did not stop there. He had a few smart bombs for you as well."

"I am honored. Like what?"

"Mr. Singer was 'pained and disturbed that the officer in charge of this investigation should feel free to stroll off down the country' while assassins are falling over each other in the Four Courts. His last shot was—you will love this—'Tell Lennon to report to me the minute he gets back.' Who the hell does he think he is?"

"I have no idea. Only my wife and my bank manager talk to me like that. At all events, Monday will be quite time enough for that little colloquy."

"Well, he certainly does not want to see me again."

"Dear me, and who says he has a choice about that? Anyhow, what did you do then?"

"I went to see the president of the High Court."

"Good. Did you ask him if he killed Piggott?"

"No, Denis. I didn't have to. He had guilt written all over his face. Seriously, what a contrast to Singer. An absolute sweetie. He insisted on making me a cup of tea with his own hands, called me 'dear lady' throughout, and kept saying how terrible it must be to find myself mixed up in such a ghastly affair. I didn't like to tell him that I have done more or less nothing except homicide for the last four years.

"We already have his statement, of course. The way he tells it, the decision to keep the press out until the body had been moved seems quite civilized. He said that in any case, and not just because Piggott was a judge, he did not see that the public was being cheated if they did not get to see the body or at least a body bag. Sounds sensible to me.

"I told him about Singer's warm welcome. He didn't let down the side—no direct criticism of Singer, which I actually thought was nice—he just groaned and offered to contact all the relevant people himself, from judges to cleaners to chuckers-out.

"I liked the way he talked about Piggott, too. He had no idea who could have killed him. 'A very unusual procedure' he called it. He said that he had never known Piggott well either at the bar or on the bench. They came, he said, from rather different backgrounds, but he said that without any trace of nastiness. 'I think,' he said, 'that Judge Piggott has had an unsettled and not very happy life.' I liked the president. In the best old-fashioned sense, a gentleman."

"Yes. Everybody says so."

"One other thing. Saunders has been trawling around. He says that the Roundstones are in deep financial trouble—mortgages, overdrafts, the lot."

"Join the gang!"

SATURDAY, JULY 18

SERGEANT MOLLY POWER WAS TWENTY-SEVEN YEARS OF age, the darling of farming parents, an elder sister, and three brothers in Fethard-on-Sea, County Wexford. She had joined the gardai straight from school. Hardworking and bright, she was a sergeant by the age of twenty-six, thereby forfeiting the short-lived undying love of Tommy, her older and unpromoted garda boyfriend, who simply could not take it.

Molly lived in a top-story flat in Harcourt Street with two other girls, Nell, a physiotherapist, and Rosemary, priestess of some computer mystery religion. The flat was comfortable, and they got on well together. Nell and Rosemary had taught Molly what to wear and how to handle boys. She was not sure what she had contributed in return, but the other two had no doubts about that. City girls, they regarded their "bog woman" as the only really sane person on the premises.

Brunette and pretty, if a bit on the plump side in an age of drug-dried anorexic fashion models, Molly would have been taken for beautiful by an artist like Rubens, who enjoyed painting pneu-matic women.

She was off duty that Saturday but awoke with a self-surprising determination to find out, off her own bat, who this Notty fellow might be. Before 10:00 A.M. she had walked through Stephen's Green and was gazing in the window of James Adams Fine Art Auctioneers. *If anyone knows,* she thought, *these people will.* But the idea of strolling in to inquire off-handedly whether they might have a few Notties going under the hammer one of these days seemed too preposterous. She funked and slunk around the corner into Dawson Street. An hour and a half of free reading in the art sections of the Waterstone's and Hodges Figgis bookshops left her no wiser.

Wandering aimlessly along Nassau Street, regretting that garda school had taught her nothing about how to find Notties, Molly walked into an idea. It was in the form of a signpost pointing toward the National Gallery. But of course! She hurried down to Clare Street, turned right into Merrion Square, and was soon downstairs in the library of the National Gallery.

Another hour and a half went by, thumbing through card indexes, tapping computer keys, skimming diagonally across encyclopedias. Net result: zero. The nearest she got was "Notte, La" in volume 7 of the Britannica Micropedia. This turned out to be a film made in 1960 by somebody called Michelangelo Antonioni, who, she presumed, was not the same as the chap who had done up the Sistine Chapel.

In desperation she approached the librarian's horseshoe counter. A horn-rimmed steel-gray lady looked up and smiled quite amicably. "Yes, dear?"

"I am trying to trace an artist called Notty. I can't seem to find anything on him."

"Notti, is it, N-o-t-t-i?"

"I thought it was *y* but it could be *i*."

"Is he a painter?" the woman asked dubiously, tapping into her own computer.

"I think so."

"You think so," the woman said, looking at her more critically. "Well, tell me something you do know about him, because I don't see anything at all coming up here."

Molly lifted her head to ponder what reply she could possibly make that would not sound totally ludicrous. She was looking straight into the green eyes of a young man standing directly opposite her on the other side of the horseshoe. He was perhaps her own age. Thin, scholarly, rimless glasses, pale, a good face, temperate, sensitive. He was . . . To her consternation, they both blushed.

"Excuse me," the librarian was repeating, "what more can you tell me about . . ."

Somehow they were standing together in the stairwell outside the library door.

"I beg your pardon," he was saying very formally. He was French, surely, or German. No, Dutch, yes, that was it: those lovely vowels! "I could not help to hear your question—about an artist called Notty. Was it Notty you said?"

"Yes. Do you know him?"

"Perhaps. I am not sure. Could it be, possibly, Notte, ending with e?"

"I suppose it could. Is there such an artist?"

"Sort of."

"Sort of?"

The young man blushed again. "Excuse me," he repeated in his punctilious English. "My name is Jan-Hein Van Zeebroeck. I am from Holland. Would you do me the honor to eat lunch in the restaurant? I will explain all what I know."

"Beautiful," Molly said. She added determinedly, "We will go dutch."

A split second. Then they both laughed out loud.

"Let's go up in the glass lift," she said with unreasonable happiness. "I've never been in a glass lift."

Jan-Hein, who was the adored only child of parents old enough to be his grandparents, could never remember doing anything wild or naughty in his whole life. To his astonishment, he found himself pulling this total stranger into the glass lift and saying, much too loudly for the National Gallery. "*Oh yes!* Let's go right up to the top . . . and down again . . . three times . . . and then . . . well . . . let's eat."

Barnaby Coughlin was a crumpled person. His clothes were crumpled. So were the cigarettes and the banknotes in his pockets. Even his skin and flesh seemed crumpled. His standards of behavior were particularly crumpled. A defrocked policeman, because he had got the distinction between poachers and gamekeepers more than a little bit crumpled, Barny was nonetheless sometimes invited, and always willing, to reincarnate briefly on the side of the righteous. This would be, of course, in consideration of an appropriate emolument. Which is why Lennon and Coughlin were having a liquid lunch together.

Information was Barny's speciality. As a garda officer he had kept several underworldly persons comprehensively briefed on what was happening or projected in police circles. Thus were suitable alibis prepared, potential witnesses leant upon, evidence recycled, and surprise police raids frustrated by the careful readiness of the unsurprised persons to be raided. For a special fee Barny would sometimes tamper with evidence already in police custody, adjusting, contaminating, or even quite simply walking away with bits and pieces in his pocket.

He had been let down lightly. If his activities had been fully investigated, and if the papers had gone to the director of public prosecutions, Barny would certainly have spent several years in jail. But he had friends, he had been discreet, and perhaps even some clairvoyant eminence had foreseen that having Barny in no-man's-land between cowboys and Indians might be no bad thing. Perhaps, too, some colleagues had personal reasons not to engage in excessive public washing of police dirty linen. He ended up with early retirement and a modest pension.

Coughlin was not a "grass." He could not be used for infiltration. But he had his ear to the ground. He heard things, and he knew who and how to ask a few questions. In the present case he would probably ask for three thousand euro and get a few hundred, with liquid lunches fore and aft of the assignment.

"Piggott had too much money, Lennon was saying.

"A very rare condition," Coughlin commented, as gravely as a Harley Street specialist.

"He may have been in some racket or other. Not drugs or prostitution, certainly. The only hint we have is about the fine art market.

"A fence?" Coughlin prompted.

"Could be," Denis said.

Coughlin nodded.

"Indeed. A growth area at the moment, though a certain expertise is desirable. That is one area where dog unashamedly eats dog. Did Piggott know anything about fine art? Personally, I doubt it."

"He may have had access to good advice. Another possibility is that he fell foul of somebody. It may have been a contract job."

"Denis, I am surprised at you. Contract killers do not kick people to death. It's too energetic, and not reliable—there would be too many indignant survivors. It is, of course, more ecological than firearms."

"There is something original about this job, Barny, what looks like a deliberate hiccup in the logic. Contract killers don't do high kicks, I agree. But junkie muggers don't find their way upstairs in the Four Courts either, and neither do they leave wallets stuffed with money behind them on the table."

"True. What about the other thing?"

"What other thing?"

"Sex, Denis. Haven't you heard of it?"

"Piggott was no stranger to the little women. From what I hear they were all glorified tarts, no deep relationship, no hard feelings, not something to murder for. Still, one never knows, I suppose. Have a look by all means."

"Leave it to Barny; he has the perfect bedside manner. You know, Piggott may have been a crook, but he was not a crooked judge. We have never had a crooked judge in this country, not since independence, anyhow. Did you know that?"

"I think it is true. A few bad ones perhaps, but not bent."

"I am happy you agree, Denis. You know how particular I am about honesty." Coughlin rolled his rubber eyes sanctimoniously toward heaven in conscious self-mockery. He returned to earth and hit it running. "Denis, we cannot do a major investigation on fresh air. I'll need five thousand. You know, expenses, travel, sweeteners to open mouths, danger money, so on."

"Barny, this is a poor country."

"I am shocked, Denis. You of all people to give me the poor mouth! Have you not heard about the Celtic Tiger?"

"Heard, yes, Barny, but he has come and gone and, sure as hell, I ain't seen him. Have you?"

They had enjoyed their meal in the gallery restaurant and, even more, each other's company. But they did not have a table to themselves, so conversation had not been too personal; nor could Molly unpack her policewoman's conundrums under the noses of casual commensals.

After lunch they sat together on a cool stone bench in the pretty courtyard outside the restaurant. Life stories were traded. Jan-Hein was from Maastricht. Aged twenty-six, a graduate in fine arts, he hoped to specialise in seventeenth-century Dutch and Flemish painting. He was touring the smaller galleries of Europe on an Erasmus scholarship concentrating on lesser-known works, mostly not on display, that had never been thoroughly researched or even catalogued. He and Molly needed to meet each other.

Which indeed was less likely: that Jan-Hein should encounter the girl of his dreams so fortuitously that morning, or that he should turn out to be perhaps the one person in Dublin who could understand and answer her cryptic question? Molly trusted him immediately, telling him what she wanted to know, and why. She omitted only the name Roundstone.

"You said that there is an artist called Notte—sort of. What does that mean?"

"Well, there was a seventeenth-century painter called Gerrit van Honthorst who spent a few years in Rome just after the death of Caravaggio. He copied a lot of things from Caravaggio's painting, especially chiaroscuro, you know, the tenebroso thing."

"Jan-Hein, talk English."

"I mean light and darkness stuff, people holding lanterns or candles, sometimes shielding them with their hands, half their faces lit up, the other half in shadow. It can be very effective, dramatic even. Sometimes you see soldiers in dark armor with the light of a torch glinting on their helmet or perhaps on the hilt of a sword. Just like in the Caravaggio *Taking of Christ* here in the National Gallery."

"I know it. There was great excitement nationwide when it was discovered a few years ago. But what has all this to do with Mr. Notty, or Notte? Where does he fit in?"

"Precisely. Honthorst painted those night scenes so well that the Italians called him Gherardo della Notte, 'Gerard of the Night.' His work is still sometimes catalogued under that name."

"Could one of his paintings be worth a hundred grand or more?"

"Grand?"

"A hundred thousand euro."

"Well, money is the bit I know least about. Besides, artists can be very uneven. Good artists can sometimes make bad paintings. But if this is by Honthorst, and if it is of the good period—then yes, it could be worth a lot of money. I know that the National Gallery was offered a picture recently by Terbrugghen—that is the same sort of work. School of Utrecht we call it. The sum being asked was half a million dollars."

"Wow! But what are the chances of such a valuable painting turning up in this country?"

"Good chances. Painters go in and out of fashion. You could have bought some pictures thirty years ago for a few pounds that now sell for hundreds of thousands. Gentry from Ireland and England used to go on the Grand Tour in the eighteenth and nineteenth centuries. They often came back with marvelous things, some of which are still mouldering away in country houses, waiting for someone to discover them. A Honthorst—or a Notte, if you prefer—could very well be one of those."

Jan-Hein and Molly left the National Gallery together two hours later, holding hands, and each more than happy with the day's discoveries.

MONDAY, JULY 20

Dear Dr. Keating,

Thank you for your recent letter. I am sorry that you have not been able to reach me by telephone. We have been very busy.

I understand and indeed appreciate your concern. I do assure you that I was personally entirely happy with the course of treatment and progress made while my son was in your care. We have got to recognize, however, that we are dealing with an adult who is no longer subject to the constraint of my views, still less of my decisions. He has decided to leave the clinic. There is really nothing I can do about it.

I have found a position for the boy with a customer of ours, cooking and housekeeping. There, he will be both in a sheltered environment and also doing what he likes best. In that respect, I must particularly thank you for all you did in the clinic to help him develop his skills in catering and home economics. That has given him confidence; it is really his lifeline.

He did assure me when we were last speaking that he

would continue to take his pills. I particularly stressed to him the possibly grave consequences of failing to do so. I also warned him, as you had told me, that he will not be able to get this medication at any pharmacy, even with a prescription. He assured me that his employer has the matter in hand and that he has been able to procure fresh supplies.

Keating read no further.

"Two-faced lying bitch," he hissed between clenched teeth, and flung the letter into a plastic tray on his desk.

Inspector Jim Quilligan was a great, red-faced, sandy-haired fellow. Scion of a well-known West Limerick family of itinerant dealers in antiques and furniture, he knew the trade intimately, both its merchandise and its practitioners. An inspired choice had placed him in charge of the garda's fine art section, where he happily and most competently pursued what he called "the three F's": forgers, fraudsters, and fences. His office in Store Street was hosting the murder squad; he had moved enough files off horizontal surfaces for Denis and Molly to sit down.

"How nice to see you, Denis. We have not met for ages. Unfortunately, fine art and murder don't often go together."

"They might do this time."

"What a nice thought."

Quilligan followed the narrative with manifest interest. As Molly was concluding the account of her extracurricular artistic researches—shorn of romantic details—he was already tapping at the Internet. He checked them all: Honthorst, van Honthorst, Notte, della Notte.

"Nothing by this chap under any of his labels has been reported as stolen, neither in Ireland nor anywhere else that feeds the Net. So where does that leave us?" Heaving back his chair, he parked two large feet on the desk. "It does seem that your judge was dealing in stolen pictures, and other things, too. A missing Sisley rings a bell. I'll look it up. But no trace of a Honthorst on the magic box. So, either the theory about Notte with *e* or Notty with *y* is wrong—or else the rightful owner did not know that he had a Honthorst, and so did not report its disappearance under that name. The picture and its theft probably are in here"—he tapped the computer irreverently with his big shoe—"but under some outlandish name, Mondrian, or God knows what. You know, half the dirty old canvases in this country have been catalogued for auction at one time or another as Rembrandt or Van Dyck. The really interesting question is this: If it is a Honthorst, how did Piggott know that, and how did he know it was worth six figures?"

"Presumably the Roundstones told him."

"No way, Denis. This is specialized expertise, which even a good dealer does not have, not the Roundstones, not even Jim Quilligan. People like us can tell you this is a fine painting, old canvas, probably seventeenth century, very much in the style of . . . That is as far as it goes. There is a missing link here, somebody who knows authoritatively considerably more than Piggott or Roundstone—and who is honest, because he is making a firm identification and a valuation that has already led Piggott to part with ten thousand and is probably about to persuade somebody else to cough up one or two hundred thousand."

"Well, Jim, I can see that those aspects of the case interest you, and indeed it is rather intriguing. Molly and I beam in on another wavelength. We simply need to know if Piggott was murdered so that somebody else could get their hands on the jackpot. The Revenue boys—they, too, will be interested, from yet another point of view.

"The Revenue?" Quilligan wrinkled his large nose quasi-daintily. "Should we have that sort of person in?"

Lennon smiled. "Let's keep to the pecking order. First, the lions; that is us, the murder squad. Then the jackals, your lot. Last, the vultures, unmistakably the Revenue."

"Anyhow," Molly added, "they like their meat high."

"Denis, I think your first idea is best. Let the Roundstones travel tomorrow. Follow them. Link up with the French police— I have an excellent contact there. The only problem is that we might get a bit cramped by what the French will wear . . . I mean in the line of procedures. Know what I mean?"

"Surely we can manage within the rule of law. I wasn't thinking of summary execution or anything like that. My strong instinct would be to have no showdown until we get the Roundstones back to Ireland. We don't need to get fouled up in any French red tape—extradition, all that stuff. Let us first see have we got anything at all on the Roundstones. If we have, is it murder, theft, receiving, tax dodging, or what? We can fight all that out later, but let's do it here in Dublin, in the Bridewell, not in the Bastille. Molly, I'd love to take you to France, but . . ."

"The chief would not hear of it."

"Don't mind the chief. My chief wife would not hear of it, either. Seriously, given all this arty stuff, I think Jim is the man to go. Jim, how is your French?"

"Extensive. *Oui oui. Bonjour.* That's about it."

"Not even *un demi?*"

"What is that?"

"To order beer—

"French beer, is it? You must be joking. I use *wee wee* for that, too. Anyway, I don't need French. Claude Ronsard is fluent in English. He is my art-cop equivalent in Paris, and a great friend."

"Will you go?"

"Dinny, I am a wandering man. I'd love to go."

Molly looked doubtful. "Inspector, if the Roundstones see you on the ferry, they may smell a rat, so to speak."

"I don't think so. They know about me, certainly, just like I know about them. But we have never met. After all, I have only been based in Dublin for the last seven months. I have no reason to think they will recognize me."

"This may be your big break, Jim," Lennon said, "so *bon voyage* and *bon amusement!*"

Irish people love going to law. In some parts of the country, one routinely sues one's neighbor every few years. At appropriate intervals, one's neighbor sues one back. It is the done thing.

In the past, causes of action were never hard to come by. A half acre of snipe grass, a tumbledown boundary wall, or a right-of-way going nowhere could inspire serialized litigation over several generations. Jubilees could be marked by something special: a disputed will, perhaps, a lively breach of promise to marry action, or a claim for restitution in respect of the fruitless posturings of an anaphrodite bull or stallion.

By the mid-twentieth century, the proliferation of motorcars and incompetent drivers had already increased the volume of litigation prodigiously. The decline of religion in recent decades has greatly compounded that effect. Tragedy and God have been replaced by justice and compensation. Misfortunes previously regarded as endemic to the human condition, or even attributable to the inscrutable decrees of divine vengeance or providence, are now routinely perceived as simple forms of human negligence or injustice for which somebody somewhere has got to be made to pay. Whole armies of fresh-faced barristers are spontaneously generating to do battle for and against all these somebodies who

make other people unhappy in such an infinity of potentially lucrative ways.

This is why transhumance has become necessary. The Irish
Bar, having overflowed the Law Library into every undefended
attic, cellar, and broom cupboard in the Four Courts complex,
has been forced at last to found colonies in Church Street and, a
strong stone's throw away, in a decommissioned malt whiskey
distillery. It was in this second premises that Mr. Albert Singer,
chairman of the Bar Council, occupied a splendid suite of rooms
on the first floor.

Short, bald, and red-faced, Singer made up in presence what
he lacked in good looks. Nobody ignored him, and he was accustomed to having his own way. People feared Singer. Physically
strong, with a mind like a razor and a tongue like a whip, he was
dangerous, whether on paper, at a meeting, or in court. In the
memorable words of one disappointed litigant whom Singer had
destroyed in a devastating cross-examination of three questions:
"a poisonous hoor."

"Come in, Lennon," Singer said curtly without rising from his
desk. "The young lady can wait outside."

"Sergeant Power is an important member of the garda team in
this investigation."

"Inspector, I have serious and delicate matters to question you
about—"

"Excuse me, sir, this is a police investigation. I am not here to
be questioned by anyone, and, with respect, it is not for you to
say which officers may participate in the investigation."

"I will remind you, Inspector, that you are now in my private
study."

"Would you prefer if I took you down to the garda station?"

Singer's head jerked backward as if he had been punched, but he stared ahead of him and said nothing. The police officers found seats for themselves and sat down awkwardly because uninvited.

"Well, Inspector?" Singer said tonelessly.

"I understand that Sergeant Power called on Friday to ask your help and advice about how to communicate with the profession, and indeed with the other groups of people working in the Four Courts—civil servants, service personnel, so on. In the event, Sergeant Power was very kindly received by the president of the High Court, who has been generous with his time and assistance."

Visibly nettled by this thinly veiled rebuke, Singer pressed his shoulders against the upholstered back of his elaborate desk chair. "Inspector, I have no function in respect of civil servants or domestics. On the other hand, you will kindly remember in future that the president of the High Court, though no doubt well-intentioned, has no standing where the senior branch of the legal profession, the bar, is concerned. In matters relating to the bar, you, and you personally, will deal with me, and with me personally. Is that understood?"

Lennon ignored the question and produced the Identikit picture of the young man who had been sighted by Frost and the Admiral on the day of the murder. Singer glanced perfunctorily at the picture, then took it up in his hands and looked more closely. He seemed to hesitate, and then to decide.

"Inspector, what is this about? You say that this vague caricature represents somebody who may have been seen in the courts on the day when Judge Piggott was murdered. Is that the best you can come up with after nearly a week?"

"Sir, this picture represents a serious effort to portray a young man who was seen by reliable witnesses a short time before the judge was murdered. He was actually in Judge Piggott's court, in the gallery, which I understand is very unusual. We are hoping to display copies in the Law Library and around the Four Courts in the hope that others may have seen the boy or can tell us who he is. He may have nothing to do with the killing, but we must check it out. That is how an investigation is conducted."

Singer thought for a moment, then flung the picture down scornfully. "There is no need to lecture me, Inspector. I am perfectly aware of how investigations are conducted, and I may tell you I am singularly unimpressed by this one." Singer stabbed the picture with his finger. "This thing is not serious. By all means show it to the domestics, if you wish. I will not have it in the Law Library, in barristers' chambers, or in any accommodation reserved to the senior branch of the profession. That is final.

"On a more serious point—and this is what I wanted to see you about before you went off down the country—I wish to express our grave concern about the inadequacy, indeed the sheer incompetence, of security arrangements here in the Four Courts. It is monstrous that some thug can walk right into a judge's private room and batter him to death."

"I understand what you are saying, sir, but I must point out that our branch has no responsibility for security."

"I see. You are telling me that the police do not care how many judges are murdered. Their only concern is to make little drawings afterward and organize these party games." He again stabbed the picture with his finger.

"I did not say that the police do not care. I said that our particular branch has no competence in the matter of security. Could I suggest that you speak with the Department of Justice or with the garda commissioner's office."

"I most certainly will, and to the taoiseach, about the attitude of the officers assigned to this case."

"Mr. Singer, may I ask where you were on last Tuesday afternoon, the afternoon of the murder?" Molly's voice cut like a whip through the conceited fug of Singer's study. She knew that the question was ridiculous, but she was determined not to leave without saying something to puncture the man's monumental arrogance.

Singer went white, then bright red. His mouth opened and closed as if he were a goldfish in a bowl. Lennon, taken by surprise, was just able to transpose his snort of laughter into an inoffensive death rattle.

The lawyer recovered his composure. Speaking with icy precision, he addressed himself pointedly to Lennon and not to Molly. "On Tuesday, July fourteenth, I was engaged all day in the Supreme Court. When the court rose at four o'clock, I repaired to the gallery of the Law Library for an important conference with a colleague about a case listed for the following day. Are there any further questions?"

Lennon said nothing. Molly replied loudly from almost behind Singer's studiedly averted head. "Not for the moment." She did not add *Thank you.*

The meeting ended with minimum courtesies. As the Police officers strolled back to the Four Courts to consult with Ben Silverman, Lennon exclaimed mildly, "Isn't that Singer guy something else!"

"He is an arch-shit," Molly replied vehemently.

Lennon was startled, never having heard such coarse language from her before.

Ben was in Court 4 representing a mass-circulation newspaper and a journalist who in his routinely scurrilous column had described a fashionable psychologist as a miserable quack. The fact was that journalist and psychologist were equally meretricious, hack and quack respectively. The psychologist quack, however, did not see it that way and had sued the journalist hack for substantial damages.

As Denis and Molly slipped into the last two seats in a crowded courtroom, Ben Silverman was concluding his cross-examination of "Dr." Dunphy, the plaintiff. "Let us turn, Mr. Dunphy, to your impressive degree, *M. Psych*. Presumably that means master of psychology?"

"Correct."

"And where did you acquire this estimable qualification? Vienna, perhaps, or was it Zurich?"

"In the States."

"The United States of America?"

"Yes."

"Well, don't be so coy, Mr. Dunphy. In which state of the United States of America?"

"Dakota."

"North or South?"

"North or South what?"

"Mr. Dunphy, there are two states, North Dakota and South Dakota. Is it possible that you sojourned in those parts and failed to notice?"

"North, North Dakota."

"And what was the name of your illustrious academy?"

"It was the . . . BBHU."

"The BBHU. And what, pray, does BBHU stand for?"

There was a long silence. Eventually the judge stepped in. "Come along, Dr., or Mr., Dunphy. What does BBHU stand for? It is not classified information, is it?"

"No, my lord. It stands for . . . Blue Bird Happy University."

There was an awful silence in court. Silverman, who had been addressing the witness through the back of his head, turned ponderously around and surveyed him in simulated disbelief. "Have I possibly heard you aright, Mr. Dunphy? Did you actually say Blue Bird Happy University?" He enunciated each word with withering deliberation.

"He did, Mr. Silverman," the judge snapped drily, "and you heard him perfectly."

"Mr. Dunphy, how long did you spend at Blue Bird Happy University? Four years at least, I assume, for a master's degree.

"Not quite."

"Three? Two? Come on, Mr. Dunphy. I cannot stand here peeling it off for you, a day at a time."

"I did not actually have to attend there physically, so to speak."

"Ah, you were there in spirit, so to speak. Do you mean to say that you never spent a single day in Blue Bird Happy University?"

"The system was different."

"So, indeed, it would seem. Well, what did you have to do? Did you write a thesis, a learned dissertation on some aspect of psychology?"

"Not exactly."

"Mr. Dunphy, I beseech you, reveal to us what exactly you did do to secure this prestigious degree."

"I had . . . I had to . . . fill out a questionnaire.

Silverman looked soulfully at the jury. "You had to fill out a questionnaire."

"It was a very detailed questionnaire, all about my vast experience and deep knowledge. No one but an expert could have filled it out."

Silverman went for the kill. "Listen, Dunphy, let's cut out the nonsense. How much? How much did you have to pay the Blue Bird Happy University for your master's degree?"

There was a long pause. Then: "Three hundred dollars."

Ben turned back to the jurors, who were smiling openly. "Three hundred dollars! Tell us, Mr. Dunphy, how much would a doctor's degree in psychology have cost you?"

There was another awkward pause before the witness answered. "Five hundred dollars."

Ben stared at him for several seconds in mock disbelief, then remarked lugubriously as he resumed his seat, "Rather cheeseparing, Mr. Dunphy, weren't you?"

When the court rose, Ben gladly accompanied the police officers to the restaurant for a quick coffee and a sandwich. Molly asked about "Dr." Dunphy's case.

"What will happen now?"

"I'll call no evidence and talk to the jury as soon as I can."

"Won't you put your journalist in the box?"

"Good God, no! He is a loathsome creature. I may not win the case, but he can be relied on to lose it. Five minutes of my fellah, and even Dunphy could rise from the dead."

They told Ben about their meeting with Singer. He shook his head in disapproval. "I regret to say this, but Bertie Singer as chairman of the Bar Council is the worst own goal the profession has ever inflicted on itself. In less than one year he has alienated the judiciary, the solicitors, the Northern Ireland Bar, the Department of Justice, the press, the general public, and now the police. Frankly, I do not understand it. He was never an agreeable person, but in the last few months he seems to have developed full-blown *folie des grandeurs*. The conversation you have outlined to me is not just bad, it is downright ridiculous."

Ben brought his big head closer. "Strictly between ourselves, I am increasingly of the opinion that Bertie is . . . not well." He touched his forehead. "Anyhow, listen. I must fly back to the Inquisition. Give me the pictures. I'll pass them on to the librarian. She, if anyone, is the person to decide whether they will be displayed or not. I don't doubt that she will post them everywhere. The simple fact is that Albert Singer has not the remotest shadow of authority to say what can or cannot be stuck on the walls of the Law Library, or indeed any other place. Be good, brethren, and keep me posted."

In the afternoon Lennon and Molly traveled out to Killiney by DART, the electric train serving the panoramic sweep of Dublin Bay from Howth to Greystones.

Judge Piggott's widow had reverted to her maiden name, Jenny Treacy, when she had left—or rather, ejected—him several years previously. She lived alone in a bijou bungalow with a tiny garden backing right onto the sea wall, so cosily tucked into the lea of the land as never to suffer high winds or inundations.

"Pretty and peaceful," she said, "and excellent protection against burglars. They are nearly always hydrophobic."

"Like rabid dogs," Lennon remarked. "How interesting! Perhaps that is why medieval fortresses had moats."

The widow was making no great show of bereavement. She installed the detectives in the garden by the sea and served iced fruit drinks. It was more a social visit than an investigation, as Molly said afterward.

Jenny was tall and slim, probably fifty-two or -three. She had auburn hair—her own, as a few wisps of gray demonstrated—fine green eyes, and fresh fair skin without makeup. Her clothes were casual but elegantly worn—white slacks, crimson shirt, espadrilles. She spoke simply and frankly.

Jenny had gone through the motions of the funeral, but in fact had had virtually no contact with Piggott for the previous eight or nine years. Initially, after the split-up, he had been troublesome about money, but, faced with the prospect of having his judge's salary garnisheed in her favor, he had accepted a civilized arrangement.

Jenny would probably qualify now for a judicial widow's pension, as they had never been formally divorced, but she was not worried about money. She lived simply. Her crafts shop in Dalkey was doing well. Besides, she had recently inherited a substantial sum from an old aunt to whom she had been attentive for many years in the firm belief that the poor creature was penniless.

She knew nothing, she said, of Piggott's domestic arrangements in recent times. She was unaware if he had a steady partner, but probably not, she thought. Stable relationships were not his strong point.

During the twenty years of their marriage he had been repeatedly unfaithful to her, and a poor provider, which was why she had opened her first shop in Blackrock village. He also drank quite a lot, though he could snap out of that when he wanted to, and he did build up and maintain a fairly good practice at the bar. His appointment to the bench was a political favor. Money may have changed hands directly or indirectly, she did not know, but, while she felt that Piggott would have cheerfully used any loophole to make money or avoid paying taxes, she could not imagine him misusing his position on the bench to supplement his earnings.

"He was not all bad," she said, smiling wryly.

"You have one son, I think."

"Yes, Inspector, John. I call him Johnny."

"He is in Dubai?"

Jenny looked at him sharply, then said quietly, "Kuwait. He has a good job in environmental protection."

"He did not come home for the funeral?"

"I could not contact him all last week. He was off on a camping trip or something in the desert. I only got through to him last night."

"He was upset?"

"Actually, he knew already. He heard it on RTE."

"RTE, in Kuwait?"

"Yes, he can get it most nights. It is bounced there by satellite, or rebroadcast from Ascension Island, something like that, I think." She smiled brightly.

Lennon was almost deflected by this interesting red herring. His question had not been answered. He repeated it more deliberately. "Was John upset by his father's death?"

"Not really. I don't think so." After a pause she continued. "They did not get on. Perhaps they hated each other."

"Why?"

"It is a long story, and irrelevant now. Sid's death is a liberation for Johnny, a monkey off his back. Is that a terrible thing to say?"

"It may be the truth," Molly said gently.

Jenny reflected, then seemed to decide. "I don't know what kind of son Sid wanted, if he wanted one at all. A drinking, whoring, boxing, rollicking rugger lout like himself, I suppose. Johnny is everything else—gentle, timid, no good at games, into classical music and nature studies. His father despised him from the very beginning. He never brought him places or told him things or taught him how to do this or that. He never gave him any encouragement or any little bit of confidence or self-esteem. Not that there were rows. It was just that Johnny was like a mouse, and his father literally ignored him.

"Things came to a head when Johnny was seventeen, in his last year at boarding school. He had never given that school a moment's trouble in all his years there, just as he had never as much as raised his voice at home from the day he was born." Jenny paused painfully, then went on. "Just before Easter in that last year, Johnny was expelled from school. He was expelled for . . . well, immorality with another boy. They were caught . . . You can imagine. I need not . . ."

"Of course," Molly said reassuringly. "We understand."

Jenny smiled gratefully. "To be fair to the headmaster, I think he would have found a way around it except that the other boy involved . . . well, he was only fourteen. The school couldn't wear that, I suppose."

"Not with all the stuff that has been going on these days," Molly said quietly, "like child abuse, pedophiles, so on."

"Well, this was a bit before all that got popular, I mean talked about, in this country, anyhow. The irony is—and you will say that this is the overprotective mother doing her thing—the irony is that even in that . . . relationship, the small boy was the dominant player, if that is the word, I am convinced. Johnny is no pedophile. He is just a big soft . . . In those days he had not enough confidence to initiate a game of marbles, let alone . . . something like that. Do you believe me?"

Lennon nodded. "Yes. It is possible, although I am bound to tell you that, in my experience, sex is the one area in which what people seem, and even what they are, is most often at variance with what they will actually do. How did John's father take his expulsion?"

Jenny's face whitened. "I was away in Galway visiting my mother. It was before Sid became a judge. They rang him at the Law Library to come and take Johnny away. He drove down that same afternoon and brought Johnny home. In the car Johnny tried to talk to his father, to explain, to apologize, to God knows what, to ask for some crumb of advice or understanding. Not one word, not a single word from his father. He dropped him at our house. We were living in Monkstown at the time. He left Johnny in an empty house and went out drinking for several hours."

Jenny was dabbing her eyes with a handkerchief, crying soundlessly. "He came back near midnight, dragged his son out of bed, and beat him within an inch of his life. It was horrible. I got back the next afternoon, knowing nothing. Johnny was in the kitchen trying to get some food. He had not eaten in nearly two days. He was almost naked, black and blue from head to toe, as his father had left him, cut, bruised. I cannot describe it. His face was so swollen, I could barely recognize him.

"I should have called a doctor. I was afraid. Any doctor worth his salt would have gone straight to the police. Not that I cared a damn about Sid, or about what the neighbors would say. With Sid's incessant womanizing, I was well used to wagging tongues. I just felt that it was more than Johnny could take—to have to tell all that to the police, the circumstances of his expulsion from school, what his own father had done to him, and then seeing all that in the newspapers. It would have broken him.

"A friend of mine, a nurse, helped me. She even had to give him stitches, which I don't think they are meant to do. He was not right for weeks afterward, I mean physically. Psychologically, in his soul, will he ever recover?"

Lennon was looking at her intently. But he did not reply.

"Anyhow, after that, I got Johnny into one of those grind schools. It was only a few weeks to his leaving certificate. He got some sort of result, not much, nothing like he would have got if he had stayed on in school, because he was a great little worker.

"His father was rarely in the house at that time. He was having one of his sordid affairs. When he was there, he just ignored Johnny completely. He never gave him a penny piece. Any pocket money the poor waif got was from me. If Sid did refer to him at all, he never even called him by his name: it was always 'the queer' or 'the ponce,' even in front of Johnny's own friends. The little fellow who was expelled with Johnny used to call around to the house quite a lot. I didn't think it was a great idea for either of them, but I wouldn't dream of saying anything. He was a sweet little chap, actually—very lost, I felt.

"One day Sid arrived when the boy was there. Well, he ran him out of the house with every filthy name—fruit-sucker, fairy, dirty ponce, worse things I could not repeat. If you saw the faces of those children—and for God's sake, that is all they were—the hurt, the fear, the humiliation. How could anyone treat them like that!

"After a year or so Johnny just left, first to London, then Dubai, Kuwait now. It was after that that I finally threw Sidney out. I could forgive or at least ignore all the rest, but not what he did to Johnny, his own, our own flesh and blood."

"Was your husband violent with you?" Molly asked.

Jenny smiled. "He tried it just once, very early in our marriage."

"What happened?"

"I broke his arm." There was a moment of shocked silence. Then all three burst out laughing. "You see, I used to teach gym before I was married. I know a few things. Like all bullies, once you stand up to them, Sid never tried it again. Perhaps if Johnny had hit him back that night, things might have been different now. Sid might still be alive."

Denis and Molly exchanged glances.

Jenny smiled sadly and shook her head. "Oh no, Inspector, I don't mean it like that. Johnny is the least vindictive person on earth." She looked from one police officer to the other. "You hardly think that after all these years Johnny suddenly disappeared into the desert, sneaked home, kicked his father to death, then fled back to Kuwait. You surely don't think that, do you?"

"At this stage I don't think anything," Denis said, "But, to be frank, you have just given an excellent outline of one possible scenario. Incidentally, what makes you say that your husband was kicked to death? Was that in the newspapers?"

"Did I say that? It is just an expression. Anyhow, the whole idea is just too fatuous. Johnny could not kill a flea. That was another of his father's sneers. Johnny would not even shoot or fish."

As they stood to leave, Lennon asked if he might have a photograph of Johnny. Jenny said nothing but went into the house to fetch one. It showed a tall young man with dark brown hair already receding at the temples. He had one plump arm around the shoulder of a petite red-haired girl.

"Recent?"

"Last Christmas. That is Sophie, a lovely girl, Norwegian. He arrived with her in tow."

"Is Johnny not still . . . gay?"

"I don't believe he ever was, Inspector. I can tell you, we had rows at Christmas about who sleeps where."

"Ah yes, it happens all the time these days." Lennon shook his head philosophically.

"Johnny won. Anyhow, I have only two bedrooms in this house, and I am not having anybody sleeping in the drawing room—even for the sake of morality."

As they walked to the DART station, Molly said, "What about Johnny? It could be Johnny, couldn't it?"

"It could. The Arabian desert is a vague enough sort of alibi."

"His photo does not look at all like the fair-haired boy seen by Frost and the Admiral."

"True, but that boy may be a red herring. We are following him up because we have not much else. There is another possibility, however, a long shot perhaps. Suppose for a moment that Mummy gave us a photo of her favorite nephew, not of darling Johnny."

"Denis, that is totally far-fetched. She does not even know that we have a description of another boy.

"People do far-fetched things. Murder, for instance, is fairly far-fetched. And Jenny is a highly intelligent woman. When we ask for a photograph, she knows, she must know, that we have a particular face in mind. She can work it out that somebody has probably seen the killer. Get Saunders to check this photograph against Johnny's mug shot in the passport office. There is another possibility, of course. What about Mummy?"

"Jenny!" Molly exclaimed.

"She has all the same motives as Johnny, even more. Also, as she herself says, she knows a few things. She used to teach gym. She can break arms. An occasional broken neck might not be too far out of her line. No?"

"You have a diseased mind, Denis."

"Thank you, Molly. That is what they pay me for."

TUESDAY, JULY 21

INSPECTOR DESMOND TWEEDY GLARED WRATHFULLY around him. He had arrived at Lennon's request to do a sweep of the public gallery in the late Judge Piggott's courtroom, only to find that the Board of Works had got there before him. It was axiomatic in Tweedy's branch of the service that he, the great ringmaster and impresario of technical experts, had *droit de seigneur* at all sites of interest to the gardai. Nobody, but nobody, should get there before Tweedy. He therefore contemplated the scaffolding that encumbered the well of Courtroom 2 with the vehement indignation of Daddy Bear discovering predators at work on his porridge.

The Board of Works, quite reasonably assuming that Piggott's successor would not be appointed until after the long vacation, there being no point in paying someone for two months of doing nothing, had moved into Courtroom 2 with paintbrushes, ladders, and buckets. It was an opportunity to make an early start on a long list of repairs and decorations to be effected in the courts during the holidays.

The place reeked with dust, paint, and cigarette smoke. While the gallery itself had probably not been entered since the day Piggott died, Tweedy had grave doubts about the evidential value of anything he might collect there now. The risk of contamination by the environmentally licentious activities of the Board of Works was all too obvious. Tweedy would say so in his report, vigorously. Meanwhile he drove painters and plasterers from the temple with knotted whips of abuse and vituperation. They left uncomplainingly and promptly went home for a day off on full pay.

At the ferry port in Rosslare, Jim Quilligan identified the Roundstones by simply hanging around the check-in kiosk until their car arrived. He had their registration number. As his own journey would be pointless unless the Roundstones traveled, he waited to see them safely embarked, then joined the happy backpackers and boarded on foot himself.

An hour after sailing, Quilligan slipped into a sofa seat opposite the Roundstones in the Mermaid Lounge. There, ensconced behind a newspaper and a pint of black stuff, he observed and listened to connubial conversation mere feet away across a low table.

An idiosyncratic observer of people, Quilligan was not much interested in accumulating details. He gave more credence to subcutaneous vibes. At the outset he could have an intuition about a person or people, an outrageous intuition perhaps, but one that remained with him obstinately throughout an investigation. And these private revelations were rarely proved wholly wrong in the end.

So, before he had twice blanched his salt-and-pepper mustache in the creamy collar of his pint, Quilligan knew with psychedelic certainty that Isabelle Roundstone was a crocodile and that Felix was her egg. He had no doubt, either, about which came first: the crocodile, not the egg.

Felix was an unprepossessing little man. Everything about him was narrow—head, eyes, mouth, chest, thighs, toes. His narrow, pointed egg-skull poked up from a nest of tarnished ginger hair. The rest of him seemed like an afterthought.

Isa Roundstone, on the other hand, was a not unattractive woman. Well proportioned and smartly dressed in a bottle-green trouser suit, she had, for her age, plenty of sex appeal of a rather menacing kind. As befits a crocodile, she had a voluptuous mouth and lots of teeth. The inspector fantasized briefly about whips, leather, and, in best operatic tradition, death at dawn for not being able to solve the riddle.

They were drinking kirs, not proper kirs like the good Chanoine Kir would have drunk, dry white wine and cassis, but the shameful vulgarity styled "kir royal." What next, Quilligan the tinker asked himself, green-plastic-bottled champagne in all the flavors of toothpaste?

Desultory and dull, the Roundstone conversation reflected little credit on the convivial properties of their tipple. Felix's proposal to take the Coast Road from Cherbourg was vetoed by the crocodile.

"No. We shall go the way we know. We don't want any unforeseen adventures."

This last remark caused Quilligan to snort uncontrollably into his beer with disastrous consequences. He had to apologize and mop up half the table with his handkerchief.

Later Felix said, "I'm still sad about Sid."

Quilligan was sad about the limp alliteration. Isabelle was not sad about anything, not even to the point of crocodile tears.

"Sad!" she exclaimed. "We are heading into the black for the first time in ten years. Just remember that. No omelet if you don't break the eggs."

A fascinating variation on the crocodile-and-egg motif, Quilligan thought. What exactly did it mean? If getting money for a painting was the omelet, was killing Piggott the breaking of the eggs? He could imagine rival counsel urging a jury to interpret these enigmas one way and another. A nice bone for Denis to chew on. Glancing at his watch, he finished his drink and stood up. Time for action. He bowed decorously to the Roundstones and sea-rolled toward the door.

The purser smiled pleasantly when Quilligan introduced himself.

"Telepathy, Inspector. I was about to call you on the PA."

"Don't do that, I beg. There are people on board who must not know that I am here."

"Won't they see you? You are certainly big enough, if I may say so."

"That does not matter. They don't know me by sight, but they almost certainly know my name and what I do."

"Dear me, and what do you do? State secret, I suppose. Never mind. The French police have just been on, requesting that we get you ashore tomorrow before any cars roll off in Cherbourg."

"Splendid. Can you do it?"

"No problem. Just come here about ten minutes before we dock. I'll take you down myself."

"Thank you indeed. I am most grateful. Meanwhile, I wonder could you help me, shall we say, more immediately?"

"Certainly, if I can. What is the problem?"

"There are people on board called Roundstone. I need to get into their cabin."

"Oh?"

"Yes, I have to steal something."

"I beg your pardon."

"I said I have to steal something."

The purser looked closely at Quilligan. There was an unmistakable aroma of beer. "That is what I thought you said. And what is it that you want to, er, steal?"

"I don't know yet, something valuable, money perhaps, jewelery. Preferably something I can put in my pocket. After all, we don't want to be caught coming away with some unwieldy object, do we?"

"I am sure we don't," the purser replied faintly. He continued more resolutely. "Inspector, this is a highly unusual request. I am not at all happy, frankly, about my own position . . . I mean . . ."

"Relax, my dear man. You see, I am really very good at this sort of thing."

"I don't doubt your competence, Inspector. The problem lies elsewhere." Quilligan smiled encouragingly. "I promise you, the Roundstones will have their property back before we reach Cherbourg. Let me explain myself. May I sit down?"

"Please do." The purser pointed to a chair.

"You give me a key. I steal something valuable from the Roundstone cabin while they are stuffing their faces in the restaurant. As soon as they discover their loss, they will be down here like avenging angels."

"Thank you. That is precisely the problem."

"But, sir, that will be your finest hour! Listen, this is what I want you to do . . ."

Twenty minutes later the purser was alternately shaking his head in disbelief and nodding it in brave assent. He punched his computer a few times.

"Roundstone. Here we are. Cabin 59, C deck, aft. It is a four-berth, but they have it to themselves." He found a key. "Here. This will open any cabin in the whole bleeding ship. I might as well be hung for a sheep as a lamb.

"Now, you listen to me for a while. Thirty seconds after the Roundstones have been in here, and I have done my thing, there will be a call over the PA for, let's say, Miss Potts, seeing you don't want your own name publicized. So you are Miss Potts. If you are

not down here within a further thirty seconds together with whatever it is that you have stolen, I am going to radio for the entire
army, navy, and air force. Agreed?"

Quilligan flung a hand across his heart, winked, and added a
thumbs-up. He had reached the door when the purser exclaimed,
"Heavens, how do I know that you really are a policeman? I never
even asked you for identification."

"Purser, Purser, don't let your nerves undermine you like this!
Anyhow, I never carry identification. It gets all sweaty limp in my
pocket, you know how it is. Just trust my honest face." He winked
again and was gone.

"Jesus," said the purser.

It was the biggest album he could get. It might have to be big. He
had selected five cuttings. Three of them had banner headlines
that had to be folded over to fit the album. He opened them out
again carefuly and read.

Four Courts Horror
Judge Slain in Courts
Judge Battered to Death

The first two were alright, he supposed; the third was melodramatic and untrue. He knew that he had never "battered" anyone in his whole life.

But why was this life of his always so strange and so difficult?
What was that thing in Shakespeare? *O cursed spite, that ever I was
born to put things right:* It went something like that. Was that what
he had to do on the face of the earth, put things right? It was not
about revenge: It was about putting things right. Piggott certainly
needed to be put right. Well, he had done it, hadn't he?

The boy stood up and stretched. He went over and lay on the bed, long fingers entwined in golden hair behind his head. Was it a kick? He could not remember. Probably a kick, quick and painless. It could have been a hand-slice, of course, especially as he wasn't very fit just now. You have to be fit for a kick.

He hoped the judge would understand, wherever he was. Blood is thicker than water, true, but judges are meant to understand justice. "May God have mercy on your soul." Isn't that what judges themselves say when they condemn people to death? He hoped that God would have mercy on all their souls.

What next? There was the priest. Would he have to die? And the psychiatrist? And his mother? *People of the Lie.* That was the name of a book. He hadn't read it, but he had seen it in bookshops. That is what they were, all of them, people of the lie, full of wrong answers. Perhaps everybody is. Their wrong answers and their lies had made him suffer, together with his own lies, to be fair, and his own wrong answers. Making other people suffer is wrong, but it wasn't wrong just because they made *him* suffer—who was he, after all? It was just wrong anyhow. *That* was why he had to *set things right.* It wasn't a bit easy doing that: it was *cursed spite.*

That must be why he couldn't remember these things very well, the *cursed spite* and the *putting things right* he had to do. The mind suppresses unpleasant memories. The shrink had told him that.

Then there was the lawyer. What about him? He rolled off the bed and went to the window. There he was, the lawyer, putting shit on his roses. He would freak if he knew. He had been furious the day the boy went to suss out the Four Courts, even though he had actually encouraged him to go there another day. For such a brainy guy he was pretty inconsistent. He was dead scared, too, for his own reputation. He was consistent about that alright. But the lawyer was no fool. How long before he copped on? And then what? Would he have to kill him?

He liked it here, freedom to come and go—not that he went out much, a nice room, good food, and work he was good at. The old boy was generous with money and presents. He would talk to him nicely and advise him. Also, to be fair, he wasn't too demanding. For the moment the boy could manage him. Jesus, he had only to finger the top button of his shirt for the stupid faggot to go weak at the knees. But later? Realistically . . .

He turned away from the window and looked at himself in the wardrobe mirror. He went close, face to face, eye to eye. His four lips opened, fogging the glass. "Did you really kill him," he whispered. "Did you? Tell me you did. Tell me you didn't. Did you imagine it? Tell me."

But there was no sound.

"Of course not," he said.

"Of course not what?" he replied.

At 9:10 P.M. precisely Felix and Isabelle arrived clamorously at the purser's office. Monstrous and unbelievable! They had been pillaged and plundered whilst ingurgitating their frugal sufficiency of seafood, rack of lamb, Limerick ham, four vegetables, three salads, five cheeses, assorted desserts, Riesling, claret, and Irish coffee.

Felix's dome fairly glistened with good food, Dutch courage, and indignation, while Isabelle spat poison like a hooded cobra.

The purser got to the dreaded bottom line as quickly as possible: What had the wretch actually taken? The answer was two thousand euro in a red wallet that had been nestling under Felix's pillow.

Sweating copiously, the purser went through his normal patter in such cases: Were they sure that they had searched properly? Were they quite certain that they had indeed left the red wallet in that exact place? Perhaps Isa had stuffed it down her bodice or Felix wherever? The locks were terribly sophisticated. Nobody could possibly have broken in. The stewardesses? Oh *no!* Unthinkable. Sweet girls, all of them, who had been with the line for years.

"Don't give me that," Isa screamed. "Student hussies on holiday jobs. You don't know the first thing about them. Deceitful, two-faced minxes, sleeping around, on drugs, all of them, beer and vodka coming out their—"

"Please, please," the purser begged, holding up suppliant hands. Having exhausted his own habitual lines, to poor effect, he set himself to cope with Quilligan's libretto. "This is a very serious matter. I am determined to get to the bottom of it. I assure you that you will have your property back within twenty-four hours—even sooner."

"This is more like it," Isabelle said, mollified. "But in twenty-four hours we could be hundreds of miles away."

"Wherever you may be, it will be our responsibility to bring you your money. We shall send a special courier. On the basis of experience I would say that your property will be found about two hours after we dock. Once we clear the ship of passengers we will search everywhere and all crew members. That is how these things are done."

"Good. But we cannot hang about, even for two hours. We have an urgent appointment to keep in Saint Germain-en-Laye."

"Just outside Paris. Perfect. Can you give me an address and telephone number? I am confident that by the time you get that far I shall have good news for you. I shall telephone and we can make a suitable arrangement."

Isabelle and Felix exchanged glances. The crocodile replied.

"Excellent. We shall be at the Galerie Ménard, Rue du Conseil des Anciens. Here, let me write it down for you, and the telephone number."

Quilligan was examining duty-free merchandise when Miss Potts was called on the loudspeaker.

"That's me, I'm afraid," he said to the young lady who had been assisting his selection.

"I must fly."

"Jesus, Mary, and Joseph," she gasped as she tidied away the lingerie, "and I thought it was for his wife."

"Galerie Ménard, Saint-Germain. Wonderful. Exactly what I need to know. And look, you even have the telephone number. You are a marvel. To think that they told us all that themselves! Never despair of people, dear purser. There is always a way to their hearts."

"The wallet," said the purser, holding out his hand.

"What wallet?" Quilligan asked innocently. Then, as the purser's mouth fell open, he took it from his pocket and handed it over. "I am very grateful. What about a drink?"

"I can't. Strict dry ship for crew on duty. Slung from the yardarm if caught infringing. But it has been fun. Can we meet sometime on dry land, and you can tell me the full story?"

"I'd love to. Here is my number." He scribbled it. "Now call poor Felix. Tell him that he left his wallet in the loo."

"Tell lies, is it? Certainly not!" The purser threw the wallet on the floor and picked it up again. "I shall tell him that somebody found it on the floor somewhere around the ship—somebody who does not want a reward. Or do you?"

"Don't bother about that bit, Purser. That pair would not give you the steam off their piss."

As Quilligan reached the door, it was thrust open in his face by a formidable old lady. Large and barefoot, she was draped in a voluminous sari, her hair in curlers under a massive net.

"Are you the purser?" she inquired belligerently, flicking ash from her cheroot.

"No, ma'am," Quilligan replied, adding with indecent helpfulness, "there he is over there."

She sailed past. "Well, Purser fellow, what is it?"

"I beg your pardon?"

"I am Miss Potts, Miss Prudence Potts."

"O Jesus," said the purser for the second time that evening.

Miss Pseudo-Potts-Quilligan fled the field.

WEDNESDAY, JULY 22

JIM QUILLIGAN HAD MET CLAUDE RONSARD FOR THE
first time two years previously in Florence at an Interpol conference about art robberies. Ronsard was a Breton, and the two
Celts had soon become friends. They shared humor, fantasy, and
the valuable corrective of common sense. Five months later they
met again in the context of a Community-wide drive to smash a
syndicate that seemed to be dealing in stolen antiques. The antiques turned out to be fake, but the heroin inside them was perfectly genuine and of high quality. For a few days during that
investigation Quilligan had stayed with the Ronsards at Pontoise.

The following summer, Claude and Véronique Ronsard, with
their two delightful children, had spent ten days with Jim and
Ann Quilligan and their three slightly older children at the Quilligan holiday home on the Dingle Peninsula. It was a wonderful
success, except for the evening when Ann had produced a pig's
head for dinner. This was a handsome pig's head, as pigs' heads
go, with elegant whiskers and a pretty pink tongue that lolled out
good-naturedly between slightly parted teeth into the dish-gravy.
Shrieks of horror and alarm from the French!

There ensued several days of frankly racist insult. The French
children ran around making violent vomiting noises and squealing,

"Peeg's 'ead! *Aaaah!* Peeg's 'ead!" The young Quilligans retaliated with equally disgusting retching sounds and cries of *"Schnails! Ughghg! Frogs' arses!"* Both recitals had to be outlawed eventually by the mutually embarrassed adults.

Ronsard was a small, thickset man in his midforties who smoked those horrible Gauloises cigarettes rolled in brown toilet paper. His highly colored, homely face, under close-cropped black hair, bore witness to seafaring origins. He spoke excellent if highly accented English and, since his Kerry holiday, even some smattering of Irish, greeting Quilligan with a creditable *Dia dhuit* and the inevitable *Céad mílle fáilte.*

An unmarked police car complete with driver was parked literally at the water's edge. As they drove away Quilligan explained that he knew where they were going, to the Galerie Ménard in Saint-Germain-en-Laye.

"Chouette," said Ronsard, "I hate tailing people. It is so boring, and tense at the same time, because you can lose them in a split second." He was silent for a moment, then said, "We are in luck, Jim. Guy Ménard is a reputable dealer. He will cooperate. In fact, I feel like giving him a ring, to find out what the score is. What do you think?"

"Yes, perhaps. You know your man. Can we trust him? Could he not be in on the fiddle?"

"It depends on what the fiddle is. These dealers have their own morality. Buying stolen property—how do you say?—doing the fence. Guy will not do the fence. For that he is honest. But tax-dodging, export licenses, all those red tapes"—Ronsard raised his arms as if to soar above such trivialities—*"il s'en fiche pas mal.* Indeed, when a foreign dealer comes to him like this, he probably assumes that there is some little story in the background. But you know, Jim, the international art market is highly competitive. If dealers are too scrupulous the business just goes somewhere else,

New York, Geneva, London. So for all these little red tapes French dealers look the other way, and, as they know well, so do the French authorities. Art dealing is like the arms trade. As Molière says, one must be *sage avec sobriété,* wise or good in moderation. So, yes, in answer to your question, I think we can trust Monsieur Ménard, in moderation."

Quilligan laughed. "Fine. Let's call him up. I even have his telephone number." He gave a colorful account of how he had acquired it. Ronsard laughed uproariously and translated the whole saga into French for the driver, who struck the steering-wheel several times with cries of *merde alors!* which apparently in his lexicon served equally well for accolade and for excoriation.

There followed several minutes of rapid French on a cell phone, which Quilligan could not understand. Eventually Ronsard clicked off. "Guy is not there. That was his son, Maurice, also in the trade. He says yes, they are expecting the Round-stones this afternoon about 3:30 P.M. with a valuable painting, Dutch—which seems to confirm your information. A tentative price has been fixed on the basis of photographs. He does not know how much, or would not say, perhaps. No money will change hands until Nick Benson examines the picture next week and gives the OK. That figures, too, with your Honthorst. Benson is the editor of *The Burlington* magazine, and probably the leading authority on Baroque painting. *Enfin,* I told Maurice to tell Papa of our interest, to be most discreet, and to expect us by three o'clock."

They stopped for a quick lunch at a pleasant restaurant terrace outside Mantes-la-Jolie.

"No pig's head," Ronsard said apologetically.

"Oh well," Quilligan replied, "I'll have to settle for what my poor children call 'schnails.'"

In fact they both had pancakes and cider, cheese, and delicious *glaces maison.* The driver meanwhile stayed at the counter lunching on the nearest thing to pure absinthe still legally available in France.

Guy Ménard was a genial colossus of a man, gigantic and gentle. A prodigious crash barrier of bushy eyebrows held back riots of chaotic graying hair from engulfing his massive red cheese of a face, which puckered all over with intelligence and humor.

"Inspectors, welcome," he rumbled, leading them through his spacious salesroom, where Quilligan caught fleeting glances of satin-lined salmon-colored walls, gilt frames, and state-of-the-art lighting. There were relatively few pictures displayed, each one in its own enchanted space, so that older and modern pieces could cohabit without clashing. What they had in common, Quilligan knew, was to be unbelievably expensive. Turnover here was probably sluggardly, but seismic when it happened.

As he passed through the door to Ménard's office, Quilligan glimpsed a solitary female customer in a secluded side chapel. Austerely seated on a hard upright chair, she was examining through a lorgnette the peaches-and-cream bottoms of some up-ended putti who put-putted about the sidelines of a Baroque apotheosis.

Monsieur Ménard's room behind the gallery was a high handsome space tastefully and solidly furnished in proportion to its occupant's culture and bulk. Glass doors gave onto a quiet courtyard with access to the street through an archway.

"The picture will arrive by this way. We shall put it here on the easel for the moment while we talk. When the Roundstones have left we shall bring it to the upper floor in the high-security lift. There is no other access to the upstairs. It is robberproof, you see. Even the windows to the rear are blanked off upstairs."

Quilligan was both relieved and impressed by his excellent if occasionally curious English.

"So, Inspectors, expose to me your little affairs."

Quilligan embarked on a colorful yet concise account of Piggott's dubious acquisition of the picture, his violent death, and the suspicion that the Roundstones might be party to either or both of these transactions.

Ménard shook his great Medusan locks, pushing out fat lips like a tender for kisses. "This is probably the fifth or sixth time that Madame Roundstone has come to sell me something for Monsieur Piggott. I have never had direct dealings with him. My impression was that he was a collector who was gradually and discreetly disposing of his pictures. One felt that there were perhaps reasons for this of a delicate nature. This could be anything, you know, a lady friend to be maintained appropriately, gambling debts, the systematic dispersal of a heritage to avoid crushing death duties for one's heirs, *des problèmes fiscaux.* The French authorities turn the blinded eye to that one, if it concerns a foreign jurisdiction, I mean. Is it not so, Claude?"

"I would not know," Ronsard replied innocently, looking at the ceiling.

"*Tartufe!* Anyway, I never dreamed of anything criminal, and certainly not murder."

Monsieur Ménard began to bestir himself about some idea of setting up a security camera and sound system so that the police could observe and even record the delivery of the picture from the burglarproof Aladdin's cave upstairs. The sudden appearance of the Roundstone Peugeot through the archway into the courtyard put paid to that project. As Felix maneuverd smoothly towards the glass doors, Quilligan and Ronsard were rather less smoothly bundled into the lift and dispatched to the upper floor.

For forty minutes Ronsard took siesta on a comfortable leather couch. Quilligan meanwhile surveyed the several pictures that were accessibly positioned for viewing in the great open space that comprised the entire upper floor. There were many more pictures in crates, on shelves, or propped heavily facing inward to the walls. He was pleased to discover that for most of those he could see he was able to suggest at least a "school of" attribution. In a few cases, a Boudin beach scene and a wild Géricault horse, he might even have ventured a few euro on his judgment.

There were a few Oriental pictures of which he could make nothing. He smiled ruefully at the thought that a theft from the Chester Beatty Collection, now housed so near Lennon's office in Dublin Castle, would leave him as flummoxed about provenance and value as the fruit-sellers in Moore Street.

The lift doors slid open. Ménard appeared. "*Alors,* we have finished. What now? Do I let them depart, or do you come down to arrest them?"

"Nothing like that, Guy," Ronsard answered, swinging his stockinged feet to the floor. "Jim wants an Irish solution to an Irish problem."

"No money changes hands today?" Quilligan asked.

"No. We have agreed a price, but nothing happens until Monsieur Benson gives his approval."

"You can let them off so."

Ten minutes later Quilligan and Ronsard were sitting with Ménard in his office, sipping pastis and gazing at the picture on its easel before them. Perhaps five feet by three and a half, it was dark and dirty, but Quilligan had no doubt, it was a magnificent painting. Besides, he recognized it immediately. Stolen two years previously from a rectory in Mallow, County Cork, where it had presided over a succession of parsons' families, it had no reliable pedigree and had been known simply as "the painting." When it had been stolen, the only photograph available was one taken at a children's party in the rectory. There in the background, off center and partially obscured by romping children and a Christmas tree, enough of the picture could be seen for identification. Quilligan remembered it clearly from his files. "What is it, Monsieur Ménard?" he asked.

Ménard dispatched a backhoe arm toward a desk drawer from which he scooped up a file. From this he took some sheets of paper. "This is Monsieur Benson's report. It is provisional of course, being based purely on photographs of the painting, but he is very reliable, the best there is. Normally, he will not have to change his opinion when he sees the original. Gaze at the picture before you, messieurs, whilst I make to you a reading of the report."

The art dealer began to read in solemn and mellifluous accents.

Physical Condition: This is an oil painting on strong herringbone-weave canvas typical of Roman studios of the early seventeenth century. Surprisingly for its age, it has never been relined, nor, in so far as I can judge from photographs, has the painting itself ever been restored.

There is paint loss, especially in the lower left corner. The painting is also very dirty and has been subjected to several imprudent coats of heavy varnish. All of this is reversible. Essentially the picture is in remarkably good condition and will respond very well to appropriate conservation work.

Subject: A night scene. A vigorous elderly man stands knocking urgently at the street door of a town dwelling. Through a wide lattice we see a maidservant holding a lantern. Instead of opening the door, she is turning away toward a secondary focus of light behind her, eager no doubt to tell people in the house of the newcomer's arrival. It seems probable that the scene depicted is the arrival of St. Peter at the house of Mary, mother of John Mark (Acts of the Apostles 12:12).

Provenance: Physically, stylistically, and thematically, this picture belongs to the entourage of Caravaggio. It is Roman and was probably painted in or around 1615. Subject to a close examination of the original, with particular attention to the brushwork, I would be reasonably certain that this is the work of Gerrit van Honthorst (G. della Notte) who was certainly active in Rome at this period. Comparison with known works by this artist yields numerous similarities, e.g.: the night encounter—dramatic but not melodramatic; masterly use of light and darkness; two foci of light, one dominant, the other subsidiary. It can be noted also that the same models, man and woman, appear frequently in other works by this master.

Valuation: Paintings by this artist rarely come on the market, as the known oeuvre is nearly all in public collections. The few pictures of this artist I know to have changed hands in recent years have all been sold by private treaty and for undisclosed prices. Having regard, however, to the painterly quality of this picture and its excellent condition, and considering also the keen interest currently being shown in painters of the Utrecht School (e.g. Adam De Coster), I would expect a price in the region of 800,000 euro. Possibly more.

Quilligan whistled softly. "Did the Roundstones see this report? Did Piggott?"

"Neither. This is how things happened, how they always happen. The Roundstones contacted me about a year ago to say that Monsieur Piggott desired to sell another picture. As always, they enclosed several detailed photographs, color and black-and-white, front and back—I mean the picture, but also the canvas backside and its stretchers. I knew at once that it was an exceptionally fine painting, post-Caravaggio and pre-Rembrandt. I sent all the photographs to Nick Benson, whose report you have just heard. I informed the Roundstones in due course that, following research, and always subject to seeing the picture itself, I was satisfied that they had a fine painting by della Notte. I made them an offer of two hundred thousand. What they did or did not tell Piggott I do not know. As agents they should have told him everything. Their appropriate commission should be five percent, ten percent at the very most.

"You stand to make six hundred thousand yourself?" Quilligan asked with brutal directness.

"Possibly," Ménard replied with equanimity. "I have a customer who will be very interested in this painting. I am not acting as agent for Monsieur Piggott or for the Roundstones. I am a dealer. I make a serious offer. They are free to go elsewhere if they think they can do better."

"They could go to auction."

"They could, but they won't. At auction the dealers would form a ring and snatch the picture for a fraction of its value. The Roundstones know that perfectly well. They are dealers themselves, don't forget."

"So they stand to get two hundred thousand euro."

"Well, we bargained a little. To get rid of them quickly I increased it to two hundred and twenty."

"Very generous of you."

"Not really, when I knew perfectly well that, with you people on their tail, they will probably end up getting nothing. They accepted, of course. The cash is supposed to be paid into a numbered account on the Grand Turk."

"Who or where is that?"

"In the Caribbean, north of Haiti. Our previous arrangement had always been that thirty percent was paid into the Caribbean account and seventy percent into Piggott's named account in Jersey. Until today I had always believed that both accounts belonged to the judge. Today they let slip that the Grand Turk account is, in fact, their own. So they have been helping themselves to thirty percent every single time. And now, this time, nothing for Jersey and a hundred percent for the Grand Turk. Winner takes all."

"How did they explain that?"

"They told me that Piggott had sold them the picture, that he needed money urgently. They did not bother to mention that the poor man is dead. I would still not know that if you two had not just looked in."

"Such a pair," Ronsard exclaimed. "Still, it does not prove that they actually murdered Piggott."

"Whoever did," Quilligan retorted, "certainly did them an enormous favor."

Monsieur Ménard went around again with his bottle of pastis and the conversation turned to the heroic virtues of French food and drink.

As he was seeing them to their car, Ménard said to Quilligan, "Very nice to meet you, Inspector. You might tell the pastor of Mallow that I am looking after his picture for him. Perhaps if he were thinking of renovating his temple or maybe putting in the central heating, I could make him a very attractive offer."

Quilligan chuckled. "Well, do you know what? I'll tell him that, surely, and he may well take you up on it. He could have sold that picture for a few thousand pounds to a fellow like myself. He will be pure ecstatic with the sort of money you are talking about. Besides, it is always difficult for religious people to be selling works of art outside the country. The newspapers black-guard them about it. But now that the picture is safe and sound outside Ireland, wouldn't it only be tempting Providence to bring it back in again?"

"Ah!" cried Ménard, clasping Quilligan to his ample breast in a high tackle that would have suffocated a lesser man. *"Vous autres Irlandais, votre logique est adorable!"*

Tinkers' horses again!

Father Tommy Meagher struck the steering wheel in exaspera-tion. He even swore under his breath. Of course, he should not swear, and he should not say "tinkers" when he meant itinerant people, who had plenty of troubles of their own. Most of them, he knew, were decent honest folk who did no harm to anyone. In-deed, he himself had often preached against the hard-hearted churlishness of the settled community toward these homeless people.

In the present case, Father Tommy realized, the real culprit was his own well-intentioned confrere, Father Clarence Mild. Father Mild, a totally impractical idealist, had established a four-acre paddock for the itinerants on their religious community's land down near the Dublin road. Here, the idea was, the wander-ing folk would be welcome to halt for a few days in their unend-ing peregrinations. Water was laid on, basic sewerage, and some other rudimentary facilities.

A commendable idea, but one needing not only implementation but also ongoing management. Father Mild had implemented and then returned to his seventh heaven of mystical contemplation. He made no serious attempt to supervise the halting site or to impose some sort of discipline. The site was small and regularly over-crowded. Inevitably some of the visitors misbehaved. There were constant complaints about thieving, fighting, and drunkenness, exaggerated, no doubt, as always happens when no effort is made to deal with the few genuine incidents that do occur.

The local farmers were anything but enthusiastic about the Holy Family Halting Site, and were nothing comforted when legitimate complaints were received with homiletic references to the hardhearted innkeepers of Bethlehem. The scriptural allusion was not only insulting, it was also counterproductive, reminding the stout farmers of the midlands that, if they did not particularly relish seeing "tinkers" in their local pubs by day, they absolutely hated like hell finding them in their stables in the middle of the night. Father Mild, a city man who understood nothing of the peasant id, would merely shake his head sadly and resolve to pray more earnestly for this "stiff-necked people."

Father Meagher's principal complaint, which he shared with most of the farmers, concerned the horses. These wild piebald animals, which accompany the itinerants everywhere, were a constant cause of grief and frustration. There could be any number from one or two to a dozen with each family of travelers. Having no pasture lands of their own, the itinerants left these animals loose to graze the long acre, as the grass to either side of the highway is called in rural Ireland.

At nighttime, too often, the horses would find their way or be driven into farmers' fields, where they would have hours of fine feeding before the enraged farmers found them and drove them off in the morning. Father Meagher had no doubt that these horses had been repeatedly driven over the cattle grid at the entrance to his community's back avenue and left to wander and fodder themselves as whim or horse sense might guide them. The avenue was a mile long. It led through forestry to the community residence and secondary boarding school. These buildings were surrounded by well-laid-out grounds and formal gardens. Here on several occasions the wild horses had wreaked havoc.

An even greater sacrilege from Father Tommy's point of view was the repeated desecration of the nine-hole golf course that he had slaved to create behind the school. An invaluable asset for the community, schoolboys, and local people, it even made a little money during the summer months from tourists. On one terrible night the first and eighth greens had suffered hoof damage so appalling that even a year later the scars had not completely healed.

It was five o'clock in the afternoon. Father Meagher was due in Roscrea an hour later for a meeting. He would just have time to evict the intruders, provided that they stayed on the avenue and allowed themselves to be shunted backward. If they veered off into the forestry he could be chasing them for hours. He slewed his car across the width of the avenue to make a barrier and got out, brandishing a golf club.

There were five animals, mad, wild, and frisky, the lot of them. The leader of the pack was a great wicked stallion, hands high, unusually massive for the breed. He disputed every yard of the retreat, pawing the ground, tossing his rebellious head, baring angry teeth, swivelling sideways to the priest, never quitting him with his glaring malignant eye, gauging the moment when his enemy would step that cat's whisker too close, that demisemiquaver between time and eternity.

They had progressed or regressed a hundred yards back along the avenue, a mere third of the distance to be traveled. The priest was becoming impatient. Time was ticking away. If he could put skids under that impudent stallion, the others would follow. *As meek as Father Mild,* he thought sardonically.

He lunged with the golf club in his hand to belabor the great animal's quarters. There was a sudden movement to his left at the same moment, which distracted him and startled the horse.

"Well, hello," he exclaimed.

It was like being hit by a juggernaut, enormous shock but no pain. He did not lose consciousness immediately. His last thought was how marvelously well everything had happened for fifty-eight years—and slight embarrassment that in the force of the impact his upper denture had shot right out of his mouth. He tried to apologize.

Barny Coughlin had left his modest residence in Finglas at 9:50 A.M. By 10:20 A.M. he had imbibed a pint of stout in his local hostelry, then two more in the city center before noon. At 1:30 P.M. he was osmotically engaged with a fourth pint and a simultaneous double whiskey in a bar at Harold's Cross.

Even for Barny, who was far from abstemious, this was a copious feed of drink for so early in the day. In normal circumstances it could only happen if somebody else were paying, in which case there were neither times nor seasons. But today was not normal, and the circumstances constituted an emergency. Barny was bracing himself for a fearful ordeal.

Researching Piggott's former lady friends had been easy going, because so had they. Nearly all had belonged to the public domain, supplying roughage and spice in the staple diet served up by mindless gossip columns. The list read, Barny told himself nastily, like an outdated edition of *Who's Whore*.

Exploring Piggott's possible connections with the underworld had been more difficult. There was no shortage of rumors, nods, and winks, but nothing solid. There were too many tale-spin doctors, gray-collar workers like himself, keen to make a few pounds out of anything except hard work. Such people would cheerfully invent for sale the information that they did not possess. Barny had to use all his skill to avoid being led up several garden paths.

One name, however, kept coming back: Tony Macklin. They had never met but Barny knew who Tony Macklin was: an accomplished burglar who plied his trade mostly in the southwest. He had been prosecuted several times but always had solid if somewhat repetitive alibis, and he was never caught with stolen goods on his hands.

Piggott had defended Macklin successfully four or five times. The only time he had been convicted, the verdict had been overturned on appeal. A cat with nine lives, Macklin was known in the trade as the one that got away, and Piggott's role in this patent injustice was duly appreciated. Whether it was an extension of this admiration into the realm of fantasy or actual reality, there were persistent stories that Piggott and Macklin had been linked both in constant friendship and in episodic felony. Contacted by intermediaries, Macklin had made it clear that he would cooperate with anybody in pursuit of Piggott's killers.

For Barny this was good news. The bad news was that Macklin was terminally ill with cancer and could be interviewed only at the Hospice for the Dying in Harold's Cross.

Barny disapproved of cancer and was zero tolerant in respect of anything that had to do with death. He hated clinics, hospitals, nursing homes, doctors' surgeries, and funeral parlors, all of which, as he saw it, were engaged in the same racket. Beset himself by hiatus hernia, varicose veins, and occasional minor ailments, he obdurately refused to consult a doctor. The only function of doctors, Barny believed, was to deprive him of cigarettes, alcohol, sex, and palatable food, and to bully him into jogging, doing press-ups, and retiring to bed on a nursery timetable. He foresaw that when his entire immune system had eventually collapsed under the cumulative weight of such torments, they would subject him to a prolonged series of ghastly "procedures," the ultimate objective being to siphon off every last cent he possessed and ensure that he died in excruciating agony.

Barny had often passed the hospice in a bus. Its great iron gates were surmounted by a central shield with bannered text. This blazon, he assumed, would portray a skull rampant, with dried bones strewn sinister and dexter. The legend could hardly fail to be *Abandon hope all ye who enter here*. His mental image of what went on behind those gates combined the worst nightmares of innocent childhood with the best hellfire sermons of lustful adolescence. Hence the morning's massive programme of anesthetization.

Still feeling distressingly sober, Barny crossed the street to the hospice. The text above the gate, he noted, merely indicated that this was Our Lady's Hospice and not Butlin's holiday camp. The central motif was a simple crucifix, a symbol of death no doubt, but somehow reassuring.

Within seconds of entering the grounds he was dizzy with normality: two pretty nurses walking toward him arm in arm chatting and laughing; attractive gardens with well-tended lawns and flower beds; some lively children playing with a football. Nearer the hospice buildings—a pleasant mixture of Georgian, midcentury, and next-millennium architecture—he came upon patients. Most were elderly and frail-looking, walking slowly, some with sticks or frames. Some greeted him cheerfully. One even thanked God for such a nice day.

In the sun-mottled reception area there were flowering plants and singing birds and, instead of a death's-head monk with scythe, a homely woman who clearly intended to survive for several decades. She thought that Tony Macklin had gone down to the pub.

"No," said a smiling nun, coming out from an office nearby. "He is expecting you, Superintendent. This is Superintendent Coughlin, Mabel. Sit down, Superintendent. We shall find him for you at once."

Barny obeyed, reflecting that if Macklin still had enough malicious humor to tell his undertakers that he, Barny, was a superintendent, the man could not be quite down and out yet.

Macklin appeared. An appropriate word, for he was almost a ghost. Thin, pale, his hair snow white, eyes sunken, he looked incredibly old, or perhaps young, as if shuffling off a skin that had served. "Superintendent, how nice to see you!" he mocked in a surprisingly resonant voice. "Let us go and sit in the sun."

"Do, Tony," said the smiling nun encouragingly. "It will do you good."

They settled on a wooden bench beside the River Poddle, which makes one of its rare surface appearances in the grounds of the hospice.

"It is very good of you to see me. I hope you feel able for it."

"On the contrary, it is good of you to come here and to give me the chance of doing something about Sid. We were friends, you know."

"So I hear. Do you know who killed him?"

"Well, for once my own alibi is above suspicion. But no, I do not know. Few people liked Sid. On the other hand, he had no real enemies. Besides, apart from some harmless marketing with me and one or two other people, he was not into anything that could make him inconvenient. So why kill him?"

"Why indeed?"

"I have thought about it a lot over the last week. I see two possibilities. First, money. Does somebody stand to gain by Sid's death, in his will, or however? The only other possible explanation is a nut case. Frankly, it looks like that to me. The killing itself is off the wall. A clout under the ear, what sort of way is that to kill anyone? It's not a gangland job. Not the IRA either. You might get the likes in a pub brawl, or out in the street, but not upstairs in the Four Courts.

"You are right. The actual killing was bizarre. Yet the gardai seem to think there was something more cunning behind it.

"Well, let them work it out. You hardly came here to pick my brains for theories. You want sordid facts. No problem. For Sid's sake, I'll tell you some stories. Half what you'll hear, I have already been acquitted of, so I can't be tried again. The other half, no problem either. I won't be around by the time the nice people can organize a trial.

"Don't worry about trials. I am sure we can arrange immunity."

Macklin laughed outright. "Don't you worry either. I'll have the best immunity imaginable. You can send six squad cars to Glasnevin Cemetery—they won't give me up. Seriously, Barny, I'll be dead in six months, max. Even if they arrest me tomorrow, I just won't be around, either to be tried or to give evidence for you. Previous engagement, like I said."

"I hope you are wrong—for your sake, I mean."

"Thanks, and well meant, too, I am sure. Anyhow, for what it is worth, here goes. I stole stuff. A chap called Moran stored it for me—I was too hot. I had to off-load the same night. When the heat was off we would move the stuff to Dublin. I had several outlets. We need not go into all that."

"No. just Piggott."

"Thanks. Well, the classier sort of things, good antiques, so on, paintings, I would bring to Sid. He had this woman called Roundstone. A shirty bitch, airs and graces. She is in the antiques trade. Low-profile stuff she would sell in her own shop. Better items she would take abroad, to London I suppose."

"Listen, Tony, you are on the ball. Lennon did not mention Roundstone to me. I don't know if he is on to her. But he did mention Sid's possible involvement in the antiques trade, in less than legal ways, I mean. Do you think that Roundstone knew she was handling stolen property?"

"Do I think! You must be joking, Barny. Of course she knew. She even did her damnedest a few times to squeeze Sid out of the action and get me to deal with her direct. She had to be careful about that, of course. She knew that Sid and I were old buddies. But she was after it all the time."

"Why didn't you?"

"Naw. Several reasons. A High Court judge is a much better customer for someone like me than a shady antiques dealer. He has enough respectability for the two of us. If the police come sniffing my tail, there is nothing better than a sweet-smelling judge to louse up their scent. Also, Sid always paid me serious money. I know he probably made much more in the end, but he gave me more than anyone else would have, and he paid up front. The Roundstone bitch— I know her type—she would throw me small change and sell my ass to the police at the first sign of trouble.

"But listen, Barny—I am thinking as I talk to you—and I can tell you this much. Last year Moran and I delivered a really classy painting to Sid Piggott. He gave me big money for it. If Sid was killed for money, I'll swear there was more of it riding on that picture than on anything else we ever handled. Perhaps he had sold it by now and got the money. Perhaps he had hidden all that money in his room in the courts, and maybe somebody got to know about it and came to collect the money. And maybe Sid got in the way. He was stubborn, you know."

"What was the picture?"

"God, Barny, don't ask me. Some dirty old fellah talking suggestive-like to this bird in the window. She is half loving it and half trying to get away. I got ten grand for it. That is the biggest money I ever made. It will pay for the funeral. I'm planning a great funeral, Barny. Don't miss it. Doyle's Corner pub, five minutes after the shoveling. Drinks on the corpse."

"What about Moran?"

"Now, Moran is an interesting case. He can't stand the Round-stone woman. She used to treat him like a criminal—and me, too, for Christ's sake."

"And sure, aren't ye?"

"And what the hell else is she?"

"True, too true!"

"Moran was arrested shortly after we delivered that picture. Not for that job, of course—they had something else on him. He is in Portlaoisc, I think. Well, here's the bit you'll like. Believe it or believe it not, no sooner was he inside this time than he caught religion, seriously. A bad case. The Charismatics got him. He had a bleeding conversion and confessed to a whole load of jobs, asking for them to be taken into consideration, as they say. They were. He is in for five years. Confession is his favorite pastime nowadays. With Sid out of the way, and me shortly to follow, he will gladly tell you everything you need to know, and give evidence. And if that includes screwing Roundstone, why, he'll be mixing business with pleasure."

The business was over. Barny said, "Did I hear correctly? Did that bird in reception say that you might be down in the pub for a drink? Are you really allowed out to a pub?"

"And why the bloody hell not? This is not Mountjoy jail, you know. I can come and go as I please. To tell the truth, I could not manage a pint now, just a short one when I feel up to it. They have me on green pills and white pills and red pills, and they were all made by the Quakers."

"How do you mean?"

"Not one of them agrees with drink." He laughed.

"Jesus, Tony. I know I shouldn't say this to a dying man, but how can you laugh?"

"I'll tell you something, Barny. As time goes by, as time goes away, you expect less and enjoy more. You learn to be grateful.

There are terrible days, too. But this is where I am at in my life now. To tell the truth, I wouldn't really want to turn back."

"Jesus, I'd die before I'd come into a place like this."

Macklin laughed again. "Then there wouldn't be much point coming in, would there?"

At ten o'clock that evening Coughlin realized that he had had no drink since 2:00 P.M. He had to run to make up the deficit.

THURSDAY, JULY 23

"DENIS, TWEEDY HERE. WE DID THE GALLERY FOR YOU IN Court Two on Tuesday."

"Oh, thanks, Des. Any joy?"

"That depends on your concept of joy. Do you realize that the Board of Works morons have been in there since last Monday, without leave or license from anyone?" How on earth are we expected to find anything with those idiots scratching and rooting and flinging their muck all over the place? God alone knows how much we have lost in the process."

"Oh dear. Well, it was worth a try. Thanks anyhow, Des."

"They are absolute savages, Denis. Did I ever tell you what they did in Longford?"

Lennon very badly wanted not to hear what the Board of Works had done in Longford, because he knew it would be but the prelude to a comprehensive tour of Ireland, not forgetting the offshore islands.

Des Tweedy loved righteous indignation like bluebottles love dung. When it had eventually become politically incorrect to wax wrathful about family or personal morality, Des had sought other irritants to stimulate his need to scratch. He had found them. Tweedy was a member of the Georgian Society and of all right-thinking environmental and conservationist groups. Even the most ardent votaries of these causes found him over the top. Everybody knew that there were certain dangerous words never to be pronounced in his presence. There were in fact many such words. They included effluent, spillage, Wood Quay, beach, oil, chemical, nuclear, architect, engineer, river, progress, tree, life, death, planet, industry, air, sea, and, most especially, Board of Works.

Lennon replied in haste. "I know, Des, I know. Well, listen, thanks anyway. I am grateful."

"No, hold on, Denis. We did manage to salvage something from the carnage."

"Oh yes? What have you got, Des?"

"Hair, Denis, human hair, capillary hair, from the head.

"Hair. Is it significant?"

"Yes, it is. We have six identical hairs, four from the front row of the gallery, two from further back, near the door. And—wait for it—we found four of the same hairs in the judge's room after the murder. That's ten hairs, Denis, nice long hairs. How about that? Your Identikit Golden Delicious was in the two places."

"Des, is this true? Ten hairs! That's a whole headful of hair."

"Isn't it! Your chap must be molting. But take my word for it: same chappie."

"Des, you are brilliant."

"Glad to oblige."

"And Des . . ."

"Yes?"

"Stuff the Board of Works! OK?"

"Hear, hear, Denis! Man after my own heart!"

Thanks to Ben Silverman's intervention, the Identikit pictures of the boy had appeared in the Law Library on Monday afternoon and at various points around the Four Courts on the following day. There had been no reaction from Albert Singer. Nobody had sought to twist his tail by posting the offending images in the Distillery Building, where he had his chambers.

The regular panel of journalists covering the courts had wanted to pass the picture immediately to their media. Lennon had bargained with them not to. If somebody in the Four Courts extended family could be found to give a better description of the boy, they could make a better picture. And the better the picture, he knew from experience, the fewer the sightings and the greater their reliability. The bargain was that, when and if there was a breakthrough in the case, the court reporters would hear of it first, *not* the newsroom boys.

Four further witnesses had come forward in response to the in-house picture. These were a typist from the Central Office, a solicitor's apprentice, and two schoolgirls who were doing some esoteric transition-year project in the Four Courts basement. None of the four had materially improved on the description already available to the police, although one of the schoolgirls did say that she "thought" the mystery man had been wearing an earring. This was a modest advance at best, and even suspect as the detail had been elicited by a leading question.

There was also Mr. Arnold St. John Smithers, senior counsel, who was in the habit of seeing visions and dreaming dreams. The elusive youth had, according to Mr. St. John Smithers, appeared to himself, in the early hours of Tuesday morning. He—that is, the youth—was attired in a long flowing robe, white in color, and had been issued with some obsolete weaponry, specifically a golden spear. His flaxen hair, gathered in a silver sweatband of the kind worn by tennis players, had grown at least eighteen inches in the week since the murder. Although he did have feet— two in number, of bronze—the youth commuted about the place by floating at low altitudes. He confided in Mr. St. John Smithers that he was actually the Archangel Gabriel and that he was currently engaged in pronouncing and, indeed, in certain cases executing "true judgment on the sons of iniquity," of whom, it was clearly implied, the late Mr. Justice Piggott was undoubtedly one.

The Archangel Gabriel had further intimated to Mr. St. John Smithers that Mr. Justice Piggott had merely been the overture, an appetizer, one might say, and that there would be several further richly deserving targets of angelic huntspersons. A list of future victims had not been supplied, but Mr. St. John Smithers had indicated his willingness—indeed, his eagerness—to compile such a list for the police from the moral dregs of bench and bar.

He had finally warned Saunders, who took his statement, not to "trifle or tinker with the awful decrees of Divine Justice" (spelled with capitals). Saunders had assured him of his determination to do no such thing and thanked him warmly for all this insider information.

Ben Silverman called Lennon shortly before 10:00 A.M. and left a message. "Denis, I am flying to a consultation. Listen, there is a young lady barrister here, Rachel Sheehan. She just got back from circuit last night and saw your pin-up this morning. Come and see her. She saw the boy and thought he was *gorgeous*—I am quoting, you understand. A clever girl, and a nice one. You can take it she had a jolly good ogle at your man. A high-grade witness, I should say. I'll see you for lunch if you are around. Bye."

Rachel Sheehan was nothing short of gorgeous herself. Legal black set off her Dresden-fine features and pure white skin to perfection. Eschewing the horsehair wig, which looks outlandish on most women, she let her jet black hair fall sheer and silken to shapely shoulders. Voice clear and vibrant, her bearing graceful, firm, and very feminine, Rachel was, in a word—well, two words—Portia Rediviva. Denis and Molly had followed her to Chancery Place, where she was appearing in Circuit Court 3.

Rachel was acting for a mother who had fed her infant for almost a week from a packet of baby food before discovering a whole colony of cockroaches foddering and fornicating in the bottom of the pack.

Unfortunately, so to speak, the infant plaintiff herself had suffered no ill effects whatsoever. Indeed, on the evidence of a bugs-and-beetles professor produced by the manufacturers of the baby food, cockroaches are perfectly harmless, full of protein, and probably quite palatable. The professor, who looked strangely like a beetle himself, even suggested that mothers could do worse than to feed their babies on cockroaches all the time. When asked about the distressing effects on less adventurous mothers of seeing cockroaches in their babies' feed, the professor replied, in effect, that he could not help it if nonscientists were not only allowed to have babies but even permitted to feed them.

Counsel for the defendants, an earnest young man called Quinn, kept a straight bat and a low profile, confident of ultimate victory. He had not reckoned with Circuit Judge Padraig Rafferty. Padraig was a plaintiff's judge. This meant that, not content with righting wrongs and punishing iniquity, he also willingly redistributed the wealth of the nation. Until the invention of the victim society, in which everyone is assumed to be routinely done down by somebody else, nobody had devoted more energy to breeding underdogs than Padraig Rafferty. He particularly enjoyed playing Robin Hood with the funds of banks, insurance companies, and the state, perhaps because none of them had ever briefed him during his long and impecunious years at the bar.

There was a further factor: Rafferty's extreme susceptibility to women. In his court, women plaintiffs got Brownie points. If they were mothers who stayed at home, they got more, and a bumper bonanza if they were pretty into the bargain.

Rachel's client, Mrs. Murphy, was somewhat on the homely side, but Rachel herself more than made up for any judicial disappointment in that department. During the plaintiff's evidence, Rafferty leaned toward her across his bench—and towards Ms. Sheehan, who was positioned near the witness box, in an attitude of compassionate solicitude.

When young Mr. Quinn very reasonably asked Mrs. Murphy whether the offending cockroaches might not conceivably have entered the open packet in her kitchen, rather than in his client's factory, the judge adjured him menacingly not to add insult to injury.

At the end of the plaintiff's case, Mr. Quinn made a dignified application for a direction on the grounds that the plaintiff had not made out her case.

"What do you say to that, Ms. Sheehan?" asked the judge, with a leer that he fondly imagined might pass for an avuncular rictus.

Rachel half arose, murmured, *"Res ipse loquitur, m'lud,"* and sank down again, seemingly exhausted.

"Exactly," said Rafferty, who could not quite remember what the Latin tag meant.

"Cockroaches in Ms. Sheehan's pantry—I mean in Mrs. Murphy's kitchen. *Res ipse loquitur.* Nothing more to be said."

A science graduate himself, Mr. Quinn was not sure what this was all about. So he tried some other points, but feebly now, sniffing defeat in the air. Rafferty did not seem to be listening.

"What do you think, Ms. Sheehan?" he asked suddenly.

What Rachel thought was that the judge was doing fine on his own. She rose delicately to her feet, looked particularly vunerable, and said, "I am in Your Lordship's hands."

The very thought entranced him. There was judgment for the

infant plaintiff forthwith, and an unsolicited rider that the entire sum of damages should be paid out immediately to Mrs. Murphy. At this the court registrar put his head over the bench and reminded His Lordship discreetly that the money should be lodged in court until the infant plaintiff reached her majority. The judge told the court registrar in plain English to mind his own business. Mrs. Murphy, he added, would soon be meeting considerable expenses, and he listed, off the top of his head, schoolbooks, rugby togs, dental braces, and a Swiss Army penknife. The child, to the knowledge of everyone in court, was fourteen months old, and a girl.

Ben Silverman laughed heartily when he heard the story. "Rafferty is an unbelievable rascal. It is like having a pirate king on the bench, or a hijacker. You never know what is going to happen next. Yet, in his own extraordinary way, he does manage to dispense a lot of rough-and-ready justice. The sound effects are terrible. The substance is sometimes not quite so bad."

Ben, Molly, and Denis met Rachel in the restaurant. She was clearly delighted with her unexpected win. They ordered food, Molly expressing the hope of encountering some cockroaches in the side salad.

Rachel said that she had indeed seen the fair-haired boy in the Four Courts, but not on the day of the murder. "No. It was a week or ten days before that. I was coming down from the robing rooms. He was outside the barristers' restaurant arguing with somebody on the flight of stairs below me, the one going down to the basement."

"Arguing, really? About what?" Lennon asked.

"I could only hear what the boy was saying. He was quite loud. The other chap was trying to calm him down."

"Was he not calm?" queried Lennon.

"He was angry, not exactly shouting, but sort of making a scene. He was saying things like 'I will go where I like,' or actually, if you'll excuse the language, 'I will go where I *effing* well like.' That was more or less the tone, truculent. The other chap obviously didn't want him around the Four Courts for some reason, and the boy was resenting that.

"Was he nice when he was angry?" Molly asked sympathetically.

"He was lovely," Rachel answered, quite unabashed.

"What about the other fellow?" Lennon asked. "You did not see him at all?"

"Barely at all. As I say, he was on the flight of stairs below me. But he was a barrister. In fact, I can go further. He was a senior counsel."

Ben gave a little jump on his seat. "Heavens, Rachel, that is not nothing. It is most interesting. But how do you know, if you did not see him?"

"The row between the two ended quite abruptly. The boy suddenly turned on his heel and stalked away through the swing doors back toward the library. I continued down my flight of stairs, three or four steps. Just as I turned the corner onto the restaurant floor, I could see the bottom half of the person below, whom the boy had been talking to. He was making for the bar, I suppose. I did not even see the bottom half of him, just from the knees down about."

"Was that enough to say he was a senior counsel?"

"Yes. I saw his tail! A senior's gown is quite different to a junior's. It is silk, heavier. It has long narrow tails that hang down from the sleeves. I saw one of those tails quite distinctly. He was a senior counsel."

Denis had meanwhile forgotten his manners. He sat with half a sausage on a fork suspended between platter and palate. "Thank you very much, Miss Sheehan." The sausage vanished, swallowed whole apparently. The inspector continued, "What does this mean? There is somebody here, a barrister, a senior counsel even, who knows this young man, who must recognize him from the Identikit pictures, but who has not come forward. Why? And this is the same boy who we now know was in the gallery of Piggott's court and in his chambers on the day of the murder. Yes, Ben, Tweedy has found matching hairs in both locations. What does all this add up to? Who is this senior counsel? Why was he so perturbed that the boy should be wandering around the Four Courts a week before the murder? And above all, why is he sitting on his hands now when we need and are entitled to all the help we can get?

Molly asked suddenly, "Rachel, did the boy have an earring?"

"Yes, he did."

"Are you sure?"

"I am quite certain. That was the tragedy. It was in the wrong ear."

Ben looked puzzled. "Wrong ear? Have we a right ear and a wrong ear?"

"It was in the right ear," Rachel said, "which is the wrong ear. It means he is probably gay."

"Do you tell me!" Ben exclaimed, astonished. "I cannot wait to get home to see which ear my young fellow has it in."

"Has Sam got an earring?" Lennon laughed. "Hardly kosher, I would have thought."

Ben turned toward him solemnly. "He has three earrings, Denis, all in the same ear. I said to him the other day that cauliflower ears are bad enough without turning them into cabbage colanders as well. But truly, one learns something new every day. Is it really so, that young men with earrings in the right ear are ipso facto homosexual?"

"Well, it is not the law," Rachel answered, "just a fairly wide-spread convention. Lots of people ignore it. But a boy as hand-some as this one cannot afford to be sending out wrong signals, if he doesn't want a load of unwelcome attentions."

Lennon rubbed his chin thoughtfully. "I don't suppose there is any chance, Ben, that Piggott might have been gay? You know, male prostitute, that sort of stuff."

"Oh, he wasn't a prostitute," Rachel protested.

Ben snorted. "Forget it, Denis. Few things are certain in this life, but one of them is that Sidney Piggott was exclusively, prodigiously, and disastrously heterosexual."

"So, was the disastrously heterosexual judge done to death by the tragically homosexual young man, who goes where he effing well likes?"

"Who said that being gay is a tragedy?" Rachel challenged.

"Well, you did," Lennon countered. "You described the boy's earring as a tragedy."

"Yes, but I meant a tragedy for me, not necessarily for him."

Lennon looked at her appreciatively and said gallantly, "Oh, for him, too, in that case, for him, too, a tragedy." He thought for a moment, then asked, "Ben, who is gay at the bar, at the senior bar?"

"Define your terms, Denis, define your terms. Percentages. Gay for a day, or gay to stay?" He added mysteriously, "When does a lettuce head become a cabbage?"

Rachel started the list. "There is Kingsley, certainly, and Toby Wilson. They say Martin Mulcahy, too, but he has about twenty children."

"Means nothing," Molly murmured.

"Then there is that fellow," Ben volunteered, "with a name like an address. What's his name?"

"Is it Melvyn Rhodes?" Rachel prompted.

"That's him. Though, come to think of it, he is not gay—just queer. There was Broderick, too. He came out—is that the expression? Yes, he came out last year. But nothing happened, so he went back in. There are even some whispers about your friend Bertie Singer."

"Oh my God," exclaimed Molly, "I cannot imagine anyone . . . I mean . . . with that creature."

Denis smiled. "Molly has an allergy to Mr. Singer. He makes her sneeze."

"He makes me throw up, you mean."

"Is there any point going back to Singer now? He might be more disposed to help us."

Ben shook his head. "He is away, I am almost sure, some legal binge in London, Gray's Inn, I think. He won't be back in the library until Monday. Anyhow, I don't think it was Albert on the stairs that day. I have never seen him in the basement bar in my life. Have you, Rachel?"

"Ben, I have never been inside the basement bar myself."

"Do you tell me? Well, ye pair of virgins, Albert and yourself."

The police officers took their leave, having arranged that the Identikit man would call on Rachel within the next day or so, to draw her fantasies. On the way out, keeping a promise, they alerted the courts press corps that an enhanced picture would be on its way soon.

He got up around midday and went downstairs in a bathrobe. He had the house to himself. The *Irish Times* was stuck in the letterbox. He took it into the kitchen and fixed some breakfast. Skipping the front page, which is usually devoted to politics and other trivialities, he imbibed cycling, tennis, and golf with juice and cornflakes. Then he leafed through to "Doonesbury," which, as often, he failed to understand: some insider Washington hee-haw!

Glancing casually at the opposite page, he saw the name at the head of a column, halfway across the births, deaths, and golden weddings:

MEAGHER, REV. THOMAS ALFRED, AGED 58.
Our Lady's Academy, Portlaoise.

Following a tragic accident . . .

It went on about deeply regretted . . . a sister . . . two brothers, community, large circle of friends . . . Requiem Mass, Saturday . . . community cemetery.

He read it through several times. "Following a tragic accident." When? Yesterday. Yes. When yesterday? It doesn't say. Shit!

He got up, paced, stopped, stood leaning on the sink, looking at nothing out the window. Where was I yesterday? I was in town . . . wasn't I? Doing what? What kind of *tragic accident*? It doesn't say. Shit! Could I ring up and ask? Don't be ridiculous! He mimicked in a high-pitched treble: *Sorry to disturb your deeply regretting, lads. Would you just check up there, did I kill* Father Tommy?

Still thinking, he took a scissors from the kitchen-table drawer and cut out the death notice, for his album.

Quilligan arrived back in the late afternoon.

"Ah, Jim," Lennon cried, "bronzed and rested from your continental holiday. How is Paris?"

"All I saw of Paris was what you can see from the Périphérique."

"A grand cultural experience, surely. Tell all."

Quilligan told all in his customary flow of spontaneous imagery and epigram. Lennon did not interrupt a single time, but when it was over he clapped his hands in frank appreciation. "Jim, weren't you the man to send! Your story is marvelous. But aren't they the scurrilous pair? From your own point of view, art robbery, receiving stolen property, so on, you must have all you need to hang them."

"Enough and more than, and not just the Mallow job, Ménard is to send me details of all the paintings he handled for the Roundstones over the last several years. I am sure we shall recognize quite a few more of them."

"Does he not stand to lose a packet himself if they all turn out to be stolen?"

"No. If he is an innocent middle man—and the French police claim that he is—he will not have to pay a cent to anyone. Besides, on his scale of operations, the Honthorst is the only really big one. He stands a good chance that the Church of Ireland will sell it to him anyhow. But what about you, Denis? What about the murder?"

"Yes indeed," Lennon murmured almost to himself, "what about the murder?" He stood up and paced the room as he spoke. "The murder hunt seems to be running on two parallel lines: the motive and the killing itself—and never the twain do meet. That is what perplexes me.

"As to the motive, the Roundstones had a major financial motive to get rid of Piggott. That is unquestionable. You yourself have just put the price tag on it—220,000 euro. They have already moved to bag that prize and salt it away in the South Sea Islands, or wherever the Grand Turk is. So did the Roundstones kill Piggott, or rather did they have it done? Or was it just, from their point of view, an enormously fortunate and well-timed coincidence that the judge got murdered just when he did? Perhaps I am jealous, Jim, but I have the greatest difficulty believing in that sort of good fortune.

"Yet, once we turn to the second line of inquiry, the actual murder, and start to link it to the Roundstones, everything starts to unravel. All the evidence—and we have collected some important pieces while you were away—all that evidence points to the fact that Piggott was killed by a karate kick to the neck, delivered by a good-looking, excitable, fair haired youth in a leather jacket, who is weird, wears an earring, and is probably gay. He sat in the gallery of Piggott's court that afternoon, then followed him upstairs to his chambers, and kicked him into eternity. Now what the hell is that all about? And where in God's name is the connection between those two lines of inquiry? The Roundstones are all cool calculation and cunning, while their supposed hit man is wild, weird, and wired to the moon.

"Who is this boy? He is not a hired profesional: The very idea is laughable. For a while I wondered was he Piggott's own son, Johnny, who apparently had excellent reasons to hate his father, and who did actually go missing in the deserts of Kuwait at just the right moment. Did he perhaps nip home on a budget flight and put in the boot, literally? We checked his photo with the Passport Office. Result—I got it just before we came out—negative. He does not look at all like the young fellow seen around the courts on the day of the killing, and indeed on another day as well.

"The boy was seen near the Law Library, several days before the murder, arguing with an unidentified senior counsel, who has not come forward to help with our inquiries. So what does all that mean? What is the connection between the Roundstones and this high-kicking clown? Is there any connection?"

Quilligan had sat quietly through Lennon's soliloquy, his chair tipped precariously backward, uninhibitedly scratching his hirsute abdomen in the gaps between shirt buttons. Now he grounded the chair and sat forward. "Your problem, you say, is to connect cunning and the clown, to find some logical correlation. Right? But the height of cunning is to know precisely when to send in the clowns, to defeat logic and point the police in exactly the wrong direction. The trick is as old as the country fair, Denis. The clown distracts you while cunning picks your pocket. You think you have solved the problem of motive. But have you? You know the Roundstones' motive. You do not know the clown's—and it is almost certainly different. A killer who leaves cash sitting on the table is hardly in it for the money. The achievement of cunning in this case has been to know the clown's motive and to harness it to cunning's own purposes. Find your clown. He is so crazy, he will probably tell you his motives before you get a chance to ask him. Meanwhile the Roundstones will be home on Tuesday, so why don't we ask them as well? Nicely, of course."

Lennon had stopped his pacing and was listening intently. He shook his head in admiration. "Thank you, Jim, thank you very much."

"For a blinding flash of the obvious."

"Yes, perhaps, when you say it, but I did not have the thing in focus. You have given me a nice bone to chew on. One killing, two motives. Neat. About the boy, yes, we are hopeful. We have an excellent new witness, Rachel Sheehan, a barrister. She got a good look at the young fellow. We have a good-quality Identikit going out at the weekend. That should stir up the pot. Listen, Jim, stay on call. I don't care what squad you work for. I need you."

Toward evening he had an idea. He got the telephone number from the back page of the newspaper.

"*Irish Times,* can I help you?"

"Listen, you have this thing in the paper today about Father Meagher being killed in a tragic accident. Well, I mean, like, what exactly kind of a tragic accident?"

"Sorry, I don't quite understand."

He had to repeat and rephrase the question several times. Eventually the bemused telephonist put him through to the newsroom. He could hear the reporter at the other end of the line researching his question. "Yeah, that priest in Portlaoise; some weirdo here wants to know what happened to him. What? Jesus!" Then, into the phone, "He got kicked."

"Kicked?"

"Kicked, mate, that's it. He got kicked. He kicked the bucket. End of story!"

He put down the phone. "Oh sweet Jesus! Father Tommy! What have I done?"

SATURDAY, JULY 25

THE ENHANCED PICTURE OF THE MYSTERIOUS BLOND youth had not been available on Thursday or even Friday. This was because the talented Mr. O'Sullivan, who usually executed these minor masterpieces, had chosen this moment to shed his appendix. Finding an alternative artist was not a problem; arranging to pay such a person was. Cutbacks on everything in the public service, except red tape, resulted in the familiar bureaucratic paradox of knee-jerk paralysis. It was nearly two days before the required sum of fifty euro could be "appropriated." The much-delayed portrait finally appeared on Saturday, at tea time, which is the expression employed by the Irish Broadcasting Authority to indicate when the plain people of Ireland consume or should consume their evening collation.

Lennon saw it on the six o'clock news and said, "That should be that," to which his wife replied that she certainly thought so. Molly said something similar to Jan-Hein when they saw it on the nine o'clock news. He was sitting on his sofa with her heels in his lap, painting her toenails with all the artistery and devotion of a Dutch old master. Thanks to Rachel Sheehan's sensitive description, the boy now looked less of a zombie and more like an actual person. He also wore his earring, in the right ear.

Saunders was in charge of taking phone calls. There were thirteen of them between 7:00 P.M. and midnight, some direct and some relayed from garda stations around the country. The sightings were too few to speak of a pattern, but Saunders did notice that two of them were from the Ballsbridge area of Dublin City, both within the previous month.

No name was suggested for the elusive young man by any caller except, inevitably, by the weirdos. A hysterical youth, sobbing into the telephone that River Phoenix had returned from the great beyond, was followed by a female caller of uncertain years who assured Saunders that James Dean was alive and well and living in Ballyfermot.

"What's the betting on Elvis and Rudoph Valentino?" Saunders asked Garda Susan Gaynor, who was helping him.

"Elvis who?" she replied.

Mr. Arnold St. John Smithers, SC, was on, immediately after the nine o'clock news, to report that the Archangel Gabriel had given him an exclusive preview of the Identikit picture the previous day, at precisely 11:20 A.M. in the Supreme Court. This, he complained, as if Saunders were to blame, had significantly dislocated an abstruse argument that he had been developing about the statutes of limitations.

There had indeed been a hiatus. Mr. St. John Smithers had been in full flight about the importance of acting *nec vi, nec clam, nec precario,* when he halted in midsentence and stood staring glazedly at the chief justice for a full minute.

Mr. Justice O'Hagan, who was deaf, observed to his neighbor, Mr. Justice Daly, in a whisper that could be heard in the Round Hall, "Smithers is going potty. Did you know that?"

Mr. Justice Daly replied equally vigorously, "Indeed. Just like his father."

"What, was the old boy cracked, too?"

"Daft as a sixpenny watch!"

The archangel, it seemed, was objecting vociferously to being depicted in the popular media sporting an earring. This was a matter, Mr. St. John Smithers stressed, which must be remedied immediately: *sine mora,* he added for emphasis, which was a bit lost on Saunders, who was not a Latinist.

Failure to comply, it was indicated, would result in unpleasant visitations from all four Horsemen of the Apocalypse, backed up by a selection of plagues and punishments. Saunders thanked Mr. St. John Smithers once again, promising to give the matter his immediate attention.

It was not clear whether the Archangel Gabriel disliked earrings generically or was complaining about the insinuation that he might be as gay in fact as in name.

It was only half past seven. Counihan's pub was still quiet. The cows would hardly be milked yet, and on a fine summer's evening there was still plenty could be done around the farms.

The singing and the real fun would start up later, as on every Saturday evening. Then fiddlers would fiddle and pipers pipe. Pints would be pulled, glassware tinkle, toes tap, ice rustle under rapid tongs, hands clap, and nonsingers sing anyhow. The bar's four tills would sing along—the sweetest of music to Tim Counihan's ears. He would tell himself again, after midweek doldrums, that Portlaoise was not the worst place in the world to bring up a family in the fear of God and decent comfort.

There were a few people in the lounge already, and a scattering in the bar, including some German tourists, come earnestly to have a cultural experience. Propping up the counter were three permanent fixtures known to all locally as the Magi.

Conversation was the usual stream of semiconsciousness: cows, weather, clergy, politics, silage, slurry, and hurling—useful exchanges on a wide range of important issues. Buffing glasses behind the bar, Tim Counihan himself acted as moderator, facilitator, and speaker of the house.

By eight o'clock, when more customers were starting to arrive, a fair-haired young fellow had installed himself on a stool at the street end of the counter. A "Dub," they all agreed afterward, from that foreign city two hours' drive away, inhabited, said the second Magus, by "Brussels sprouts, who would not know a rosary beads from a cow's tit." The young fellow was drinking a glass of stout— a glass, not even a pint—without apparent relish, competence, or conviction.

Abruptly he spoke up. "Did any of you know Father Meagher?"

Heads turned. He was inspected. Somebody answered. "Is it Father Tommy Meagher abroad in the college, the decent poor man that was buried this very day?"

The young man nodded. "Yes, him. I read it in the paper."

They did not like that "yes, him." Tim Counihan sought to put down some necessary markers. "Musha, sure we all knew him, and all belonging to him. Why wouldn't we? Wasn't he born and bred and lived and died in this very town?"

The third Magus appended panegyrically, fixing the stranger with a threatening eye. "A decent, holy, powerful, good, and saintly man."

The boy fell silent. The Magi sank their noses in their pints again. Everybody sensed that it was not over.

"Was he then?" said the boy suddenly. "That is not my memory."

Heads turned again. Magi noses surfaced. Tim Counihan put down the glass in his hand. "Mind yourself now, sonny," he said, not unkindly. "Father Meagher was one of our own, and proud we were of him. Remember now, the man is not cold in his grave."

"I knew him before," the boy persisted. "What happened to him? The newspaper said he died in a tragic accident."

"And didn't he surely?" Tim answered. "Wasn't he killed stone dead?"

"Who do you think killed him?"

"Yerra, nobody killed him. What are you talking about, boy? Wasn't he kicked by a tinker's horse?"

The air was suddenly electric. People felt it seconds before it happened. Even the German tourists, who had not been listening, put their glasses hurriedly back on the table.

The boy sat motionless, his face ashen white, then blazing red. He staggered backward off his stool, stood legs flung apart, his beer glass clutched in his hand like a weapon. "A tinker's horse," he cried, "a tinker's horse! Is that all you know? You brainless bog-trotting turd!"

His invective became frantic and incoherent. Suddenly he flung the half-empty glass with all his strength at the mirror behind the bar, where it smashed into a thousand pieces scattering liquid and shrapnel in every direction. "A tinker's horse," he shouted again in rage. "Do I look like a tinker's horse? *Do I?*"

Eyes blinked in terror or stared in astonishment. Then in a second he was gone.

"Holy God Almighty," Tim Counihan gasped.

"Jesus, Mary, and Joseph," the first Magus added.

"Sweet Mother of God," said the second.

"Well, I'll be buggered," exclaimed the third, who disapproved of profanity.

"What did we say, or what did we do? Am I dreaming or what?" Tim asked.

"He must have drink taken," the second Magus said censoriously.

"Sorra the drink," Tim replied. "Nothing only the half glass of stout you saw in his hand. And look at the most of it all over the mirror and my clean glasses."

"It just goes to show," summed up the third Magus. "As the poet says, a little drink is a dangerous thing."

"What poet was that?" laughed Pat Henry, the garda sergeant, who had just arrived with his wife for the *ceoil,* as every Saturday when he was not on duty.

The bar was filling up. Extra staff began to appear: three girls and two boys, students on holidays, glad to earn a few euro and be part of the fun. Everyone who arrived was told about the lunatic boy who flung the glass and wanted to know whether he looked like a tinker's horse.

"He must be possessed by the devil," said Mrs. Henry, blessing herself.

"A Dub, was it?" asked another voice. "Arra, what would you expect? They are all pure crazy up there, out of their minds with drugs and sex."

"A blondy-haired, nice-looking fellah, in a leather jacket, is it?" asked Joe Geoghegan, the barber, who had just come in. "I seen him out the road this minute. He is abroad beyond the prison thumbing a lift for Dublin."

"Is he now? Well, 'tis inside the prison he should be, or maybe the loony bin." This from Kate Kearney, the chiropodist. She added, "We can do without his kind around here. And wasn't it queer and awful to be shouting like that about tinkers' horses— and poor Father Meagher hardly settled in his grave."

"But that's not the worst of it at all," exclaimed Tim Counihan. "The worst of it is what could he mean by all that he was shouting, except that t'was himself and no horse that killed the priest."

"Sacred Heart of Jesus," squealed the chiropodist, who did not know when she had last enjoyed herself so much.

"You're right, Tim," said the first Magus, "and raging furious he was at all of us for giving the credit to the tinker's horse."

"Do ye know what?" the third Magus exclaimed suddenly. "I seen that young fellah before somewhere, I'm telling you, and recently, too."

"Well, you didn't see him in here before," said Tim Counihan firmly, "and you'll not see him in here again either."

"And where else would he ever see anything?" Kate Kearney jibed unkindly.

Conversation flowed on. More people came in. The music and singing started up in the lounge. Cash registers chimed. Barmaids and boys darted between the tables discharging and recharging their circular trays, emptying ashtrays, mopping surfaces, smiling and chatting, savoring their own speed and skill as much as the customers enjoyed their drinks and the music.

At nine o'clock on the dot the third Magus lifted his nose from the pint glass and announced *urbi et orbi*, "I know where I seen him, Tim. I seen him in here alright. I seen him right there on that television set above your head. And if ye'll wait nice and patient, ye'll see him again for yerselves before the news is over. Sure isn't he the harum-scarum that murdered the judge up in Dublin stone dead? And haven't they his picture, portrait, and description broadcasted and inseminated to every corner of the country?"

A hush fell on the whole bar. Disbelief struggled with fascination. It was as if the old toper had said that the devil himself had appeared to him in the gents, and he minding his own business and having a quiet leak.

As if on cue, the Identikit picture was flashed on the screen. There was a loud communal gasp. A voice exclaimed excitedly, "Jaysus, Jerry, you're on the ball. More power to you. It's him or I'm a whore!"

Everyone started talking, putting two and two together all over the room with results ranging from one to a thousand but evening out quickly at something like four.

The judge had been killed by a blow to the head. Father Meagher had died in the selfsame way. Everyone had presumed a tinker's horse had done it. There were horses around at the time, and blaming the tinkers was second nature. But here was this boy that the police were scouring the country for, the very boy that had slaughtered the judge, a certifiable lunatic as all could plainly see—here he was in Counihan's pub, raving like a devil out of hell, insulting Father Meagher, and shouting "Am I a tinker's horse?"—admitting, even claiming the terrible deed for himself.

"Quick, Nora," Tim Counihan shouted to one of his barmaids. "Get Pat Henry in here from the lounge. Tell him it's desperate urgent."

Sergeant Henry was a quick-thinking man, even after a brace of pints. From the family sitting room above the pub, he telephoned the prison and got put through to the fortified pillbox out by the Dublin road. By good fortune he knew the man on duty.

"Yerra, Pat, sure there is always young fellas out here thumbing a ride. There is two girls there at the moment—smashers, one of them anyhow. Let me think now." He thought.

"Begod, Pat, do you know what? There was a black Toyota here, it'd be half an hour ago. I'm taking terrible note of the Toyotas these days because I'm thinking of buying one. Well, do you know what? I'd nearly swear he took up a young fellah like that. He definitely stopped. It is the car I was looking at."

Pat Henry thanked him hastily, disconnected, and rang the garda barracks. "Nuala, good girl, get me the super as quick as ever you can . . . Sir, Pat Henry here." He told his story.

"Good man, Pat," said the superintendent. "I'll get onto Kildare this minute. They just might get out in time with a roadblock, there or nearer Dublin. Black Toyota, you say. Well done, Pat. Go back to your pint now and the singing."

The boy was dozing, vaguely aware that they were well launched on the motorway. They should be passing Kildare soon. Such a fool he had made of himself in that pub, he thought, coming fully awake, practically telling the peasants that he had killed their priest.

"Tinker's horse, for Christ's sake," he muttered savagely.

"I beg your pardon," said the driver, who, if he had been hoping for congenial company on his journey, had been thoroughly disappointed.

"Nothing," the boy replied sourly.

Something was wrong. He sensed it. They were slowing. A traffic jam was starting. Then he saw them, just after the service station, police, a roadblock. *So what?* he thought, but he knew, he just knew that they were looking for him. Somebody in the pub had known, had understood, or guessed.

"Let me out here."

"What? I thought you were going to Dublin."

"I've changed my mind. Stop. I want to use the jacks in the service station."

"No problem. I'll wait for you."

"Don't. I take ages."

"It's alright—"

"Oh look, there's my girlfriend. What a coincidence! I have to talk to her. Don't wait."

There was in fact a pretty redhead in slacks, aged about fifteen, sucking a lollipop outside the garage supermarket. The car had slowed in the traffic almost to a halt. The boy flung himself out.

"Thanks. Take care." He banged on the roof in rough token of appreciation and turned quickly away. He was conscious of the driver staring after him.

Must act natural. Mustn't arouse suspicion. Act cool, he said to himself—and to the girl, "Hi, Mary. Howya doin'?" He seized her by the arm. The girl dropped her lollipop in astonishment.

"Take your hands offa me. I'm not Mary. Let go, willya!"

Disconcerted by the idea that he was being watched, growing wilder, he tightened his grip on the girl.

"Mary, come on, willya. See, I got out of that car just specially to talk to you. Let's go down here."

He was pulling her by the hand toward the gable end of the buildings. The girl was frightened now and started to struggle.

"Come on, you stupid bitch. Act natural. I won't do anything. Honest, I promise."

As they reached the corner he looked back to the roadway. His car was stopped only four back from the police barrier. The driver was gazing at him openmouthed. He dragged the girl round the corner and started down the side of the garage. It was dark and deserted.

"Mary" had had enough. Remembering the prescient instructions of Sister Joan, her athletic convent headmistress, she suddenly yielded, turning in toward the boy's body as if to snuggle him. He could feel her sweet lollipop breath on his cheek. Then, just as he relaxed in her softness, she brought her right knee up into his groin with all the jolly hockey force she could muster. Sister Joan would have been proud of her.

The boy gasped in agony as the entire contents of his scrotum seemed to splatter against the inner surface of his skull.

"Oh Jesus," he moaned, staggering away, clawing his way along the wall with one hand, clutching anything left in his crotch with the other. He paused to vomit, then vomited again at the smell of his own vomit.

He stumbled on, away from the bright lights of the forecourt, back into a quagmire of diesel oil, old tires, bits of rusting farm machinery, scurrying rats. The Toyota would be level with the roadblock by now.

It was surely him that they were looking for. His own fault, too. Portlaoise, for Christ's sake, such a place to make a fool of yourself, a town crawling with police and prison warders, all trained to spot killers. They would be on his back now in seconds.

Dragging himself through a broken wooden fence at the end of the garage yard, he landed in a muddy lane running parallel to the motorway. He staggered along as best he could, still hurting and nauseated from the Sister Joan special.

Soon the garage was behind him and he had drawn level with the checkpoint on the Dublin road. As he feared, the Toyota had pulled in. The driver was standing outside the car, pointing toward the back of the garage. Already policemen were running across the forecourt.

He ran further along the lane, panting and sobbing, bent double in panic and in pain. He sensed the police in the lane behind him already. They were hesitating, perhaps wondering which way to turn or whether to take to the fields. He fled on, swerving into a farmyard on his right, for no reason except the instinct not to be the nearest moving point on a straight line.

A wicked black and white collie came barking and snapping cruel teeth at his fingers. He kicked out full belt in the dog's face. It keeled over and lay motionless between his feet. One up for the tinker's horse!

The door of the farmhouse was thrown open. He ran down to the back of the yard, through the remains of some stinking manure, over a barbed wire fence where he tore his trousers, into a wide field bald as a billiard table dotted with great black plastic-wrapped rolls of newly cut silage.

He half ran, half crawled twenty yards to two rolls pushed to-gether and squirmed into the crevice between those monstrous black buttocks. He lay there motionless.

It was Saturday, 10:40 P.M. The early edition of the *Sunday Inde-pendent* had gone to bed or been put there. Kevin Wallace, acting editor for the night, was not happy. It was the silly season when nothing ever happened. For the third week in succession he had screaming headlines about nothing. This time, yet again, it was the sordid little pleasures of incontinent clergymen. Market-driven, hag-ridden, he hated it.

"Jesus, lads," he groaned to his team, "is there really nothing else? What do you think we are, some kind of gutter-rag?"

Journalists looked at each other, and away. Nobody answered. A voice came over the PA.

"Hey, Kev, there's a hot one coming in."

"Too late, for Christ's sake. We're gone to bed."

"It's a hot one, Kev, real hot. It's a scoop. Angela Keegan, she is on live."

Wallace looked up excitedly. Nobody ever said no to Angela.

"Put her on sound."

Angela Keegan was an ex-full-timer, now a brilliant freelance, who combined a large family with hawk-eyed instincts for a good story. She worked when it suited her and still managed to make high-profile bylines several times a year in national and even inter-national media. Quick, critical, always newsworthy, Angela never sold you a pup.

"Angela, Kev Wallace here. Let's have it."

"Hi Kev, hi gang! This is in rough. All happening as I speak. Work it up as I talk."

Wallace pointed. "Paddy, compose. Dick, headline, subhead." Angela went on.

"Goldilocks sought by police for murder of Judge Piggott, see Identikit, surfaces in Counihan's pub, Portlaoise, eight this P.M. Claims to have killed local priest, Father Tommy Meagher, same way, kick to head. Priest buried same A.M., died Thursday, presumed kicked by itinerant's horse—but nobody saw it."

"Good God!" Wallace exclaimed. "Hold a moment, Angela. Betty, redeploy whole top front page. Stick it where you like, or out. I need the whole top front. OK, go again, Angela."

"Boy clearly identified from police Identikit—after he left, of course. Flew into rage about the itinerant horse story, started breaking up the place—real looper—shouting 'Am I a tinker's horse?' Half an hour after he left, locals made the connection. Traced to front of Portlaoise prison, where he got a lift for Dublin, black Toyota. Police have roadblocks, near Naas, Newbridge, or somewhere, now, as we talk."

"Hold, Angela. Mike, check with the gardai. Get a camera out there. Angela, sweetheart for life, it's a byline, of course. We'll pay gold bars. How did you get it, for God's sake?"

"Simple. Counihan's is our local. Bobby and I just went in for a nightcap.

"Angela, darling, how do you do it? Every time! You're poxed with luck!"

The boy looked at his watch. A half hour to midnight. It was dark, insofar as it ever gets dark at this time of year. There was no moon. The roadblocks had been removed, but police reinforce- ments had arrived and were systematically scouring the fields and farms all around him.

A line of them had passed within yards of his hiding place, one fat garda pausing to piss copiously, practically into his face. The sour stench of urine remained to remind him that somebody was thinking of him.

The field where he lay hidden was so flat, bare, and open that the searchers had passed through it quickly. By good fortune the boy had found what he now saw was the only possible bolt-hole in an expanse of ten acres, because nowhere else were there two bales of silage rolled together.

He could not estimate the number of searchers deployed, not less than twenty, perhaps as many as fifty, poking and rooting in ditches and hedges, through farmyards and outbuildings. A lot of skills acquired in the fight against paramilitary organizations were being aired again in his honor.

The search party had passed in a wave from the road and was moving west and south. To the east, farther along the motorway, he could see the bright and busy lights of a hotel and a car park. If only he could make it that far, there might be a chance. It would mean covering hundreds of yards across flat, open fields, two more at least, as bare and exposed as the one where he lay. There was still too much police activity on the hard shoulder of the motorway. It would be well-nigh impossible to move such a distance across open country without being spotted from the roadway. Unless! There was one slim chance.

If he could somehow cover the sixty yards from his hiding place to the motorway—if, in other words, he could go straight to- ward the police undetected—he just might be able to sidle along inside the thick hawthorn hedge separating the field from the road- way, so near the police that they could not see him. A high-risk strategy. The alternative carried no risk at all, only certainty: Stay where he was until morning and be picked off like a sitting duck.

He wriggled from the plastic womb of his hay-mother, beginning again the hazardous adventure of living. Not walking tall, nor small, nor even crawling, he crabbed his way along, using elbows, shoulders, knees, toes, keeping his head and ass down, eager to be the lowest form of life on planet Earth. He took a diagonal, longer than the direct route but invoking the shelter of some more silage bales along the way and of a bulky thorn tree on the boundary, which would obstruct the view of anybody looking from the roadside.

Fortunately, any who were looking were taking the long view, following the movements of their companions two and three fields away by the light of powerful lamps, which had opened up suddenly from the hedgerow when the boy was still only halfway to the boundary. For a hideous five seconds he had thought he was finished. In fact, the lamps were on his side, their powerful beams making inkier shadows of everything outside their tunnel-visioned ken. He was three yards into that safe lateral darkness.

It was twenty minutes from his redoubt to the hedge, twenty minutes during which he scarcely dared to breathe. Once there, he found to his joy that he could fly along. The hedge was thick and high. After a hundred yards the hard shoulder of the roadway tapered away; he was able to straighten up and run toward his objective, the hotel.

A simple wire fence fronted by twenty-foot conifers divided rural Ireland from the urban oasis. In the shelter of these trees he rested and sussed out the scene.

First of all, himself. He looked down at his clothes. No way could he get into the hotel without attracting critical attention Torn trousers, silage, slurry, cow shit up to his knees, a cut hand, dried vomit on his shirt; no doubt, a dirty face as well, and straws in his hair—*as befits a proper lunatic,* he thought.

He surveyed the car park. Quite a bit of activity. One or more parties seemed to be breaking up, people making for cars, shouting, laughing, talking silly at the top of their voices. Two exits to the road, both with garda checkpoints. Not a Breathalyzer in sight, he noted. Free run for tonight's drunken killers who would make shit of themselves and God knows how many others half a mile down the road. Orders for the night were obviously simple: Forget the pissed—screw the fair-haired ponce.

Then he saw it. A Ford minibus parked outside a sort of functions room. He could get to it without crossing the hotel entrance or coming out into the main car park. He ran down behind the trees to the nearest point, just ten or fifteen yards from the vehicle.

Already some boisterous young people were pouring out of the building, milling around the van. He broke cover and scampered over and in among them.

"I espy strangers," intoned a pimply youth.

"Hey, buddy, where are you going?" asked somebody vaguely official-looking standing at the door of the van.

"Just coming off duty in the kitchen . . . missed my lift . . . I was wondering if . . ."

The guy was already shaking his head. Suddenly, from behind, two fat hot hands seized the boy around the waist.

"Why, *Justin,* how *are* you?"

He gazed into the dislocated features of a plump girl, disastrously clad in a sari with wide horizontal bands that made her look like a zebra crossing. *Drunk as a skunk,* he thought.

"Oh, *hi!*" he replied. "Howya doin'?"

"Long time no see," she yelped, dragging him into the bus and down onto a seat.

"Yeah," he shouted back, "must be eternity."

The police waved them through without trouble.

"Where are we going?" he shouted.

"Mecca," the girl wailed. "We're going to Mecca."

The whole van took up the refrain to the music of "Dixie."

We're goin' to Mecca, We're goin' to Mecca.
Are you from Mecca? Yes, I'm from Mecca . . .

After which they ran out of lyrics.

"Mecca, like in Morocco, or wherever?"

"No, you nerd. Mecca like in Leeson Street—the nightclub."

"Oh, terrific!" It was. He could easily get to Ballsbridge from there.

"You are not really Justin, are you?"

"That was your idea, wasn't it?"

"So who are you?"

"I'm Jonathan, Jonathan O'Keeffe."

"That's a lie, too, isn't it?"

"Maybe. Perhaps nobody knows who they really are. Do you?"

"Oh yes. Unfortunately."

She laid an unsubtle hand on his thigh. "I think you are cute. No, start again. I think you are very nice. You've got soul."

"I'm gay."

"Does that stop you being cute, or nice, or having soul? Anyhow, I don't think you are gay."

"No? Why not?"

"You're sending out too many vibes—you know, signals, real sex rays. Are the police looking for you? They are looking for you, aren't they?"

"Yeah. I wet the seat in the hotel loo."

She was silent for a while. Then she asked him again more soberly. "Justin, or Jonathan, or whoever you are, why are the police looking for you?"

"OK. I give in. I'm a serial killer. You know, *Silence of the Lambs*, BAAAAAA, all that crap."

They both laughed. She did not ask him any more questions.

From Leeson Street he went down along the canal and turned into Baggott Street. A van dumped off a pile of Sunday newspapers at the deserted kiosk on the junction of Pembroke Road. He went over. The *Sunday Independent* was top of the heap. It had banner headlines.

SERIAL MURDERS: JUDGE—NOW PRIEST
POLICE CLOSE NET ON BLOND KILLER

A not-bad-at-all drawing of what could be his face was splattered across four columns. The entire top half of the front page was given over to the drama, from Counihan's pub at 8:00 P.M. until "near midnight" when the police were "closing in" on Ireland's very own "serial killer." *Why don't they give my name?* he wondered.

He was taken by the statement that "the whole town of Portlaoise is devastated." *Not bad going,* he told himself, *on a half glass of beer.* There was a rehash of Piggott's murder for those with short memories. The boy marveled at big money's genius for getting so much detail right and so much substance wrong. "Jesus, I look good," he murmured, admiring the picture.

He rummaged in his pocket and found a two-euro coin, which he left on the ledge of the boarded-up kiosk.

A joke occurred to him as he crossed the Dodder at Ballsbridge, still reading his newspaper.

Question: What did the police find when they closed the net?

Answer: Cow shit!

He laughed out loud.

SUNDAY, JULY 26

NOBODY HAD ROUSED LENNON DURING THE PREVIOUS night's manhunt. Colleagues knew about his major heart surgery and were protective. "If we catch the lad, we'll still have him in the morning," they reasoned, "and if we don't catch him, why bother Denis for nothing?"

Molly Power called him first thing in the morning and read him the newspaper story over the phone.

"Holy God!" Lennon exclaimed. "What is our boy doing down in Portlaoise? A simple country priest! What has this killing got to do with Judge Piggott, or with his painting, or with the Roundstones? Nothing! This boy is just a loose cannon, a nut case on the rampage."

"I wonder. The method of execution is the same as in Piggott's case. The executioner is the same."

"But where does it fit in? You are not going to tell me that the priest, too, had a priceless picture lodged with the Roundstones—so they sent down their Karate Kid to stave in *his* head as well?"

"Let's find that boy. Then we can ask him."

"Amen to that!"

Major surgery and a long convalescence had taught Lennon the value of priorities. He attended to his Sunday devotions, then went home to a leisurely brunch with his wife. In the afternoon he drove in to the Harcourt Street garda station, where the hunt for the golden-haired youth was being coordinated.

As Lennon feared, their quarry was being seen all the time and everywhere. Each reported sighting had to be recorded, evaluated, and graded into degrees of interest: low, high, and priority. There were seventy-eight reported sightings that day between 8:00 A.M. and 10:00 P.M., the great majority of them in the Dublin metropolitan area. The searchers' task was complicated by the fortuitous presence in the river of two sizable Norwegian naval vessels, which had arrived the previous day and were docked in Alexander Basin. Big numbers of flaxen-haired cadets and ratings were roaming the city, many of them in mufti, with the result that the high-kicking judge-slayer was being accosted, sometimes in clusters of three or four identical clones, everywhere from Butt Bridge to Dolphin's Barn. That evening, back in the ships, the Irish police were voted even worse than their Turkish homologues when it came to importuning Scandinavian sailor boys.

In some cases, names and addresses of possible suspects were being offered over the phone. Molly and Saunders knew that they would have to spend a day or more checking out several of these delations face-to-face; which would not be pleasant, as innocent people usually resent being taken for serial killers. Besides, as the two sergeants had been warned by experienced colleagues, several of the informants would turn out to be either pranksters or downright malicious.

The sillier an idea, the faster it travels. This rule, propounded *a posteriori* by Quilligan, was amply verified in the event, when some nasty-minded urchin phoned in the name of a school companion who had fallen for the craze of dying hair pink, mango, or albino. As the city was full of such youths with close-cropped heads, the shape and color of overbleached lavatory brushes, bogus denunciations swept like wildfire throughout the child-raising suburbs, fueled by apocryphal but hilarious stories of terrified pixies being dragged away by the police for interrogation under torture.

To the credit of youth culture, it was widely condemned as immoral thus to trigger indecent rejoicing among parents, who immediately weighed in with cries of "There! We told you. With your head like that, any decent person would take you for Jack the Ripper!"

As evening nudged toward night, Lennon went off with Molly to be introduced to Jan-Hein and have a bite to eat. They avoided talking shop in the presence of a "layman"—that is, until Quilligan joined the party. His hello was the quintessence of discretion.

"Well now, Molly, so this is John Hind! Trot him up and down there till we have a look. We've heard all about you from Miss Molly, John Hind. I'm told you're a divil entirely for the women."

Molly turned beetroot. Quilligan continued unperturbed.

"Did you ever hear such shenanigans in your life, John Hind? I bet you don't have the likes of that over in Belgium, or wherever it is you come from."

Jan-Hein's first thought was to say nothing, which he did successfully. Quilligan turned his attention to Lennon.

"Well, what do you make of it, Denis? What is that lad of yours up to now?"

"Crazy stuff, Jim, crazy! In Piggott's case, OK, there is a link through to the Roundstones, and you get a motive. But now we have this priest, and things fall apart."

"How do you know? The Roundstones probably have nothing to do with the priest. But as for the boy, we still don't know why he did anything. You don't know why he killed the priest, but you don't know why he killed the judge either, do you? So what else is new? Come hell or high water, we have got to find that boy."

Everybody nodded assent. Molly spoke up.

"Denis, the Roundstones get back from France the day after tomorrow, Tuesday. Are you going to take them in?"

"I wonder. They have no idea that we know about them, I mean about the painting, and no inkling that we suspect them of murder. If we lie low and keep watch, they may lead us to this young man. That may be the best way to find him. But what about the pictures, Jim, do you want to go in?"

"No hurry. Why not wait until Ménard digs up all he can about other pictures over the years? On the other hand, if they have any lead to that boy, we want it. Who knows where or when he may strike again!"

"That's it," said Molly. "I think you have got to grab the Roundstones as soon as they set foot on Irish soil. Pull their toenails out, whatever it takes. We must find out who that boy is, and where we can find him."

MONDAY, JULY 27

For Lennon the week began badly. He had to spend
eternity listening to his superior officer, Chief Superintendent Flynn, enumerating all the things he *absolutely* could not
understand. These were many, and the cataloguing was conducted in a tone of prolonged peroration.

The many matters that Chief Superintendent Flynn could not
understand *absolutely* came down in practice to one, to the fact
that almost two weeks after the murder of Mr. Justice Sidney
Piggott, his presumed assassin was touring the country on a note
of low comedy, drinking openly in public houses and laying claim
to further, worse, and even sacrilegious enormities.

Lennon outlined patiently the various steps and stages of the
inquiry. He acknowledged himself disappointed and perplexed
that the golden-haired young man continued to elude him. He
asked the chief superintendent pointedly several times whether
he himself might not have something concrete to suggest. Flynn,
like a good missioner hired to preach at all six Sunday services,
merely laid back his ears and started all over again. "The one
thing I absolutely cannot understand . . ."

Lennon stopped listening, waiting resignedly for his superior
to either desist or die of old age. Eventually, after as many false

endings as a Beethoven symphony, and guided less by reason than by the unsatisfactory state of his prostate, Flynn did stop, to flee in one direction, while Lennon made good his escape in the other.

Albert Singer took the early morning flight from Heathrow. Executive class, of course. His few days in London had been most agreeable. The Benchers of Gray's Inn had received him very hospitably. He had been congruously grateful, but no more than that. Albert Singer, chairman of the Bar Council of Ireland, was not one to be fobbed off with postcolonial patronizing. He had made that much clear. He had also told them a few home truths about their own inadequacies, for which, he assumed, they were duly grateful, though, he noted with some disappointment, they had not exactly said so in so many words. Typical Brits, afraid to show their feelings!

There had been time, too, for various exhbitions and to revisit the National and the Tate—the *adult* Tate, of course, not that juvenile collection of blobs and glugs, and dirty knickers glued to cardboard. Sunday night's concert, Wagner from start to finish, had been superb. It had spoken to his soul. Somehow Wagner's music always moved Singer. He supposed it was accessible only to leaders (of men, naturally). It was a bit naughty of him, really, to stay on for the concert. He should have flown home the previous day to prepare for a number of weighty court engagements in the last week of term. No matter. He had little doubt that he would cope more than handsomely in these cases, as indeed in all cases and circumstances.

Albert had made an important decision during this short interlude abroad. Piggott's death had been unpleasant, of course, but there was no reason to wait longer. Besides, truth to tell, Piggott would not be missed. A shallow fellow with a plebeian mind, he had been no ornament to the Irish bench. In deciding to apply for the vacancy, he was quite satisfied both that he would get the appointment and that the immediate result would be to raise the whole tone and standard of the Irish judiciary.

It would mean a substantial drop in income. He was currently earning at the bar at least four times what he would be paid as a High Court judge. But he had made his money. He was comfortably off, and he had no dependents—well, except David. But if, as Singer saw things, every man had his price, so every man was also expendable. David would not be around for much longer.

It was the right time to move. Indeed, Albert had almost had to leave it too late. The president of the High Court was due to retire in eighteen months. By then Albert would have had just enough time to establish himself as the obvious successor. With calm satisfaction, he ran over in his mind the twenty or so serving judges of the High Court. There were some quite clever fellows among them—he could not put it any higher than that—but not one to hold a candle to Albert Singer.

And then, the chief justice would be retiring in three years' time. Traditionally, the president of the High Court had first refusal on that exalted position. Albert would not refuse. He had the satisfaction of knowing that, over the last year as chairman of the Bar Council, he had whipped the profession into shape—and put a lot of people in their places in the process. He looked forward to doing the same for the judiciary: They badly needed a good shaking up. He felt sure that he was just the man to do the shaking.

Professionally successful—if success consists in being paid large sums of money to inspire fear and dismay in others—Albert had not been happy in his domestic life. His mistake, as he saw it, was to have married beneath him, an unintelligent woman who had never appreciated his exceptional qualities and her own good fortune. Her final tasteless act had been to put her head in the gas oven. He had been embarrassed rather than grieved. He still had the unpleasant impression that food cooked in that oven was slightly tainted.

Albert's elder daughter had gone completely off the rails: drink, drugs, sexual promiscuity, abortions. She called herself an actress. She was that alright, though he marveled that anyone would actually pay her for it. To his considerable relief she had hightailed off to America ten years ago with some crazy fellow—he would need to be, wouldn't he? She had not been heard of since.

There was a second girl, a mousy, spiritless creature, just like her mother, with bad skin and no figure. Left alone in the house with her father, she had tried her best to please him. The harder she tried the more she exasperated him with her graceless, hangdog ineptitude. Eventually, in an age when no sensible girl would have contemplated such anachronistic behavior, she had fled to a convent, where, by the pitiable standard of such happiness as she had known until then, she was happy.

Albert Singer remained a profoundly lonely man.

It might have been different. If Billy had lived. But Billy, his darling son, had died aged seven, a lingering, painful, and utterly pointless death from encephalitis. That was many years ago. Albert could still hear those tiny tortured cries . . .

After that, Albert did not care, did not allow himself to care for anyone. Nobody would ever again have the power to hurt him so profoundly. He had become, in the most exact sense of the word, a repulsive man.

It was through sheer loneliness that in recent years he had got involved with a succession of young men. These had been shallow affairs, which perhaps was their interest from his point of view: pleasure, some companionship, no real relationship. Besides, all these lovers, if one may call them that, had quickly shown their venality. They shared his board and his bed, not because he was handsome, romantic, or, still less, pedagogical in the best Greek tradition. It was simply because he had money. One after the other, they had prized as much of it as they could out of him before departing or, in grosser cases, being sent upon their way. Then there had been David. His coming had been something of a miracle.

Albert Singer had been collecting Irish silver in a small way for several years, which was how he had come to know Isa Roundstone. He had bought some nice pieces from her. When one of his more disreputable young men, who had departed with a George III silver sugar bowl under his oxter, offered it for sale to Roundstone Antiques, Isa had recognized it immediately as one that Albert had pipped her for at auction some months previously. She told the young man to come back next day, and telephoned Singer. He had meekly paid the youth a hundred euro—a nominal sum, admittedly, for such a fine piece—and retrieved his property. Initially astounded by such mildness, Isa had quickly understood.

Albert himself had no doubt that Isa knew perfectly well the nature of his relationship with his former houseboy. He had been considerably surprised, therefore, when some months later David arrived on his doorstep with a letter of introduction from Isa in which she proposed the boy as "an excellent cook and houseboy."

David was both, and so much more besides. Hardworking, intelligent, imaginative, scrupulously honest, he rarely left the house and never asked for money. Albert had to insist that he take a weekly wage.

There was another side to the boy. He was, Isa Roundstone had said in her letter, "successfully recovering from a mild schizoid episode." He did not, she added, need medication, but he might at times become "a little agitated." These upsets could be soothed by "patience and reassurance." To his own amazement, Albert had been prodigal of both. Not since darling Billy died had he been so joyfully patient, so generously tolerant, so ready to forgo his own convenience for another person. The fact was that, after an infinite ice age, and against all his expectations, Albert Singer had rediscovered something like love. One sublime proof of this was his spontaneous recognition that he would never use David grossly, as he had done with others before him.

It was true that the boy did become a little agitated from time to time. In a sense, Albert almost enjoyed these episodes. They brought him to life. When David grew fiery and tempestuous, there were angers for him to soothe, fears to allay, terrors to exorcize, old wounds to heal, a child's tears to dry.

It was awkward, of course, when these scenes—the word, alas, was not excessive—took place in public, as on that embarrassing day in the Four Courts when David had been quite beside himself. Luckily, it had happened in a relatively secluded place. Albert himself had not been observed. But David obviously had, and some busybody had given his description to the police as someone seen "behaving suspiciously" around the Four Courts. The fact that this had happened at least a week before Piggott's murder made no difference to such a numbskull.

Long experience of dim-witted witnesses had taught Albert how utterly inaccurate they can be. Some nonentity eager for notice could so easily conflate what he had half-seen on the back stairs one day with what he had not seen at all on the day of Piggott's murder. Anything for a moment in the limelight. Well, it is an ill wind that blows nobody any good. Singer had learned on reflection that even such idiocies can be turned to good account.

More intractable were the hallucinations. David was highly suggestible. He was a truthful boy, certainly, but one could never be quite sure that he had been where he said he was or had seen or done what he thought he had. The official diagnosis of his condition was paranoid schizophrenia. Whatever David himself might think, he would almost certainly be better off to take his medication. He was quite determined not to. In such a condition, he was easy meat for any predator.

The police, having come up with absolutely nothing themselves, were hawking David's image around the Four Courts like down-at-heel vendors of dirty postcards. Lennon should know better. He should also keep a leash on that impertinent little hussy who followed him around like a poodle, speaking out brazenly, even asking *him* questions as if she were a man. Insufferable! The police were fools. He was quite satisfied that David had never murdered anyone.

Singer bought an *Irish Times* at Dublin Airport, to check the legal diary. As he had expected, Brownlow and Hudson V Mercantile Agents International was listed before the president. He was reasonably well prepared. A taxi straight to his chambers near the courts: that would give him nearly an hour to look at his post and go over the main points of his argument. There was quite a queue for taxis. He glanced at the main headlines. He saw the enhanced Identikit picture.

Inspector Diarmuid Clancy telephoned Lennon from Portlaoise.

"That was your boy we had down touring the provinces last Saturday evening."

"Yes. So it seems."

"He is a phony, Denis. All talk and no action."

"Are you out of your mind, Derry? That boy is a killer."

"Perhaps he is and perhaps he isn't, but he didn't kill anybody down here. That's for sure."

"What about your priest, Father Meagher?"

"Denis, we did a postmortem."

"Really?"

"What do you think this is, the Wild West? Of course we did a PM, and there will be an inquest."

"Sorry, I didn't mean it that way. I am just saying that PMs don't find out who killed somebody."

"Perhaps not up in Dublin. Down here they sometimes do."

"How?"

"Easy, if it happens to be a horse."

"A horse?"

"A horse, Denis. That's an animal with four legs and a tail. Listen, the pathologist here is furious. He is being pilloried in every newspaper this morning as a total idiot who wouldn't even realize when somebody has been murdered. You people seem to be actively supporting that libel."

"Derry, calm down. Our boy has an unusual way of dispatching people."

"Is that so? Does it include iron shoes on his feet?"

"Iron shoes? Well, I don't think so. Of course not."

"And can he kick with two feet at the same time?"

"Is it like that?"

"Exactly like that. Father Meagher got two hind hooves full belt in the upper body. The right hoof broke his shoulder; the left one stove in the side of his head. There was a hoof print on his face as plain as a scorch mark on an ironing board."

"God! What did he die of, broken neck?"

"Massive brain hemorrhage. I can tell you, the hospital is putting out a statement confirming the findings of the PM and referring all further inquiries to the coroner."

"Should they put out a statement, Derry? I thought—"

"They have no choice, Denis. Donough O'Meara, the pathologist, showed them a personal statement he was going to put out himself if they did not rally to his defense immediately.

"Hard to blame him. It is true, the whole country is saying he screwed up the autopsy. I suppose his statement was strong."

"Strong! You must be joking, Denis. Every second word began with *f*." They both laughed.

After Clancy rang off, Lennon got Quilligan on his mobile. Quilligan was in poetic humor.

"A horse, a horse, my kingdom for a horse, as the Fairy Queen would have said."

"She didn't."

"Well, I doubt if a horse did for Piggott either. In fact, I've never seen a horse upstairs in the Four Courts, Denis, have you?"

"No, nor downstairs. But where do I go from here?"

"Cheer yourself up, Denis. Ring Tweedy. Ask him why didn't he test Piggott's room for horseshit. He'll love it!"

"That's what you think! But seriously, Jim, this case is impossible. Nothing stays true for more than five minutes."

"I tell you what, Denis, I am down in Monastrevin, spot-checking on a fine art auction. Would you like me to go on to Portlaoise? I could visit Father Meagher's place. I just might pick up something."

"Would you? See if there could be some connection between Piggott and the priest."

Rumpus Hall was one of those stately homes sold off for a song by nervous Anglo-Irish families in the early years of the Irish Free State. A Victorian folly, which would have suited a budget Harry Potter just fine, it had, like many similar houses, fallen into the hands of a religious order and become a boys' boarding school. The Congregation of Gospel Messengers was extensively engaged in African missions. At home they ran schools that contributed usefully towards the educational needs of the infant state while also offering a pied-à-terre to malaria-drained missionaries returning on leave from the tropics. These schools, in their turn, were rich veins of vocations for the congregation. Each year throughout most of the twentieth century, dozens of youngsters, inspired by the remains of idealism and the beginnings of disillusionment in a postrevolutionary Ireland, had heard and heeded that higher call. Tommy Meagher had been one of these boys.

Quilligan, unlike Harry Potter, did not have the option of arriving by broomstick. Instead he nursed his axles gingerly around and over a mile of lunar potholes, which at least had the merit of demarcating an avenue through the dense shrubbery to either side.

Entering on these grand estates stirred embers of memory for Jim Quilligan. He had been eleven years old when his parents, abandoning the open road, had joined the settled community. He could still feel vividly what it had been to arrive in those earlier days: barefoot and ragged, yellow hair swirling chaotic around his nut-brown face, strong little hands and knees clutching and clamping the mane and backbone of a wild piebald pony, the kind that had done for Father Tommy Meagher. He could still smell the uneasiness, the dislike, the fear even, of the narrow-eyed house-dwellers. The tinkers had come to ask for food, not as beggars, but as of right. Jim had never ever felt inferior to anyone in his entire life. Pride was inbred, the pride of those who have nothing except their freedom.

The tinkers were proud people. Turned out of their native homesteads by force of arms, supplanted by waves of loutish mercenaries and adventurers—the unpromising premises of a new aristocracy of scullions and stableboys—they had been sent to wander and die on the highways and byways of Ireland. They had wandered, for hundreds of years, but they had not died. Neither had they taken soup or the king's shilling, and they did not tip their caps to any man.

"Father, did Judge Piggott's son go to school in this place?"

The old missionary's eyes widened. He smiled. "Inspector, you certainly get to the point, don't you! Well, indeed yes, Johnny Piggott came here."

"What kind was he?"

"Nice boy, shy, quiet. His leaving was a disaster."

"How so?"

"You obviously know."

"Did you people have to throw him out?"

"Tommy Meagher was the last man in the world to throw anyone . . . anywhere."

"Well, why . . . ?"

"Listen, Inspector, let me tell you a story. It is about a boy called Morrisey. He was a senior here when I was in first year. That's back in the thirties. Tim Morrisey was the Renaissance man of our little world: footballer, athlete, hurler, singer, actor, a born leader, and scholarship material. Tall, good-looking—all the etceteras you fancy. The school hero.

"Well, one day, Morrisey came back from a cross-country run, tired and hot. He dived into the lake you see out there through the window, got cramps, and was drowned. The first death we ever had in the school—we've had four or five since, I'm sorry to say, thanks to the proliferation of the motor car—anyhow, Tim was drowned. You can imagine the scenes.

"The whole school cried for a week, adults and children alike. The funeral was incredible: the bishop, all the local politicos, parents, past pupils. The memorials went on for ages afterward, people writing poems, planting trees, all that stuff. They even called a new art room after Tim, the Tim Morrisey Art Room. That was a bit of a joke actually; the one thing poor Tim couldn't do was draw a straight line.

"Well, all of that was, let's say, the *official* version. The boys had their own story, which was whispered from class to class and from year to year, down to my own time and beyond. Perhaps the kids still talk about it now, more than sixty years later. According to this version, Morrisey was queer—well, that's the language we talked in those days—Tim had been misbehaving with some juniors, that's the story, and somebody had found out about it. They were going to out him that very evening. So that is what Tim did. He jumped in the lake, and he stayed there."

"Mother of God!"

"Well, that is the principal reason why Johnny Piggott had to go. For his own sake. I see you are surprised, Inspector. Take my word for it, an all-male boarding school is about the most homophobic milieu on earth. Adolescent boys are so insecure about their own sexuality, they make life hell for anyone even suspected of being homosexual."

"Do you think young Piggott murdered his father?"

The priest coughed a dry laugh and shook his head. "Forget it, Inspector."

"What about the other boy?"

"Which? You mean the gossoon sent walking with Johnny, David?"

"David who?"

"David Roundstone, of course."

"Of course. You mean Roundstone, as in Felix and Isa?"

"The antiques woman. I don't think the husband is the father. Anyhow, veil of discretion over that, and so forth. I haven't seen David for ten years. A nice poor child, vulnerable. I don't think the home scene was very . . . nurturing, shall we say. And yes, you need not ask, David is the chap who was down here last Saturday claiming to have killed Tommy Meagher. Poor boy! He is off his rocker, but I could not imagine him murdering anyone."

"People change."

"Ah yes, and above all, life can be rough. I pray for those boys, all of them, every day of my life."

Quilligan was touched. As they walked to his car, he said, "Can you really love *all* of them?"

The old priest replied sadly, "Nowadays, a priest could hardly dare admit to loving *any* of them. I am not sure anyhow if love is the right word. I *pity* all of them. Life can be lonely and cruel, and each of them has so little to throw into the struggle, just that little bundle of bones, gas, and guts, and a few bits of brains, for whatever that's worth. I think compassion is all that we can do. That is love, in a way, isn't it?

All of a sudden, every dog in the street seemed to know about David Roundstone. Even as Quilligan was hearing about him from the elderly missionary in Portlaoise, people were queuing up to tell Lennon the same glad tidings. First off the blocks was Jenny Treacy, Piggott's ex-wife. At two o'clock the previous night she had woken up abruptly, possessed of the idea of a connection between Piggott, Father Meagher, her own son Johnny, David Roundstone, and death by kicking.

"Inspector, I am not saying that David killed either Sid or Father Meagher. I hope he didn't kill anyone. But he *is* blond, and there *is* all that unhappy history in the background linking him to both of them, and they both died the same way, didn't they? Poor little fellow . . . It is very hard to imagine. Well, of course, it is several years since I have seen him."

Lennon had barely time to send Molly out to the Roundstone

home in Donnybrook, in the vague hope of finding David in pajamas and dressing gown attacking his cornflakes, when the telephone rang again. This time it was Albert Singer. He informed the inspector peremptorily that he required to see him urgently. Having declined to say what about—"I do not deal with important matters over the telephone"—he added, typically, "I shall be in the president's court. You can wait for me outside. Good-bye."

Next up, this time in the flesh, was Dr. Dan Keating, a psychiatrist. Slight, sandy, and seedy. "I run a private residential clinic in Arklow."

"Ah yes, Dr. Keating, I have heard of your clinic." Lennon tried to remember what exactly he had heard about Keating's clinic; canteen chatter, no doubt, and not complimentary. Canteen chatter usually wasn't.

"To come to the point, the young man whose picture you have been circulating is a former patient of mine. He had been with us for four years, doing well on appropriate medication. About two months ago, his mother took him out of the clinic without discussion or notice. I was away in the States at the time."

"What age is this young man?"

"That is the point. He is twenty-three or -four. His mother says that he discharged himself. Technically, that is correct, but my staff assure me that while I was away, David's mother came to see him several times and talked him into leaving. The boy's name is David Roundstone."

"I know."

Dr. Keating looked displeased. He tried harder. "I can tell you two other things that are certainly relevant to your investigation."

"Please do."

"Firstly, David is black-belt standard in tae kwon do."

"In what?"

"Tae kwon do. This is the most lethal form of karate. David was taught it by one of his gay friends, a Korean called Kim who works in the inner city. David is gay, you know. Well, a kick in the head would be no bother to him."

"And what is the second thing?"

"The second thing is that if David Roundstone has not been taking his medication, he would be very volatile. He might do . . . anything."

"Anything?"

"Anything, and he might be confused about what he had or had not done."

"Is he very disturbed?"

"At this precise moment, probably, yes. But this has less to do with his underlying condition, which was coming along quite nicely, than with the sudden discontinuation of medication, which he still needs and which, in any event, would always have to be withdrawn gradually and carefully monitored."

"What is wrong with David Roundstone?"

"Skipping the technicalities, essentially a mother who never wanted to have him, and a father who never acknowledged him when she did have him."

"Felix and Isa?"

"Not Felix. Isa and Mr. X."

"Does he know who Mr. X is?"

"Yes, and *was*, not is."

"You mean Mr. X is dead?"

"You mean you don't know? Good Lord! But that is precisely what we are all on about just now. Mr. X was Sidney Piggott. I presumed you knew that. This is patricide, unadulterated Oedipal. I don't mind telling you, Inspector, it is a big moment for a psychiatrist, when you get it in the pure state."

———

Albert Singer's opponent before the President's Court that morning was Tommy McGonigal, perhaps the only colleague who could seriously disconcert him. When in good condition, Tommy enjoyed a precision of thought and language that few practitioners could rival. He was a brilliant lawyer and, some said, the greatest advocate of his generation.

This morning, being in less good condition, Tommy had several times interrupted Singer's erudite submission with observations as dignified as they were outlandish. When, for instance, Albert had referred the president to the case of Darling v. Semperhill (1857 House of Lords Law Reports), Tommy had struggled to his feet to assist his learned lordship.

"A most excellent case, m'lud. I was in it myself."

"Thank you, Mr. McGonigal," said the president with the utmost civility. "The court appreciates your assistance."

Albert had not been pleased. Irrespective of Tommy's state of health, his appearance in court invariably triggered deep-seated anxiety in Albert's soul. This could be traced to traumatic events dating to his own professional childhood.

When still a very junior barrister, Albert had been briefed to appear with Tommy McGonigal and other eminent counsel in a matter of considerable importance. Convoked to a consultation on the eve of the trial, he had presented himself punctually at Tommy's Fitzwilliam Square mansion, pink with pleasure and white with excitement. Ushered into an exquisite Georgian dining room where a galaxy of important people was already seated around a splendid mahogany table, he took his seat and looked timidly about him. Having recovered a little from the dizzy exhilaration of simply being there, Albert was surprised to notice that all items of furniture in the room, with the exception of the table and the chairs where the company sat, were covered in dust sheets, several of which were bespattered with what looked very like bird droppings.

The reason for this arrangement became clear when Albert observed, to his astonishment, a large and truculent-looking bird of prey, perched atop the elegant Adam fireplace. This, it seemed to him, must be a vulture or some sort of eagle—a rather bald one. It was, in fact, a parrot of great antiquity who had lived in ménage à trois with Tommy and his wife for many years. From the moment Singer caught the bird's eye, he knew, he just *knew*, that the creature had it in for him.

The consultation was soon going famously. Albert became interested, then quite absorbed. He relaxed and forgot about the parrot. But the parrot had not forgotten about Albert. Suddenly, Nemesis flapped its ragged wings and launched its yellowing carcass into the air. Nobody else seemed to mind. Banking NNW, the beast came zooming into Albert's airspace, where it circled, then swooped several times back and forward along the parting of his hair. Albert, who had served in the SAS and was reputed to have killed men with his bare hands, shriveled into an uncontrollable blue funk.

With its target softened and demoralized, the bird alighted on Tommy's bald head, the better to size up its quaking quarry seated three chairs away. The consultation continued serenely, nobody else apparently thinking it odd that Tommy's cranium should serve as a parakeet helipad.

Schlump! With one buccaneering leap the predator had landed on Albert's forearm and was digging cruel talons into the veins of his wrist.

"*Aaaah!*" cried Albert in wild alarm.

"Oh, look!" exclaimed Tommy, delighted. "He likes you, Singer!"

By now the bird's vicious hooked beak was three inches from Albert's horrified eye.

"No! Tommy, no! Get him off!"

"He likes you, Singer. I can see it clearly. He really likes you."
The bird was gurgling and salivating.

"No, Tommy, he doesn't like me at all. He detests me!"

"No, Singer, no. He really likes you. Scratch his head. Go on, Singer, he wants you to scratch his head. He'll be offended, mind you, if you don't."

The parrot was now leering obscenely, rocking its can-opener head from side to side in crude parody of Albert's awful dilemma. Caught between a rock and a hard place, the priority had to be not to offend the brute. So, stretching out a trembling hand, Singer unfolded his least favorite finger, advancing it timorously, all of one centimeter, then another centimeter, a third, a hair's breadth to go . . .

Squawk!

They took Albert away in an ambulance. Tommy never referred to the incident afterward, and Albert was never again invited to a consultation in Fitzwilliam Square.

With his hawkish nose and bewigged crest, Tommy himself looked oddly like a bird of prey. No wonder that Singer was never quite himself after a morning spent in his company.

Singer saw the police briefly and brusquely at the luncheon interval.

"Inspector, as you are probably aware by now, David Roundstone is the name of the young person you are seeking. He has been in my employment for the last six weeks or two months. To suggest that he murdered Sidney Piggott, or anybody else, is, of course, perfectly ridiculous, and I regret to find that you are still pursuing this futile line of inquiry."

He made no reference to the difficulties he had created when the police had wanted to display their Identikit pictures.

"I should like to point out that I have been away for a week or so. Accordingly, I had no inkling until this morning, when I saw a newspaper at the airport, that David is probably the young man whom you are so misguidedly pursuing. Have you been to my house?"

"We are indeed looking for David Roundstone. We have not been to your house. We were not aware of the . . . connection."

Singer colored at the studied pause.

"Mr. Singer, we need to interview Mr. Roundstone immediately. We also need to get into the house."

"For what?"

"Sir, it must be obvious. If this young man is indeed implicated, there is probably much we can learn by visiting his . . . habitual living space."

Singer laughed sarcastically. "David suffers fools less than gladly, Inspector. I doubt if he will let you in."

"We were rather hoping that you would let us in."

"Were you indeed? Well, I'm sorry. I am detained in court until four o'clock, after which I have a meeting of the Bar Council."

"You can pass us your key."

Singer's eyebrows shot into his wig. "I shall do nothing of the sort."

"Very well, sir. We cannot wait until this evening. I shall get a search warrant and enter . . . as best we can. We may have to break in."

Singer zapped Lennon a laser glance of pure malevolence. His thin lips enunciated icily, "The gardener is there today. He has a key. He goes in to make his lunch. If David is not at home, the gardener will let you in. David's room is upstairs, at the back. Keep your noses out of everywhere else."

"We shall go everywhere, and only where, we have to go. I will need a written authorization, if you would be so good."

Mr. Singer said a very rude word.

Mrs. Marjorie Connolly was sitting at the open upstairs window where she had spent most of her waking hours since her stroke seven years previously. When not supervising the neighbors, she was discussing them on the telephone with a coterie of leathery octogenarians, pickled in gin like herself. She did the *Irish Times* crossword every day, the hard one; the one for simpletons was quite beyond her. She was nevertheless convinced that Crosaire, who invents the clues for the hard one, was well into his second childhood, so she changed half the clues each day to make her words fit. She never looked at the solutions in the next day's newspaper, since she had discovered that the editor, too, was senile and invariably published the wrong set of solutions.

Marjorie's neighbors on the right, the Lallys, were "sweethearts." Those on the left, the Roundstones, were "tramps," whom she "would not have in the house"—not that they had ever manifested any great desire to enter it. Animosity dated back all of eighteen years, to the demise of a favorite tomcat, Pickles, whose urine, Isa Roundstone maintained, was damaging her seedlings. Marjorie was quite convinced that Isa had fed the beast poison.

Further border incidents had followed: overhanging boughs cut or not cut; a front door, the Roundstones', painted an offensive color, "like a house of shame," Marjorie declared, having never seen a house of shame in her life. Isa had even sunbathed topless in her back garden. "The slut," declared Marjorie, who nearly fell out the window trying to make an adequate sighting.

Marjorie's dislike for the Roundstones was most essentially based on her accurate perception that they, or at least Isa, treated David badly. She knew that his mother beat him, and that he was a sad, lonely little boy growing up. She sensed that Isa had forbidden him to visit her, but when the Roundstones were away, which was too often, he sometimes slipped through the hedge and came to see her.

He never complained about his parents, but his almost abject appreciation of any little kindness spoke volumes of how things were at home. Marjorie's daughters were already married. She had no son. At times she wanted to take David in her arms. He was such a lovely child, so gentle, so lost, so touching. But she was an intelligent woman, too, who realized that to gratify her own maternal longings with caresses and kisses might be just another form of the selfishness that had already robbed the child of so much.

She knew, later on, that David was said to be homosexual. That would have shocked her terribly when she was younger. Now, it was not that her ideas or principles had changed—she was a fairly conservative person—but she continued to relate to the boy as she knew him, somebody loving and lovable. To speculate, let alone judge, about what was intimate and personal to himself would have seemed to her mean-minded and prurient, a violation.

When Marjorie had become incapacitated, David, by then old enough to do as he pleased, had indeed been like a son to her. He ran messages, did jobs around the house and garden, or simply sat and kept her company.

The trouble had started when David lost his job. From about the age of sixteen or seventeen he had worked in the Blue Moon restaurant in Rathmines. He was a natural for it, and he loved the work. One of her daughters had taken her there one evening for her birthday. David had been so proud, waiting on them with great poise and panache. He so needed to be affirmed. He could cook, too, so Denis Tierney, the owner, told them. Denis was such a nice man. When he died, some fast-food idiot had taken over the restaurant and fired David. It was a devastating blow. He needed that job, just to keep his head together. How fragile we are, really!

When he began to deteriorate, she had noticed it with growing anguish. He would still come to see her, but less often. When he did come, she could see him trying to sparkle, to entertain, to tell her things—and just not being able. Two invalids: each painfully reaching out to the other, each stubbing and scorching out-stretched fingers against an invisible but impenetrable membrane between them.

He had been gone for four years. Then he had reappeared briefly at home. She had seen him once or twice in the garden, but he did not come to visit her. Then he was gone again.

Suddenly, the police were next door, then at her door. A pretty girl, Molly something-or-other. Hard to imagine her as police. Where were the Roundstones? Who knows? Who cares? Been gone for a week, probably abroad: Irish Ferries sticker on the car. *Doesn't miss much,* thought Molly. What about David? Gone for years, back for days, gone again for months. Why? Nice boy. Why do you want him? Thanks for your help. Nice day. Byyyyye!

She heard it on the 1:30 P.M. news: David Roundstone, blond, this height, that color eyes—green, weren't they? Wanted (dead or alive?). Help police with their inquiries. Murder of Judge Piggott.

Sacred Heart of Jesus, have mercy! Has the whole world gone mad?

What could she do? If she were younger, she would have gone down to the garda barracks in Donnybrook and talked to the su-perintendent. If he did not listen, she would have boxed his ears.

She rang the Carmelite Sisters in Malahide, asked them to storm heaven: Everyone knew that Carmelite prayers were the best. She would get nice Mr. Lally to bring ten euro down to Father Conway and get mass said for David. What else could she do, only hope and wait?

If there was a murderer next door, it wasn't poor David, nor that gormless imbecile Felix: It was that scarlet woman, Isa Roundstone. Hadn't she murdered poor Pickles! Why hadn't she told Molly that? She would telephone immediately!

David heard the radio news, too. He had known since Saturday night that they were looking for him, that his picture had been all over the media for days, and now his name as well. How had he managed to move around so much before being recognized? Perhaps he was invisible some of the time. He had often thought that, when he was a child. It had seemed as if nobody saw him, as if he existed in a world all his own. He remembered his excitement when he read in a book at school about warriors of some savage African tribe who could become invisible in battle. They had to take off all their clothes and perform secret rituals. They also had to abstain from women. Perhaps he qualified. Perhaps he was invisible—at certain times. Who could say?

Of course, he had been out of circulation for four years. Few people were familiar with his appearance or knew his whereabouts. There was little need to worry about the neighbors where he now lived. It was one of those places where people avoided their neighbors. Separate entrances, high walls. They went to each other's funerals. That was about it. The house on their right was vacant and for sale. The other side was a busy medical practice frequented by people who came and went, preoccupied with their own bodies, not looking at anybody else's.

The two people who did know where to find him were the lawyer and his mother. The lawyer was away, but it could be awkward when he came back. Even then, the lawyer would not give him away. He was a prude and a hypocrite: He would be the last to invite police or press into his parlor, if he could possibly avoid it.

His mother? He pressed his teeth together and frowned. If he were never seen again this side of doomsday, that would suit her fine. As far back as he could remember, he had always been in the way. Never more so than now, when he had really screwed up—he must have—and been found out. She would not like that. His mother was not the kind to wait for things to happen. She shaped events. What, he wondered, would she do now? Where was she? Why had she not been in touch? These questions troubled him.

David stood up from the kitchen table. Leaving his lunch unfinished, he walked out of the house and into the street. From fifty yards away, he watched the squad car arriving and parking opposite the house. "*Merci, petit Jésus,*" he muttered, a French child's grace after meals. *Where did I learn that?* he wondered.

Having failed to find David Roundstone at his Donnybrook home, Molly Power was sitting in her police car with Garda Tim Fahy, discussing what to do next. Her mobile phone sounded. It was Lennon.

"Molly, still on the south side?"

"Sure. Empty-handed. David hasn't been seen around here for months, according to the neighborhood watch next door."

"I know. Well, head for Ballsbridge, 22 Willow Drive. That's down Anglesea, turn right at the bridge, second or third off to the left. You'll be there quicker than I can."

"What's there?"

"Prestigious address. Your friend Mr. Singer lives there. So does David Roundstone."

"Denis, you are joking. But that means . . ."

"It means a load of things. Just get down there. Are you armed?"

"Of course not."

"Don't attempt to go in. I'll get there as soon as I can. I am just leaving the Four Courts, going back to the castle for firepower and authorization."

"Necessary?"

"Probably not, but we can't be sure."

"Bring me something."

"Sure, a nice boarding-axe. Stay out of there, do you hear me?"

"Yes, sir!"

Lennon got there by two o'clock. He and Molly quickly ascertained that David Roundstone was not in the house. Admitted by the gardener, they found his half-eaten lunch in the breakfast room and the radio still playing. The inspector read the scene rapidly.

"He heard his name on the news, and he did a runner. He knew we would be round in no time."

"Singer probably tipped him off, as soon as you left him."

"There's a thought. Anyhow, straight into action! You stay here, Molly, with Fahy. Search the place—for anything, whatever you can find. I'm straight for the DART."

"Drive carefully."

He did not, and got to Sydney Parade much sooner than he should have. Parking clumsily just beyond the level crossing, he ran in to the ticket office.

"Yeah, sure," said the ticket-seller, "there was a lad like that here moments ago. He seemed in a great hurry—but he had to wait twenty minutes all the same. There was a train broken down on the line. He has just gone this minute."

"Which way?"

"Into the bright lights. Pearse Street he said, I think."

Lennon got on his mobile. Fast police footwork. Minutes later, two garda were waiting on the platform at Pearse Street station. David got out. He saw them and they saw him. They lunged. He jumped back in the train just as the doors were closing. At Tara Street, the next station, he made a dash for it. Down the stairs, along the quays, into Hawkin's Street, up to College Green, then zigzag through Temple Bar, past his mother's shop, without thought of stopping. He was making for the old city. At the bottom of Fishamble Street, where, two hundred and sixty years before, George Frideric Handel had first presented his *Messiah,* he was confronted by a solid garda: not the brightest blade in the pack, God knows, but one who knew a blond head when he saw it.

"Hold on there now, young fellah. Where would you be off to in such a hurry?"

"Uh!"

"What's your name?"

Think quick: quick think.

"Me no understand . . . *Ich bin Berliner.*"

"What?"

"Jajaja . . . Morgen ist auch ein Tag."

"So you're a foreigner, are you? What about the passport?"

"Der Frisör schneidet Haare . . . Der Schumacher macht Schuhe."

"Alright, sonny, alright."

"Wohl Gespeist zu haben . . . Vater unser im Himmel."

"Tá go maith, tá go maith!" Off you go, now, off you go."

"Viele Dank, Dank, Dank. Auf Wiedersehen. Sieg Heil!"

"Right. *Arriver-durchy . . .* and *Haben-vous an gutten jour!"*

"Prostate!" cried the fugitive, raising an imaginary glass.

"Slán!" replied the other, not to be outdone in glossolalia. They shook hands, and the boy was gone.

Left alone in the house, Molly went straight to David Roundstone's bedroom, which was upstairs, overlooking Singer's rose garden at the back.

A large, airy room with a generous window and a high ceiling, it was comfortably furnished, yet simple. Molly liked the cleanliness and tidiness of everything. A few austerely beautiful posters and small ornaments reflected the tastes and personality of the occupant. *He can't be all bad,* she thought.

There were some books: poetry, she noted with interest, Dostoevsky, *The Catcher in the Rye,* something called *Songlines* by Bruce Chatwin, and *Giovanni's Room* by James Baldwin. There was also Bret Easton Ellis's *Less Than Zero* and, to her surprise, a book about prayer by some sort of monk fellow with a long beard. On the bedside table lay what seemed to be current reading, *The Secret History* by Donna Tartt. *Hell of a name for a girl!* she thought.

Catcher and *Less Than Zero* were the only two Molly could remember reading. Somehow the others now seemed interesting and desirable. She would watch out for them.

She found the album. It had press cuttings about Piggott's murder, as well as the newspaper death notice for Father Meagher, an article from a provincial weekly calling down imprecations on tinker horses, and the *Sunday Independent* splash about the Portlaoise episode.

In the margin of the item about horses David had written in his clean hand, *Delegate: You can't do everything yourself!* Momentarily puzzled, Molly burst out laughing. So he had delegated to the horses! Black humor, but it confirmed that he had not killed Father Meagher. Well, they knew that anyway.

She opened the fine Swedish-wood presses. Clothes, some of them fashionable and new, others frayed and faded, all clean, impeccably hung or folded. Trousers, shirts, sweaters, reflecting moods and seasons, underclothing, last veil of the mysteries, shielding desire and vulnerability: taboo. She smoothed with soft fingers, guiltily.

The leather jacket was there. Heavy, yes, but beautiful. She could understand him wanting to wear it, even in hot weather. His wash things were still on the handbasin. *Wherever he is now,* she thought, *he probably has nothing but the clothes on his back.* All of a sudden, she was holding a purple cotton shirt to her cheek, tears pricking at her eyes.

"Oh my God," she said, angrily thrusting the shirt back on its shelf, "if Denis could see me now . . . or Singer!"

She commandeered a small suitcase and bundled in the album, the leather jacket, and some other bits and pieces. Then she left the room quickly, still furious at her own lack of professionalism.

"Who is the weirdo in this thing anyhow," she hissed vehemently, "him or me?"

A gentler thought came as she crossed the landing: Jan-Hein would understand perfectly.

About to go back downstairs, she turned instead on an impulse, into the master bedroom, Singer's. *Wouldn't he just freak,* she thought, *if he knew that a mere woman was poking around his boudoir! What am I doing here anyhow? Is this bit any more objective and professional than the last bit?* She glanced around, rummaging desultorily, uninterested, unattracted by anything. The décor and furnishings were luxurious and expensive, perfect for trendy magazines or art deco catalogues, but soulless, empty, like the man himself. *Frankly,* she thought, *I couldn't care less what he has under his bed.*

What an odd expression! "What he has under his bed." Why had she thought that? It was like a jack-in-the-box phrase, something wholly surprising springing ready-made out of her subconscious, a scarce-formed memory, an image hardly registered. She saw it or sensed it fleetingly again, no more than a gray shadow, an impression. Yes, there *had* been something under David's bed. She had just about glimpsed it out of the tiniest corner of her eye. She ran back to his bedroom.

There it was, a dark, low-lying oblong. She scooped it out. A battered green ring binder. David Roundstone's name was written on the front in bold block letters, and underneath it, in titillating fire-engine red, *Aggression Fantasies*. Printed on the inside of the cover was *Mountainview Clinic, Arklow, Co. Wicklow*. Molly flicked through it rapidly. As many as one hundred pages in David's precise script: narratives, it seemed, about incidents and conversations involving David with members of his family, school friends, teachers, other acquaintances, and sometimes total strangers. It was obviously some kind of therapeutic journal-writing organized by the clinic's headshrinking handlers. *Could be interesting,* she thought, recognizing clearly this time that there was as much voyeuristic relish and sheer prurience in her interest and motivation as professional ardor. She was really learning things about *herself* today!

Hearing the inspector downstairs, back from his hot and fruitless pursuit, Molly stuffed the folder into the suitcase and went down to meet him.

Lennon's only satisfaction was to have sighted in the back hall of the house, just then as he came in, an excellent and obviously recent photograph of David Roundstone. He was about to rush off again to make copies for the media. Molly checked herself from asking for a copy. Rachel Sheehan had been so right: David Roundstone was indeed gorgeous. Hell, if this went much further, she would be on the murderer's side!

———

"Kim!"

"David! Holy God, what have you been up to? There is nothing else on radio and TV these days."

"I know. Can I come in? I'm on the run, I suppose."

Kim held the door wide. "This door will never be closed to you, David. You know that. Come in, you bloody lunatic."

"I have been hiding in John's Lane Church since three o'clock."

Kim smiled. "In a church. Brilliant. I guess they never think of looking in the churches. Too bad! They are probably full of murderers."

David had taken a shower. They had made food and eaten. Now they sat opposite each other on beanbags, some of the scant furnishings that Kim allowed in the open-plan top-story space from where he looked down on the Dublin Liberties. It was a comfortable apartment, quiet, bright, and unbelievably cheap: Somehow the developers had overlooked it.

Korean, tidy-sized, and fine-boned, Kim, like many Orientals, was ten years older than his lissom frame and child's face suggested. He worked in an inner-city health center, putting obese business people of both genders through their paces. They liked him, and he was a splendid teacher, though few had the discipline to acquire or maintain his perfect fitness. He and David had become friends at a time when neither of them had many others.

"David, I taught you tae kwon do as a means of self-defense against muggers, gay-bashers, and rapists. I was not teaching you how to go around murdering people."

"I know, Kim. I am sorry."

"So why did you kill Piggott?"

"Kim, how can I explain it? It must be a compulsion—that is the only word for it—an obsession. I am horrified and hypnotized.

It sucks—like those movies about vampires. They sink their teeth into this beautiful, innocent girl, into her throat. She struggles and screams. In the end, she, too, becomes a vampire. That's it, Kim. I think I have become a vampire. It is like sex."

Kim laughed outright. "Wow! Enjoyable?"

David shook his head sadly. "I mean . . . inescapable." Suddenly he was crying. "Kim, help me!"

"Jan-Hein, just listen to this!"

Jan-Hein was at the sink, making cannelloni-something. Molly, lolling in an armchair, her legs dangling over the side, was doing her homework out loud, giving readings from David Roundstone's *Aggression Fantasies,* which lay cradled in her lap. The journal was, in fact, a sort of let-it-all-hang-out archive, in which patients at Mountainview Clinic were encouraged to confess the angry things they had said and done and express their violent fantasies and feelings. Psychologically, these seemed ninety percent normal, even if socially or politically incorrect. Starting with potty-rage, then yelling at nannies and teachers, they continued through pulling little girls' pigtails, fistfights, dirty tackles and stamping in football matches, and on to smashing mirrors in bathrooms that showed too much acne. Heavier stuff were Oedipal pogroms on the home front, and fits of hate and jealousy between lovers. More awesome still were passionate death wishes—for self or for others—murky sado-masochist stuff, and one or two vicious scenes of explicit physical violence.

"Jeepers, it's all in here, Jan-Hein. Just listen!"

He was sitting on the couch putting on his socks. He had had a shower. It was a hot day. He looked up, surprised, I suppose, and annoyed. I said, "I am David Roundstone, your son." He turned scarlet, not with embarrassment: with sheer rage. "How dare you walk in here," he said, "you guttersnipe?" That is what he called me.

I started shouting then, about myself and my bitch of a mother, about Johnny and his lovely mother, about school and being expelled, about being a pervert, and a queer, and a nut case, about Keating, that prick, and his shitty clinic, about him—my fucking Daddy. (That's not a joke: It's literally all he ever did for me!)

He was in a rage, but nothing like the rage that I was in! It all just burst out of my head. I really hated him. I wished that he was dead. He went on putting on his socks, then his shoes. He looked furious, and dangerous, and . . . what is the word? Contempuous. Yes, contemptuous, that is it. Then I thought of something really awful. I thought: This man is my father, My Father! And as far as he is concerned, I don't even exist. I am nothing except dirty dregs in a thrown-away condom!

It was like he was reading my mind. "Listen, you guttersnipe." He called me that again. "Listen, you guttersnipe, get this into your thick head. You are not my son. You are a mistake." A MISTAKE!

Then he told me, he actually told me—this is so sick-funny, I just could not believe I was hearing it—he actually told me that he and Isa, my loving mother, had fully decided on an abortion in England . . . I mean I *was* to be aborted. For Christ's sake, what way was that bad bastard dragged up? You don't go around the place saying that to people, do you?

But I wasn't aborted, because the stupid bitch broke her leg and ended up in hospital with her leg wired to the ceiling.

So, in spite of all the good planning, I got born. Isn't that just wild? Isn't that just the funniest joke anyone ever heard?

"There is a big gap here, Jan-Hein."

"Like rubbed out?"

"No, a gap. He is not writing. He is crying."

"How could you possibly know that?"

"I know."

"Intuition?"

"Why do you guys always have to say that? It is so boring."

Jan-Hein came and looked over her shoulder at the page. He kissed her on the top of the head. "OK. He is crying."

"Oh sweet Jesus! Listen to the end, Jan-Hein. Two lines." She read:

I lashed out, once. I knew he was dead. I wiped my shoe on the carpet, and I went out.

Jan-Hein gave a low, slow whistle, ending in one of his carefully learned Dublin expressions. "Holy mackerel, Molly! That is as good as a signed confession."

"But it was written in the clinic, two years ago. It is dated. All the entries are dated. It cannot be a description of what happened a few weeks ago. Besides, there are several discrepancies. For instance, it says that Piggott was sitting on a couch when he was killed. He was not. He was sitting in a chair. In fact, as far as I remember, there is no couch in that room. And what is all that stuff about taking a shower? I don't think there are showers in the judges' chambers."

"Well, if it is not a confession, it is even worse. It is a detailed and amazingly accurate plan. That is disastrous from your dreamy boy's point of view. In what you read out, he makes the killing sound like a spontaneous lashing out, in answer to unbearable provocation. But look at the reality: This murder was premeditated and carefully planned, two whole years ago."

He put a comforting arm around Molly's shoulder. She looked as if she might be going to cry, too. "How do you say?" he added less helpfully. "His goose is really cooking!"

"I don't understand what you are telling me, David. It doesn't make sense. You talk as if this stuff has happened dozens of times, I mean the urge, the inescapability, the compulsion. But how many people exactly have you murdered?"

"I don't know."

"You don't know! More than one? I mean, you didn't murder that priest, did you?"

"I don't think so."

"You don't think so. What in God's name is that meant to mean? David, are you sure, really sure, that you murdered anyone, the judge, for instance?"

"The papers say I did."

Kim reached out and took David's chin between his thumb and index finger. He turned the boy's face toward his own and looked into it attentively. "Dave, do you know what your face is saying, and your eyes?"

"What are they saying?"

"They are saying, *Cloud Cuckoo Land,* loud and clear. Have you got any of those pills left?"

He did not answer immediately. Then, reluctantly, he pulled a battered wallet from his back pocket. From that he took an even more battered bubble card and threw it on the floor. "Eighteen. A week's supply of shit, nine days actually. Kim, I'm not going back on this stuff. I want to be well. Four years in Keating's kip is enough. Enough is enough."

"You want to be well. And how well are you, Dave? Are you any way well at all?"

David lowered his head but said nothing.

"Listen, I am no medic, agreed, but I do work all the time with people who want to be well, and I have learned some things about what you can do and what you cannot do in that line. A lot of these guys, when they come, have some pretty filthy habits by way of chemical dependency. It can be anything—alcohol, cigarettes, drugs, any of a million different medicines. More generally, when they start with us, they are eating too much, and all the wrong things, or drinking. They are overweight, their blood pressure is in a mess, cholesterol over the moon, and, above all, they have not been taking any regular exercise.

"So what happens? They arrive at the center on a tidal wave of good resolutions. No more booze or cigarettes, no more pills, no more sex, red meat, spuds, no more anything. Instead, ten-mile jogs every day, two thousand press-ups, weight lifting, exercise bike, you name it. Result—unless you stop them in their tracks—massive coronary, cardiac arrest, stroke, whatever, the guy is dead on the floor. Conclusion: Too much good health can *kill* you!"

They both laughed.

"So there is the message: Even if you should never have been on those pills, after four years, you cannot just drop them like that. You have to go slowly, under medical supervision. Look at what has happened since you went off them, for God's sake, David, you don't even know, for sure, what *has* happened. You don't even know, for sure, what you have or have not done yourself. In a few short weeks, you have totally lost the plot. In fact, David, at the moment, you are *not* well, and you are *dangerous*. Isn't that true? Isn't it?"

David dropped his head again. There was a long silence. Finally, he whispered, "I guess."

Kim searched for words. "David, take these pills. Get your head working again, I mean working full-time. Stay here for a while. Lie low. In a few days you will know the next step. God will show you."

"God? I don't know if I believe in God anymore. He misses too many appointments."

"Does it matter what you believe? The only important question is whether God believes in you."

David looked up, surprised. "I never heard anyone saying that before. Do you think that I . . . I mean, do you think that God . . ."

Kim colored slightly. "Believes in you? I don't see how he could possibly do otherwise."

They looked at each other, eyes saying what words could not. After a while Kim said, "Listen, you spent hours in that church today. Perhaps God listened to your prayer."

"I wasn't praying."

"Are you sure? Perhaps God listened to your heart."

There was another long silence. Then David said, "Thank you, Kim. Get me some water, will you? These things taste like rattlesnake's vomit."

TUESDAY, JULY 28

Two calls came in soon after 3:00 p.m., both from surveillance. The Roundstones were back in town. Isa had just walked into her shop, and shortly afterward Felix, who had presumably dropped her off, had driven up to their house in Donnybrook.

"Neat." said Lennon. "The merchant princes have landed and are conveniently apart."

"Divide and conquer, as the Fairy Queen said. Let's hit the beaches."

That was Quilligan. He and Saunders drove out of Castle Yard and headed for Donnybrook. At 3:20 p.m. they were comfortably ahead of rush hour traffic, which an hour later could have quadrupled the ten minutes it took them to complete their journey. Meanwhile, Denis and Molly crossed Dame Street and entered Temple Bar.

Roundstone Antiques looked as it should: a bow-windowed boutique in deep purple and gilt. The window showed Irish glass and a mishmash of art deco whatnots. Inside was better: something called seashell-green paintwork backing well-designed showcases. There was some nice silver, a fine longcase clock, *Spy* cartoons, and some quite decent small items of furniture. An attractive girl was showing silver napkin rings to a Japanese couple. Lennon murmured in her ear. She excused herself to the customers and ushered the police into an office behind the shop. Isa, dressed cooly in a smart lime-colored summer frock, rose to meet them.

"Inspector, Sergeant, please sit down. Well, I hope I am not in trouble."

Lennon ignored this conventional greeting of the innocent and of those wishing to be thought so. "You have just returned from France, Mrs. Roundstone. May I ask what you were doing there?"

Isa's eyes widened. "Certainly, Inspector. I have no difficulty about that. It might be more polite, however, if you were to tell me the purpose of your visit." Lennon said nothing. After a slight hesitation she continued. "In the meantime, seeing you ask, my husband and I were on a mini-break to Paris, a purely recreational activity."

"Were you not engaged in business, Mrs. Roundstone, in buying and selling?"

Again, a fractional pause, calculation, a sarcastic smile. "Yes, Inspector, I believe I did buy some postcards, and a blouse, and we did, of course, require to eat from time to time."

"Did you visit antique shops or commercial art galleries?"

"Inspector, I do feel that by now you have overstepped the bounds of common courtesy. I have been away. I am now quite busy catching up. Do please tell me what we are talking about. If there is a problem, let us clear it up quickly and conclude our conversation."

"You will be aware, Mrs. Roundstone, that we are searching for your son in connection with the death of Mr. Justice Piggott."

Isa's face reddened slightly, but she kept an impassive expression. "Poor Sidney . . . He was a friend of ours, you know. I am certain that David had nothing whatsoever to do with his murder. Why would he?"

"You took David out of his psychiatric clinic five or six weeks ago, didn't you?"

"No, Inspector, I did not. David is twenty . . . he is twenty-something. I have no authority whatsoever to put him in or take him out of any clinic. He got fed up in there, and he came out himself."

"You paid him, most unusually, a number of visits in close succession around that time, during which, according to the clinic staff, you encouraged him to leave. And he did leave, with you."

"Inspector, I would suggest that I know better what transpired between my son and myself than do the slandering skivvies in Dr. Keating's insanitary clinic. Why don't you ask me what happened, instead of pursuing these will-o'-the-wisps in such a needlessly offensive manner?"

Lennon did not reply nor even look sheepish. Isa continued. "Three months ago I took on the excellent girl whom you met in the boutique. That gave me, at last, a little more leisure time, which I was happy to spend with my son. He was happy, too, and yes, if you like, it did encourage him. He decided he wanted to leave that clinic. It was his idea, not mine."

"Did you discourage him?"

"No, Inspector, I could not say that either. I counseled prudence, but I did not try to push him in one direction or the other. David, for all his mildness, is very strong-willed. I suppose he inherits that from me. If you attempt to drive him one way, he chooses the other. Besides . . ."

The pause was beautifully timed, Lennon thought. She was probably a formidable liar. Fortunately, there was one tiny vein in her forehead pulsing away and telling the truth, possibly the only organ in her body accustomed to do so. He helped her along.

"Besides, Mrs. Roundstone?"

"Well, I don't like saying this, but I had been hearing stories about Dr. Keating, the director of the clinic, that he had been experimenting with medicines, using new drugs which had not been fully authorized for treatment of . . . well, for use on people."

"Is that why you encouraged David to stop taking his drugs?" He could see her weighing up which way to jump. "Did Dr. Keating warn you of the dangerous consequences if David did not take his medication?"

"Dear me, Inspector, that is quite an avalanche of questions all together Well, I most certainly did not discourage David from taking his medicine, though I will admit that I am something of an antipill person. Dr. Keating, I should say, was not there when David discharged himself, but he did contact me afterward to say that David should continue with his medicine. All doctors say the same. It is a bit of a cliché, don't you think? But yes, of course, I did ask David about it a few times. He assured me that he was taking his medication regularly."

"Did Dr. Keating tell you what might happen if David did not take his tablets?"

"Nothing that I remember. I suppose he may have said that he might become a bit depressed or excitable, that sort of thing."

"Did he not tell you that he might become paranoid, obsessive, highly dangerous, even murderous?"

"Oh no, Inspector, heavens no! That is nonsense. David is the sweetest boy. He is incapable of violence."

"Would you live with him in the house if he were not taking his medicine?"

"The telltale pulse on Isa's forehead gave a double thumbsdown. She replied, "Of course, Inspector. I love having him with me."

"But you don't have him with you, do you? Where is he living?"

"To be perfectly honest, I do not rightly know. I have not seen him for over a month. As I told you, he is very independent. Look,

Inspector, you are forcing me to go into private family matters which are really none of your business. The fact is that David, much as I love him, is homosexual. He spends his time and even lives with that sort of people. If David did have anything to do with Sidney's death—which, personally, I do not believe—but if he did, it must have been under the influence of these people. They are notorious for their rivalries and jealousies. Don't you think that you should turn your attention to that area of investigation?"

Molly cut in across the flow of words. "Didn't you hand him over yourself, bound and gagged, to Albert Singer?"

"You are an impertinent young woman! I did not hand David over, bound and gagged, to anybody. Mr. Singer is a customer of mine. He employs houseboys. You can understand that in whatever way you wish. David is skilled in the area of catering and housekeeping. The fact is that I did not feel he was ready to go back into working in a public restaurant, as he used to do. So, yes, I did get him a job with Mr. Singer. I felt that Mr. Singer would—how shall I say?—look after him. Now . . . There was a message on my answerphone when I got back from Paris an hour ago. From Mr. Singer. It seems that David has . . . disappeared. As you should understand, I am worried."

Before she could say anything more, Molly had another question. "How many times have you done trips to Paris or London to sell stolen artworks for Judge Piggott?"

Isa's face was transformed instantly into a perfect death mask, white, hard, and ugly. She did not have, at that particular moment, the makings of an attractive corpse.

Lennon decided it was time to step in again. "Never mind, Mrs. Roundstone, we already know the answer. I must tell you that you seem to be in very serious trouble. Our first priority, however, is to find your son. I am asking you directly, where is David Roundstone? It is absolutely essential that we find him."

"Isn't he with Singer?" she asked hoarsely.

"As you have already told us yourself, he is not."

"Well then, I have no idea. That world of his is a labyrinth."

The police stood up to go. Isa followed them to the door. "What do you mean, Inspector, when you say that I am in serious trouble? I haven't done anything wrong."

Lennon turned slowly to face her. "Apart from such relatively less serious offenses as receiving and marketing stolen property, and various revenue irregularities, our main concern is that you used your mentally ill son to murder Mr. Justice Sidney Piggott."

"We must not keep you, Mrs. Roundstone," Molly said brightly as she and Lennon turned again to go. "You must have lots to do and think about."

Isa took rapid steps after them. "But wait, Inspector, this is utter nonsense. It is absurd. Your insinuations are outrageous. What possible motive could Felix and I have for wanting to murder poor Sidney?"

Lennon stopped with his hand on the doorknob. He looked her straight in the eye. "Mrs. Roundstone, neither of us has so much as mentioned your husband. How very interesting that you should do so in the way that you just have. As for a motive. Well, what about 220,000 euro, tax free, salted away on Grand Turk Island?"

He opened the door, allowed Molly to pass, and closed it again softly behind them.

"Felix. The police have been here."

"Yes, darling, they are here, too."

"What, how could they? They have just left here."

"They must be different ones."

"Felix, tell those bastards nothing. Do you hear me?"

"Darling—"

"Stop talking and listen."

"Darling—"

"Shut up, I said. What have you told them?"

"Isa, they are sitting here—right beside me."

"Shit!"

"Whatever you say, darling. Good-bye."

Felix had recognised Quilligan the minute he opened the door. When it was announced that they were police he felt faint and smelled rodent. They went to sit in the drawing room, a suitably elegant salon for fashionable art dealers.

"Have a nice time in France, Felix?"

"Yes, thank you," Felix replied, wincing at the intruder's familiarity.

"Business or pleasure?"

"I beg your pardon?"

"Were you traveling for business or for pleasure?"

"Oh. A bit of both, I suppose. But, Inspector, are you not going to tell me why you are here?"

"In due time, Felix, in due time. Sometimes one has to wait to know these things. Life is like that. For instance, on the boat I was just dying to know where you and Isa were heading."

Felix winced again at the sustained familiarity, now extended to include his wife. She would not approve.

"I had to be patient and wait," Quilligan went on, "until you very sportingly told me yourselves, through the purser, that is. God works in marvelous ways, doesn't he? So do the police."

"Please, I don't follow," Felix stammered.

"No? Well, the point is that we *did* follow, the whole way to Monsieur Ménard's. In fact, we got there before you. We saw and heard everything. By 'we' I mean myself and the French police, *laze flicks,* as we call them in the vernacular."

Felix did not have much chin. His lower jaw now sagged forlornly on his lumpy Adam's apple. He was pea green. Looking behind him mentally, he saw the menacing figure of Isa, and stumbled forward onto enemy bayonets.

"Inspector, I am very surprised. Indeed, if I may say so, I am a bit annoyed . . . or almost annoyed." He stopped, unaccustomed perhaps to such extensive liberty of speech. Quilligan smiled sweetly and said nothing. Saunders seemed absorbed in silent prayer. "We were selling a painting to Monsieur Ménard. We deal in paintings and that sort of thing. This one is by an obscure artist, not worth very much. We may eventually get a few thousand euro. Monsieur Ménard will send us a check if he manages to sell it . . . You know, you cannot sell . . . unless you have a buyer."

Quilligan was still smiling pleasantly and saying nothing. Saunders was excavating his toes through the apertures in his sandals. The telephone rang. It was Isa with her encouraging message. Felix was feeling quite ill.

"Isa, was it?" Quilligan inquired. "I hope she is well, and telling the truth. But where were we? Yes, you may get a few thousand pounds. Well, good for you, Felix. But what about the poor old judge, what will he get?"

Felix's coloring disimproved further, to frozen celery. "What judge?" he faltered. "I do not understand."

"Ah, how quickly they forget!" said Quilligan mournfully. He got to his feet and came to stand over his interlocutor. Felix gazed up like a rabbit ogling a wolf. "Come on, Felix, why talk yourself down? A good Honthorst is worth more than a few thousand euro. Do you know how much I would ask for it, if I were you?"

"How much?" Felix inquired faintly.

"Two hundred and twenty grand, Felix, not a penny less. And do you know what I would do with the lolly when I got it?"

"No," Felix croaked.

"Straight to the Grand Turk, *cher ami*. No place like it for money. Nice discreet climate."

Felix retrieved his lower lip from down around his clavicle and bit it, perhaps in self-punishment.

Quilligan asked in a gentler voice, "Did you see David's picture in the paper this morning?"

"Yes. We saw a paper in Rosslare. I . . . we are very upset. David would not hurt a fly, normally . . . He is not well . . . He is mad."

"That makes it worse, don't you think?"

Felix lowered his head. A tear splashed on his clenched hands. Quilligan dropped suddenly to his haunches and seized those hands in his own. "Where is David now?"

"I do not know."

"He has not been treated fairly in all this, has he? Come on, Felix, has he?"

Felix shuddered but said nothing.

"Did Isa set him up to murder Piggott?"

"No!"

"And if she did, and if push comes to shove, whose side will you be on?"

Felix blundered to his feet. "Listen, Inspector, I don't know what you are talking about. I hope with all my heart that David has not murdered anyone, and if he has, it is not his fault. That is all I have to say. Now please leave."

"And what about Isa?"

"I cannot talk to you about my wife. You have no right to do this, Inspector. Please go!"

They went.

"Why did you let him off the hook, sir?" Saunders asked.

"Did I?" Quilligan countered unheatedly.

They were stalled in rush hour traffic at the junction of Waterloo and Morehampton.

"Well, you had him in tears. A little more and you could have cracked him."

"I don't think that 'cracking' is what questioning is about."

"No? What is it about, so?"

"It is about finding out."

"We didn't find out much, did we?"

"I think we found out that Felix doesn't know much more than we know. He is fond of David, more so than Isa is. He is afraid that David may have killed Piggott, and he is afraid that, if he did kill Piggott, Isa was behind it."

"But, sure, we knew all that."

"Not quite. I think that Felix told us the truth."

"Big deal!"

"No, small deal, Saunders. But detection is a matter of small deals. You must learn that."

If the training of garda recruits has some small deficiencies, these probably include failure to teach hurlers and football players how to perch artily cross-legged on high stools in gay bars extracting useful information.

Training or no training, Lennon had felt constrained to try something. So he had propelled twelve emissaries into the highways and lowlife byways of Dublin's gay culture. Their mission was to seek and find David Roundstone. Nine of these apostles were men, three were women. None, insofar as he knew, had either predisposition or the slightest natural talent for the task. Quite to the contrary, all exuded acute discomfort in these unfamiliar surroundings, bordering in one or two cases on hysteria or panic.

They were seen coming a mile off. Some gay people were

offended by this irruption into their bars and clubs all over the city and by the inference, as they saw it, that Piggott had been slain because he was homosexual, or else because he was not. The fraternity's estimate of Piggott was that he had been unsympathetic and ill informed about them, one of those judges who seemed to assume that most homosexuals are pedophiles and that all pedophiles are homosexual.

Other gay people took a lighter view and settled down to the entertainment of baiting the invaders. This mostly took the form of high camp to the point of absurdity, right in the face of the intruders, whose heroically contained yet perfectly evident revulsion provided splendid amusement for the regular clientele. One or two old queens did evince a genuine interest in some of the more winsome gardai, dropping indiscreet hints or even hands. Especially in the latter instance, shrieks of terror and indignation blew whatever meager cover there might have been.

Some people did help, appreciating, even better than the police, that this was about murder and not about sex. Virtually nobody knew David Roundstone. He had been away for several years. Even before that, he had never really been on the scene. But people did know Kim, and eventually somebody was able to put the two names together. Even then they were linked not as a current item but as news from the past. An address was produced: St. Patrick's Close, behind the cathedral. It was a former address. By the time the gardai had been there and had been redirected, Kim had been alerted by telephone. It was after midnight when they got to his new address.

"Sir, sorry to wake you up. It's about this gayboy you are looking for."

"Who is this?"

"Garda Alphonsus Murphy, sir, Tallaght. I've been drafted in for this search. I don't think you know me."

"Have you found David Roundstone?"

"I'm not sure. We are here, myself and Pat Hanrahan, with this Chinaman. We are after being sent from Billy to Jack the whole night. These gayboys have a fierce impudent sense of humor. Anyhow, we've ended up with this Chinaman. He says he knows where Roundstone is but that he won't tell us."

"Whose telephone are you using?"

"The Chinaman's."

"Did you get his permission?"

"Permission?"

"Put him on to me."

"Put him on to you."

"Are you going to repeat everything I say for the rest of the night? Put him on."

He did.

"You are Kim?"

"How did you know?"

"I should have guessed. Listen, I am sorry about my friends. Give me your number, please. I'll tell them to go. Then I'll ring you back in a few minutes and we can talk about this. My name is Denis Lennon. I'm trying to deal with this case. OK?"

"Yes."

Kim gave his telephone number. Lennon talked to Garda Murphy again. "Well done, Alfie. You can leave it with me now. Mr. Kim will cooperate. By the way, he is Korean, not Chinese."

"Sure they're all the same, sir: slitty-eyed, tricky little bastards."

"Get the hell out of there, Murphy, this very instant. Go home!"

"He knows he has to give himself up, and he will. He just needs a little more time for the pills to work."

"How long?"

"Say, two days, Thursday evening."

"Where is he now?"

"Don't ask."

"Where was he when the police called?"

"On the roof."

"Well done! Can I talk to him?"

"That is not a good idea, not yet."

"So Thursday evening, where?"

"St. Patrick's Cathedral. In the garden, 8:00 P.M."

"I'm trusting you, Kim."

"Not half as much as I am trusting you, Inspector."

"Listen, will you ask him one question for me, just one?"

"What is it?"

"Ask him how he got into the gallery of the court, the day the judge was murdered."

"I don't understand."

"He will understand."

"OK. Hold on."

WEDNESDAY, JULY 29

THE RADIO NEWS HAD IT IN THE MORNING THAT THE search for David Roundstone had been called off. Lennon went on the air to deny this, explaining that the search had entered a new phase that made a citywide dragnet no longer necessary. The police, he added, were following a definite line of inquiry and were confident that David Roundstone would be helping them with their investigation within a few days. Mercifully, Chief Superintendent Flynn was away having his prostate done and did not ring up to add to the list of the things he absolutely failed to understand.

Singer was on the phone at 9:30 A.M. demanding to know why the search for David Roundstone had been stood down.

"Because we know where he is. Anyhow, I thought you said that we should not be chasing him in the first place."

"These stop-go tactics are getting us nowhere. If you know where he is, why don't you go and collect him?"

"We will."

"Lennon, your answers are offhand and impertinent. So allow me to concentrate your mind. Friday, the day after tomorrow, is the last day of the legal term. The higher courts will not sit again until October. We will not disperse without firm reassurances that something serious is being done in the wake of this most serious attack on our entire system of justice, the murder of a High Court judge *in situ*. I must tell you that there is widespread dissatisfaction with the way this investigation is proceeding, or indeed not proceeding."

"Who is having the widespread dissatisfaction?"

"The senior persons concerned with the administration of justice."

"Really? I haven't heard from any of them."

"You are hearing from me!"

Lennon made a slight snorting sound and said nothing.

Singer, an accomplished snorter himself, understood perfectly and was furious. "Very well, Inspector. Listen to this, then. I am convening a meeting for Friday next at 11:00 A.M. in the Board Room at Distillery Building. I expect the chief justice and the president of the High Court to be present. Also the attorney general, and such other persons as I shall call upon to attend. I shall, of course, preside, in my capacity as chairman of the Bar Council. I expect you to be there and to give an account of your stewardship in this most serious matter."

He hung up.

Lennon discussed this conversation with Quilligan later in the morning over coffee.

"Denis, the lad is off his rocker. Could you imagine the chief justice or any of those dudes going to such a meeting? Delusions of grandeur, how are you!"

"Well, let's go ourselves, anyhow. It might even help, to have to pull all the threads together under critical gaze. Suppose I do the overall thing, the general presentation. Then you cover the arty side of the story: theft and receiving, trips to Paris, the actual painting, Roundstone, mother and son, OK?"

Quilligan nodded his big head. Lennon continued. "Whoever

does come to Singer's meeting, we are bound to have some pretty good legal minds in there. A brainstorming with those guys might produce something. We actually need it. I cannot shake off the feeling that we have missed something. Do you know what I mean?"

"Don't I just! It's like mountainy sheep: You might have fifty horny lads up there—I mean sheep, Denis!"

"Oh!"

"Well, you could have half a hundred up there, and just by scanning the side of the mountain from a mile off, a good sheep farmer would know if there was one missing."

"Go on out of that!"

"God's truth, Denis!"

"And you think we are missing a sheep?"

"I am sure of it."

"A horny lad!"

"That's it."

THURSDAY, JULY 30

LENNON TOOK THE DAY OFF. HE AND HIS WIFE TOOK their two eldest grandchildren to the zoo.

Molly took the day off. She and Jan-Hein went to the beach at Silver Strand and got burned.

Quilligan took the day off and took his children up into the mountains to live in a tent for a long weekend: a sort of Sukkoth for another wandering people.

Saunders took the day off and stayed in bed.

That night, Ben Silverman rang Lennon.

"I'll see you at Albert Singer's party tomorrow."

"How so? I thought only the great and the good got invited to that treat."

"Oh, I wasn't invited. In fact, Albert is as sour as a lemon that I'm coming. The whole thing is ludicrous. Singer expected all the crowned heads of Liffey-side to turn up, instead of which he gets the likes of me!"

"And who else?"

"Wait till you hear! The chief justice just said, 'No: not

appropriate'—which is transparent code for 'Who the hell do you think you are?'"

"Quite right, too."

"The president of the High Court was more polite. He said that, as one of the first on the scene the day of the murder, he might be a witness, so he couldn't go to any meetings. He appointed Jack Porter, who is due to retire in November, to represent him, or the judges' neighborhood watch, or whoever it is the president was meant to stand for. The attorney general, as leader of the bar, asked me to go for him—in terms I had better not repeat—so that is how I get to be in there, and I invited Rachel Sheehan to assist me, whatever that means. I just thought she would like it."

"She could be a witness, too. She saw the boy on the back stairs."

"Good point. Well, leave Singer to sort that one out. He'll probably declare her unconstitutional."

"Or have her stoned! Ben, is this guy off the wall, or what?"

"Either that, or he really is the messiah! But wait, I haven't told you the best bit yet. Singer invited Tom FitzPatrick, the president of the Incorporated Law Society, that is, the solicitors. Now Singer has done nothing except be rude to the solicitors since the day he was elected. Tom is a joker, and he saw his chance. He said he couldn't come tomorrow because it is Fair Day in Ballinamuck or wherever, but that he would nominate a representative. Guess who?"

"I wouldn't have a notion."

"Mr. Arnold St. John Smithers!"

"The visionary?"

"Correct. Prepare your soul for signs and wonders."

FRIDAY, JULY 31

IT WASN'T QUITE THE BOARD ROOM, BUT STILL A MORE than generous space for the size of the assembly. Singer throned, rather than sat, in the presiding position. Mr. Justice Porter sat on his right, Ben Silverman on his left, with Rachel, the mere woman, and Smithers, the lunatic, as far away as Singer could get them on either wing.

The police were seated on hardbacked armless chairs facing this tribunal. They had not even been supplied with a table on which to write or place their documents. Singer had personally seen to these arrangements. To his intense annoyance, Quilligan had come in, taken one look, gone out, and returned with a table the size of a tennis court on his back. He had also procured a carafe of water and glasses for his colleagues, which was more than even Singer had on his pinnacle.

Quilligan was now sitting beside Lennon. He was strangely quiet, as if preoccupied. Just before the session began, he stood up abruptly and grabbed Lennon's arm.

"Denis, is that room open, the judge's room?"

"Piggott's? I haven't a clue, Jim, why?"

"We forgot something. This could be vital!"

"Where are you going, Jim? Come back!"

"It's the horny lad, Denis. This could be it!"

"Jim!"

"Keep it going, Denis. Keep talking till I get back!"

And he was gone.

Before Lennon could gather his wits, Singer rapped on the table and embarked on a terse introduction to the proceedings. In this he neither welcomed nor thanked anybody, but declared his own understanding of what was to follow: a kangaroo court with the dual purpose of excoriating the police force and demonstrating Mr. Albert Singer's superiority to everybody else in the entire legal firmament.

A curt nod instructed Lennon to begin. He stood up, wondering what on earth Quilligan was up to. "I have been asked to make a presentation of where we are at with the investigation into the death of Mr. Justice Sidney Piggott. I am happy to do so.

"Sidney Piggott was murdered in his chambers at the Four Courts, Dublin, between 5:00 and 6:00 P.M. on Tuesday, July fourteenth, just over two weeks ago. Death was caused instantaneously by a powerful blow to the neck, delivered by a kick or by some heavy instrument, and most probably by a person skilled in one of the martial arts.

"The police investigation was soon concentrated on a young man who had been seen around the courts on at least one occasion before the day of the murder, and who was seen again on the day of the murder, in the public gallery of Judge Piggott's court. I do not need to point out that this was an unusual and irregular place for a member of the public, or indeed anyone, to be seen. I have devoted some thought to understanding why this young man would have chosen to present himself in this unusual place when, in fact, there was ample space available for members of the public downstairs in the body of the courtroom."

"Indeed," Singer interjected dryly, "and has your thought on that topic yielded any significant result?"

"You will have an opportunity presently to assess that matter yourselves. For the moment, I will content myself to say that whereas one might spontaneously expect that a person would place himself in that gallery with a view to being inconspicuous, the effect has actually been the opposite: to make sure that he was noticed."

Singer looked up sharply. "What do you mean? Are you saying that this boy—and let us not beat around the bush, we are talking about David Roundstone—are you saying that David Roundstone put himself in that gallery for the purpose of being seen?"

"No, I am not saying that this was his purpose, but I am saying that it was the effect."

"So it was a random effect."

"It might have been somebody else's purpose," Ben Silverman interjected, "somebody else who steered the boy into that place, wanting him to be seen."

"Nonsense," Singer snapped. "Why would anyone want to do that?"

Lennon smiled thinly and continued. "As Mr. Singer has just mentioned, the boy in question was undoubtedly David Roundstone. He will be positively identified by a number of credible witnesses. It must also be mentioned that some blond hairs found in the public gallery of the courtroom match hairs found in Judge Piggott's chambers after the murder, quite a large number of hairs in both cases, I must say. I should add that as recently as Monday we removed similar hairs from David Roundstone's bedroom in Mr. . . . eh, in the house where he was living."

"No need to be bashful, Inspector." Singer interrupted. "In my house."

Lennon went on. "Dr. Tweedy has confirmed to me, half an

hour ago, that these hairs match exactly those found in the courtroom gallery and in Judge Piggott's chambers. There is also the
question of the earring."

"Aha! Yes, the earring!" exclaimed Mr. St. John Smithers,
counsel for the Archangel Gabriel.

Lennon continued hastily. "A gilt earring, of the kind often worn
by young people these days, was found near Judge Piggott's body
on the day of the murder—or, more accurately, on the next day.
David Roundstone was known to wear such an earring."

"So you are saying" Mr. Justice Porter summarized, "that the
presence of these hairs and of the earring, taken together with
the physical viewing of Roundstone in the vicinity of the murder,
show that he was in that room, in Judge Piggott's chambers, that
very day?"

"It would appear so."

" 'Appear,' " Singer repeated acidly. "Until now you have been
obtrusively insistent that he *was* there. Are you less sure now?"

"Until now, Mr. Singer, you have been very insistent that he was
not there at all, that day or any day. Have you changed your view on
that?"

"Get on with your report, Lennon, will you?"

"We should also note that David Roundstone is highly trained in
a particularly lethal form of martial art, called, I believe, tae kwon
do. I hope I have that right."

"You have," said Molly out loud. Singer looked as if he would tell
her to be quiet.

"So," exclaimed Porter the summarizer, "first, he *was* there. Second, he *could* do it. He was trained for it. What about thirdly, *why*
would he do it?"

"Motive," said Silverman, as if explaining to children.

Lennon sipped from a glass of water and started on the motive.
"It seems that Judge Piggott was indeed David Roundstone's father.

Apparently, he never acknowledged this son and never contributed in any way to his upbringing—I don't just mean financially, but in the wider sense of parenting. David, it is clear, was deeply resentful about this."

"Why am I not surprised?" Ben Silverman asked nobody in particular. Judge Porter threw him a disapproving look, which bounced off disregarded.

"Dr. Keating, Roundstone's psychiatrist, will be able to give evidence on that point."

"If the court allows him," Singer corrected. "The doctor/patient relationship is an area of privilege. This is a complex area of law, which we have not time to explain to you now, Inspector. Just leave these difficult questions to competent lawyers."

Ignoring this sneering put-down, Lennon pressed on. "We have discovered among David Roundstone's possessions documents in his own hand in which he acknowledges having murdered Judge Piggott. We have also found what could be described as a complete blueprint for that murder—and that blueprint was drawn up fully two years before the event."

"Great heavens!" said Porter. "*Mens Rea,* if ever I saw it, the guilty mind."

"The thing about this document is that it is quite explicit, and indeed vehement about the motive. Young Roundstone was very resentful of his father's neglect. There seems even to have been an occasion when Judge Piggott told the young man that it had been his parents' intention to abort him. I mean he told him this indiscreetly.

"Tell me, Inspector," Ben asked in his best cross-examining manner, "how could one ever impart such intelligence *discreetly?*"

Lennon smiled, fully aware that Silverman was rubbing in his point for him. "Well, exactly, sir. It does not mean, of course, that David Roundstone was justified in killing his father. It does mean that he had a motive. Another whole aspect of this affair is that David Roundstone has a history of psychological problems. I understand that the prognosis in respect of these is quite hopeful. The difficulty seems to be that during the last several weeks he has not been taking medication which he should have been taking."

"Why not?" snapped Smithers. "There could be a duty in law to take one's medicine."

"One of the main issues in this case is going to be to trace any influences that were brought to bear on this young man before he perpetrated this deed. Did somebody induce him to leave the Mountainview Clinic, where he was safely, if not perhaps too happily, lodged? Did somebody deliberately induce a state of instability in him by persuading him, or encouraging him, not to take his medicine?"

"Why would anybody do that, Inspector?" Smithers asked. "Parsimony, perhaps?"

"Parsimony?"

"The price of the pills. These medicines cost a fortune, you know. Had the boy a medical card?"

"I have no idea."

"Don't you think you should find out? That's probably the cause of most of the crime in this country: The wrong people get the medical cards."

Rachel, diffident in the strange menagerie that made up the inquisitorial side of the table, plucked up her courage to ask a question. "Inspector, are you suggesting that somebody may have induced or aggravated a state of mental fragility in this boy, so that he would murder Judge Piggott?"

"Since the outset of our investigation we have had reason to suspect that this may be the case."

"Do you have somebody specific in mind?"

Where the hell was Quilligan? This was where he was meant to come in. Lennon drank some more water and looked at the door. It did not oblige. "The answer to your question is affirmative. I had hoped that Inspector Quilligan would be here to deal with this aspect of the investigation. It is half past twelve now. Could we possibly break for lunch, and—"

"No," said Singer, so churlishly that no one thought to challenge him.

Lennon started into the whole story of Tony Macklin the burglar, Piggott the receiver, Isa and Felix Roundstone the accomplices. He described in detail the saga of the Honthorst painting, conscious that Quilligan would have made a much more exciting narrator.

"This is not a court, and I do emphasize that the information I have outlined to you is very strictly confidential. The director of public prosecutions will decide whether and which charges will be brought on foot of it. I am aware that a number of charges will very probably lie in relation to receiving and trading in stolen property, also in relation to revenue questions. My colleague Inspector Quilligan is more concerned with these aspects of the case."

Singer, who had been listening to this part of the inspector's presentation with particular interest, now intervened. "But in relation to Judge Piggott's murder, you believe that there is strong evidence that the Roundstones, or that Isa Roundstone, induced her mentally disturbed son to leave his asylum, then deprived him of his medication, enflamed him against his unloving father, and, in effect, contrived that he would murder that father—"

Porter the summarizer, unwilling to see his prerogative pass entirely to another, completed the argument. "And they, or she, did this so that they could dispose of Piggott's very valuable painting and divert the entire purchase price to their own use and benefit?"

"Yes, sir, that is the hypothesis."

Singer spoke again. "Inspector, as you know, this young man has been in my service for some weeks. I had no inkling or idea that all this was happening. Of course, he was a servant and I did not get very involved in his affairs. That would not be correct."

"Such bullshit!" Molly said, just low enough not to be heard on the other side of the table.

"Besides, one does not often suspect that a person needs to be protected from his own mother," Singer continued.

"What about Hamlet," exclaimed the visionary out loud, "and Alexander the Great? He had a terrible mother."

"But I must compliment you on your good fortune. You seem to have stumbled on the solution to this case. You may not know this, but it was Isa Roundstone who prevailed on me to take this young man into service. That was clever of her. In that way she distanced herself from what it now seems she had programmed him to do. Anyhow, by good luck, more than by skill and hard work, you have solved this case."

"Mr. Singer, may I ask you a question?" Lennon asked.

"Of course, Inspector," Singer answered, surprised into good manners.

"Why did you introduce David Roundstone into the upstairs gallery of Judge Piggott's courtroom on the day of the murder?"

There was quality silence.

Singer replied in his steeliest quiet-before-the-storm modulation. "I did not do any such thing. Where did you get this nonsense?"

"David Roundstone said it."

"To whom?"

"To me, through an intermediary. I should have mentioned that Mr. Roundstone has been in custody since last evening when he turned himself in voluntarily. I have not had the pleasure of meeting him yet, because of this meeting."

"Well, let us not deprive you any further of that pleasure, Inspector. You will find Mr.Roundstone, as you call him, a pleasant conversationalist. Sadly, he is a lunatic. So you have stumbled on the solution to the mystery and Mr. Roundstone has handed himself in—out of sheer commiseration, I don't doubt, seeing that you were quite incapable of apprehending him. I think we have achieved what we set out to do. Thank you all. There will be no need to reconvene in the afternoon."

Rachel spoke up immediately. "Excuse me. I believe strongly that we should meet again after lunch."

"I agree with Miss Sheehan," Ben Silverman said loudly.

"So do I," said Mr. Justice Porter. "We have not concluded our business."

They all looked at Smithers. He was having one of his visions. "Inspector, this painting that the injust judge owned, did it portray lewd and nude young women?"

"I have no idea, but I don't think so."

"You are wrong. See how grievously the spirit of fornication is punished in a judge of lewd eyes! I see them in my vision, lewd and wanton women, dancing and cavorting."

"Well, count your blessings, old chap," cried Silverman, clapping the visionary heartily on the shoulder, as he stood up to go for his lunch.

Emerging from the conference room, Molly took Lennon by the sleeve. "You were great, Denis, really excellent. It is terrific to see you right back in form."

He gave her a grateful smile. "Thanks, sweetheart. What happened just now? Something is happening. Don't you feel it?"

"Look, here comes Jim. He looks excited, too!"

It was an understatement. Quilligan descended on them like

the Night of the Big Wind. "Jesus, Mary, and Joseph, Denis, Molly, you won't believe it!"

"Well, Lazarus, how are you?" Denis asked.

"And where have you been? Come and have some lunch," Molly said.

"No, we can't. We've got to go somewhere quiet, with an electric plug."

"You mean now?" queried Lennon.

"I mean right now."

The group reassembled outside their meeting room at two o'clock. They were now plus Quilligan and minus Singer. The reason they were outside the room was that Singer had informed the porter's desk that the meeting was over and that he should lock the door.

"Incredible behavior!"

"Beyond belief!"

"Arrogant bastard!"

"Get that door open. We are going on with this thing!"

They got it open. A heady atmosphere of conspiracy, almost recklessness, pervaded the group. Even Smithers caught the mood. "This feels like Paris in '68, the Student Revolution, you know. We were *très naughtie,* believe me!" And he actually winked at Rachel, very naughtily indeed.

Spontaneously, they all drew up their chairs around the same table.

Mr. Justice Porter took up the running. "My friends, nobody quite knows how we all got to be around this table. As a group we have no legal status whatsoever. Yet I feel that what was done this morning should not be left there, like that, just hanging in the air, unfinished."

"Hear, hear!" boomed Silverman.

"So, Inspector Lennon, if you are ready, would you like to continue?"

"Thank you, my lord. I should say, at once, that there has been a dramatic development during the morning, which will cast a very new light on much of what was said earlier on. I will come to that in a short while. In the meantime, let us return to where we left off.

"This morning, we envisaged two possibilities. The first is that David Roundstone killed Judge Piggott because he had been a bad and neglectful father, indeed cruel, not a father at all. The second hypothesis is that David Roundstone killed Judge Piggott rather as a marionette, manipulated by his mother, who stood to make a great deal of money if the judge disappeared."

"In either event, the poor chap has been miserably served by his parents," Silverman observed.

"That is probably why he is a homosexual," Molly said suddenly. There was an awkward silence. Then, as Smithers was clearly about to have a technicolor vision of Sodom and Gomorrah, Porter cut in hastily.

"Please, I don't think we'll go into that aspect today."

Rachel got back on course by remarking that the truth could be a combination of Lennon's two possibilities: David had probably killed for his own reasons and, as steered by his mother, for her reasons. She added, "In either case, he was obviously in a very fragile state psychologically."

"Indeed," said Judge Porter. "I cannot see him being convicted of murder."

"Manslaughter at the most," Ben suggested.

"If even," said Rachel. "This boy has been treated disgracefully." She and Molly exchanged sympathetic glances.

Lennon took a drink from his glass of water and said, "Fine. Now, if you please, I have asked Inspector Quilligan to continue with the presentation from this point."

None of the lawyers knew Quilligan. They turned with interest toward the yellow-haired giant who was already lumbering to his feet. He began without preamble.

"Of course, there is another possibility. It is that young Roundstone was never in that room and never murdered anyone at all."

People exchanged good-natured smiles. It was a legitimate exercise. They would be back to reality soon enough.

Quilligan continued, "Don't mind all those words that he wrote in his book and in his album. Wasn't he half out of his mind, the creature? Sure, didn't he claim to have killed the priest down in Portlaoise as well, and don't we all know it was the purest figment of his imagination? Wasn't he pure starved of his pills, and he not knowing hardly what he was writing or saying? Wasn't he more like a farmer at a fair with a feed of drink inside him?

"And what about the hairs of his head, you'll be saying, weren't the hairs of his head found here, there, and everywhere? They were, to be sure. But was he attached to them? He was not. 'Tis easy get a supply of somebody's hairs, and to sow them wherever you like. There is even too much of them around for comfort in this case, great wads of hair above in the gallery and abroad in the judge's room. Doesn't that make you suspicious, like as if somebody is making assurance doubly sure that the hairs will be found?

"And the same for the earring. Can't you buy them in every shop and market? But it was a notable trademark and patent for this particular young gentleman. That is why it was put in the judge's room, to tie in with the hair and with the physical sight of his very self in the courtroom."

"He was certainly in the courtroom gallery," said Ben Silverman.

"He was, sir. Put in, on display, and to be well noted."

"Did you say, Inspector Lennon, that Roundstone says it was Albert Singer who put him in the gallery?"

"That is right."

There was a pause. Then Porter asked, "Inspector Quilligan, listen to my question carefully, think, and answer it carefully: Are you saying that Mr. Singer, our colleague in these proceedings until almost now, collected this young man's hair, presumably at home in his own house, off the boy's hairbrush or wherever, supplied himself with a suitable earring, and then deposited these things in Judge Piggott's chambers?"

"I am, and I think he probably put a share of the hair in the gallery, too, to top up the supply, just in case the young fellah didn't shed enough of it when he was in there himself."

"Are you also saying that Mr. Singer deliberately put Mr. Roundstone into the gallery, so that he would be seen, and that he did all these things in order to frame Mr. Roundstone for the judge's murder?"

"Yes, I am."

"Why?" Ben asked. "Why did he frame Roundstone?"

Lennon took up the running again for a while. "Because he knew that Roundstone, if ever he went back on his medication and got his wits back together, would be able to work out who had, in fact, murdered Piggott. The neatest way to neutralize that dangerous knowledge was to frame Roundstone himself for the murder."

"How would David be able to work out who had murdered Piggott?" Rachel asked.

"Because, two years before Piggott's death, David had written the screenplay for the murder in his own journal of aggression fantasies. Molly found that script in David Roundstone's room. David very probably gave it to Singer to read, perhaps in the context of asking for his help with his own psychological or spiritual problems. Alternatively, Singer may have found it himself and read it. Whichever it was, when the murder was committed, in the way that it was committed, David would know that Singer had read that blueprint and had acted it out himself."

The proverbial pin hit the floor.

"There was silence in heaven for half an hour," intoned Smithers, quoting the Book of Revelation appropriately.

Porter asked the direct question. "Inspector Lennon, are you saying that Albert Singer murdered Sidney Piggott?"

"Yes. That is what we are saying."

"Denis, you will never prove that." This was Ben Silverman. "How could Singer not be believed, in preference to this poor demented young man? Remember, too, the boy is an expert in karate, or whatever it is. He knew how to do it."

"Albert Singer is ex-SAS. He knew perhaps even better. I doubt if he used a kick, at his age, but a rabbit punch or something. He looks like a fit man.

"But what possible motive could Singer have, as against all the motives swirling around the heads of the Roundstones?"

"I'll answer that in a moment. I would first like to put one other element in place. This concerns Singer's attitude to David Roundstone being seen around the Four Courts. Miss Sheehan gave us an interesting insight into this when, during our inquiries, she described the row which she witnessed between the two of them, a week or ten days before the murder. At that time, no doubt for reasons of propriety, and out of concern for his own reputation, Singer was very reluctant for David to be seen around the courts. I have not yet checked on this, but I am sure that Roundstone will confirm that Singer was indeed the senior counsel whom Miss Sheehan saw on the stairway on that occasion.

"If we are correct in saying that Singer induced Roundstone to appear in the gallery of Piggott's court on the day of the murder, precisely so that he would be seen, we have a notable change of policy on the point of visibility. I think the reason for that change was that Singer had meanwhile read the boy's fantasy of the killing and had decided to make it a reality. Knowing that Roundstone would eventually realize what had happened, he decided to affix the guilt to him, as I have already said. Accordingly, having previously sought to hide Roundstone from view, on the fatal day he contrived the best means to make him appear, and in close connection with Piggott."

Molly had a question. "Why, then, was Singer so uncooperative when it came to posting David's picture around the Four Courts?"

"That was clever. He knew perfectly well that he had no authority to stop the pictures appearing, and he knew that they would appear—which they did. So he got the best of both worlds. On the one hand, he was busy planting hair and earrings and pushing his stooge into the front row of the gallery while, at the same time, he was creating the impression with us that he was shielding the boy because he knew or suspected him to be the real murderer. Instead of allaying our suspicions of David, he succeeded in redoubling them."

Mr. Justice Porter shook his head from side to side several times. "Inspector, this is a wholly ingenious interpretation of all that has happened. You would have made a marvelous historian. I don't doubt that you could successfully reinterpret practically any era or episode in history, if you put your mind to it. But you have not one particle of hard evidence. It is pure speculation."

"Indeed," the visionary interjected, "as the noble Festus said to St. Paul, 'much learning hath made thee mad!' That is what is wrong with this case. We are beset on all sides by lunatics. Clever lunatics, I grant you, but lunatics nonetheless."

"Starting with yourself," growled Molly.

Lennon nodded. "I came in here this morning with several doubts in my mind. On balance, however, I was convinced that David Roundstone had killed Judge Piggott. I also believed that he had done this, as I think Miss Sheehan expressed it, out of a mixture of motives, his own personal reasons and the impact of his mother's motives."

"I think that is about where we had all got to by lunchtime," Rachel said.

"Even Singer thought that was the bottom line," Silverman added.

"It is certainly what he would have wanted us to think," Lennon remarked, "but, as I mentioned at the beginning of this session, there has been a new and surprising development during the morning. If I may, I would like to ask Inspector Quilligan to speak to you about this."

Quilligan did not stand up this time but pushed back from the table where they were sitting and perched solidly on the edge of his chair. From this podium, untrammeled on all sides, he performed like a true maestro, conducting the orchestra of his thoughts and words with great movements of hands, arms, and torso.

"It was the same with myself as for Denis, right up till this morning: convinced and not convinced, sure but uncertain, certain but doubting, until—lo and behold—and we just under starter's orders, and all ready to go, this very day and morning—lo and behold, I say—there he was, the horny lad, staring me straight in the face!"

"What horny lad?"

"'Tis a metaphor. The lost sheep, I mean, the missing link. The third tape."

"What third tape? We never even heard about the first and second tape either," exclaimed Smithers plaintively.

"They were the ones with Judge Piggott's judgments recorded on them. The very reason he stayed back in his room that fine and fatal afternoon was to finish those judgments for the end of the law term, which is this very day today! They were found there ready on his desk, two judgments, I think it was, on two tapes.

Once the registrar had all the judgments he needed on the two tapes, nobody cared a trawneen about the third. It was left sitting there in the recording apparatus high and dry on his elegant, eloquent desk. The Registrar told us it was just a talk the judge was going to give. So it is, and *two* talks actually. The fact that the registrar said one talk, when there were two, shows that he more than likely didn't listen to the whole of it. Besides, ninety minutes, two sides of a tape, is a bit long, even for two talks—I mean, on such boring legal subjects. What could you be saying, for God's sake?"

Judge Porter snorted, "Well, that is a point of view!"

"Whatever and howsoever, didn't the idea float down from heaven and into my head this very morning, and I thought to myself: If it is a thing that this tape ran right through and down to the precise and mathematical end of its tether, couldn't that be because, though there was somebody there, in the shape of the judge, to turn it on and to talk into it, there was nobody there in the end to turn it off when he had his last words said because, somewhere in the middle, the judge had been dispatched and was gone to meet his Maker?"

"I don't believe it," breathed Silverman, awestruck. "I don't believe it!"

"What's this?" asked Smithers. "A dying declaration, is it? There are special rules about that, you know. I hope you know the special rules, Inspector."

Quilligan was pulling the tape recorder out of his briefcase and hunting for a convenient plug. "As I said, this seems to be a talk that the judge was preparing to give, about defamation and the right to free speech, and how to balance the two—that sort of thing. I'll skip the first side, which is actually a talk about something else, bail or something. I have fast-forwarded a little on the second side—unless some of you want to hear it—he is just going on about the different points of view. No? Alright, let's start here."

He pressed the button and sat down. Every eye was riveted on the small black box on the table. For those who knew, it was unmistakably Piggott's rasping voice.

". . . iary damages. Defamatory material contained on film or on tape is regarded as libelous rather than slanderous, even though it consists of spoken words. This is because the offending words do not disappear into thin air, once spoken—as spoken words normally do—but are preserved in permanent or, at least, more durable form. This could have important results in relation to the requirement to prove special damage. As I ex— What are you doing here? Did you knock? Listen, Singer, I have had enough of this, do you hear?

"You have had your chance, Piggott. I warned you."

Piggott gave a harsh bark of laughter. "Did you, then? Listen, Singer, you pathetic imbecile, is there any point talking to you? How can you imagine that we could ever let a megalomaniac idiot like yourself on the bench? You would be a total disaster!"

"Piggott, you are talking to the best legal brain, the best advocate, and the best chairman of the Bar Council in living memory. Everybody recognizes that."

"Jesus!"

"The entire profession is crying out to have me on the bench, and I will not be stopped by a malicious, mean-minded nonentity like you. Besides, as you well know, just one of the reasons why so many people want me on the bench is to make short work of lazy, good-for-nothing peasants like yourself."

"Singer, we have been through all this a dozen times. It is

utter garbage. All of this exists only inside your own sad sick, hallucinating little head. You are a sad, sick bastard. Now get out of my room or I'll call the guards."

"Not till I have done what I came to do. You have used your political influence at least three times to deprive me of a judicial appointment. Is that not so?"

"It is perfectly true, you pompous ass, and I'll use it five, fifteen, and twenty times again, if necessary. You will get on the bench of this country, Singer, over my dead body!"

"Exactly, Piggott. You have pronounced your own sentence."

"Look! Will you get to hell out of . . . eh! . . . What are you doing with that thing? ALBERT!"

There was a dull thud, a cry, a pause, another dull thud, and no cry.

The seconds ticked away in silence. Quilligan got up quietly, walked to the table, and pressed the stop button.

"It continues like that for another twenty minutes. Silence. Just at the end, you can hear what I think is Ned Frost, the crier, coming in. Then the tape runs out and switches itself off automatically."

FRIDAY, NOVEMBER 13

EDITORIAL
Singer Walks Free

Albert Singer, accused of the murder of Judge Sidney Piggott in July of this year, walked free from the Central Criminal Court yesterday afternoon when the trial judge, Mr. Justice Kevin Price, ruled that, on the evidence adduced by the prosecution, it was not open to a jury to find the accused guilty *beyond all reasonable doubt*. He accordingly directed the jury to find Singer not guilty.

There is no appeal from this decision. Even if further convincing proof of Mr. Singer's guilt were to be discovered, he has now stood in jeopardy once and cannot be tried again on the same charge. This outcome has caused widespread disquiet.

It is not our wish or intention to comment on the merits of this particular case or to call in question the fact that Albert Singer has been found not guilty of murder. As the law stands, that is his entitlement. It is nonetheless a cause of grave concern that, in this or in similar cases, a judge's decision to withdraw a case from a jury and, in effect, to decide the case himself is without appeal or surveillance of any kind.

In criminal cases, whereas the decision of a lower court on a question of law can be appealed by the prosecution to a higher court, at least by way of *case stated,* not even that limited form of appeal exists in respect of a decision by a judge in the Central Criminal Court, whether on a point of law or even as to whether or not a jury should be allowed to decide a case at all. The only form of appeal allowed to the prosecution from the decisions of this court is in respect of a sentence which the director of public prosecutions considers to be unduly lenient.

No one would welcome the spectacle of frequent appeals by the prosecution against verdicts of innocence pronounced by juries. But there should, surely, be some possibility of judicial review where the decision to acquit is made effectively, not by a jury, but by one solitary judge, and on the basis of an assessment of the evidence which, to say the very least, does not impose itself.

With due respect to the learned trial judge in the present case, it must be recorded that his decision on the one point on which the whole prosecution case stood or fell was the occasion of unprecedented critical comment, openly expressed by many highly qualified jurists in the immediate aftermath of yesterday's outcome. Individual members of the jury, too, were outspoken in their dissatisfaction that evaluation of evidence about the vital tape recording was not left to the twelve good and true men and women of the jury.

Mr. Singer conducted his own defense. He did it with superb effectiveness and not a little ruthlessness. One will not easily forget his treatment of young David Roundstone in the witness box. It cannot but be a matter of satisfaction to all right-thinking people that the director of public prosecutions took the highly unusual step of issuing a statement immediately after yesterday's verdict, to the effect that no charges are contemplated against David Roundstone, either now or at any time in the future. That, at least, was Justice done.

"Denis, I just cannot believe it!"

"You win some, Molly, and you lose some."

"But this not a game. I mean, it is about justice."

"Big word, Molly, 'justice'! Sometimes we just have to settle for law, and be glad to get that much."

"Well, I am *not* glad this morning, not the smallest little bit. We had him, Denis, we *had him*. We had the whole bloody murder *on tape!* When did you ever hear of that before? What more can a court reasonably expect?"

"What indeed! I guess the judge just got it wrong."

"So how can it possibly end up like this?"

"Are you sure it is over? asked Denis.

"Of course it is over. Every newspaper, TV and radio show, every lawyer and commentator in the country is agreed about that. Now, even if we discover Singer on film, bashing out Piggott's brains with one hand, and giving us the finger sign with the other, there is not a thing in the world we can do about it."

"God is not mocked," he said seriously.

"I am not worried about God, Denis, he can can look out for himself. But *I* certainly *am* mocked. So are you and Jim. So is just about anyone who gives a damn about justice. Is there *nothing* we can do?"

"There is. Lets all go on holidays and stay there as long as we can."

"Denis, how can you?"

"Old dog for the hard road, Molly: I've been here before."

Despite his stiff upper lip, Lennon was deeply perturbed. Price had simply thrown out the tape as evidence. His reason was that the High Court official who had listened to it immediately after the murder insisted that there was nothing on that tape, when he heard it, except Judge Piggott's legal ruminations. The prosecution, who had felt duty-bound to present the evidence, were not allowed to cross-examine their own witness. The judge did press him strongly on the point. He would not move an inch: He had listened to every word on both sides of the tape, and there was no voice to be heard except Piggott's.

He was asked by the trial judge why, if he had really listened to both sides of the tape, he had reported that it contained "a," that is *one* talk by Piggott, when in fact it contained two. The registrar replied that, as he had no interest in the subject matter of the talk or talks, he did not pay close attention to the detail and had obviously missed the transition from one topic to the next. But he was sure that Piggott's rasping voice was the only one on the tape.

When applying for a discharge at the end of the prosecution's case, Albert Singer had reinforced the registrar's evidence with bitter complaints that this tape had not been taken into safe custody until weeks after the murder. It had been left lying in Judge Piggott's chambers where anyone could have gone in and tampered with it, or even taken it home for days on end to doctor it at his leisure. "Is it not ironic," he had asked, "that the same deplorable laxity that allowed some ruffian to enter that room and batter Judge Piggott to death has also permitted the same or another criminal to enter that same room weeks later to corrupt and contaminate the evidence in this trial?"

When asked by Mr. Justice Price who could possibly have wanted to do such a thing, Singer had withered him with sarcasms and indignation: Was it really *his* job to answer that question? Did his liberty for the rest of his mortal life really depend on his ability to guess, locked up in his prison cell, why, or how, or by whom, this, that, or any other thing had been allowed to happen by the crass negligence and stupidity of police officers who, having got their man—or at least having got *a* man—clearly could not care less what happened to that man so long, of course, as he ended up convicted? The evidence in this case had been adulterated and polluted, through the gross negligence of the police, and in a way gravely prejudicial to himself, while he was locked away like a convict, unable to lift a finger in his own defense. And now *he* was being required to explain how or why this had happened.

The fact was, Singer concluded, pounding the table in front of him, that this tape had been tampered with. The registrar was categorical in his evidence: days after Piggott's death, none of this incriminating material was on that tape. In the face of that clear evidence of forgery, and of the extreme carelessness of the police in relation to custody of the tape, the jury could not possibly decide, *beyond all reasonable doubt,* that he, Albert Singer had murdered Sidney Piggott. The learned judge *must* direct the jury accordingly.

The learned judge did what he was told.

Lennon shook his head. The registrar was an obstinate idiot who could not admit that he was wrong. Singer, for all his absurdity, was an advocate of consummate ability. It was a fearful and fatal combination.

Despise not thine enemy! Lennon admonished his image in the mirror as he checked his collar for dandruff.

The Lennons and the Silvermans had dinner a few evenings later.

"What do you think, Ben?" asked Denis.

"Price should have let it go to the jury."

"Aha, good! That is what I wanted to hear."

"You are lucky that he didn't."

"Lucky! How? Lucky?" asked Denis.

"Price would have had to give the jury all sorts of warnings about the tape. Singer would have done the rest, and in the process he would have made sausage meat of the police."

"What, all that stuff about not locking up a tape which we had been told authoritively contained nothing of any interest? You might as well say that we should have taken the coal scuttle and the lavatory brush into custody—just in case."

"Much worse than that, Denis. I can just hear Albert addressing the jury."

Silverman's mimickery was eerily accurate:

"Do they think you are fools, ladies and gentlemen of the jury? Do they think that you cannot see through this miserable deception? This absurd tape, the tape that grew a beard overnight, the *bespoke* tape! It is what we call a *deus ex machina*, or in layman's language, a rabbit out of the conjuror's hat. Wasn't it an answer to a policeman's prayer, this tape? It disappointed them first time around, true, before they got their hands on it. But never mind that, isn't it a wonderful tape now after a few weeks in police custody?

"For instance, ladies and gentlemen, what did you make of Inspector James Quilligan? An unusual man, don't you think? An unconventional man, a man who doesn't always, or even perhaps often, play the game according to the rules. A bit of a gypsy baron, I'd say, an adept of the three-card trick, I don't doubt. No stranger to the quick buck and the country fair. It is in the blood.

"Well, here you have the bold Inspector Quilligan, ladies and gentlemen. Pity the poor man! He is a bit short of a necessary commodity in this case, a commodity called evidence. So lo and behold, what happens? I'll tell you what happens: Inspector Quilligan has a brilliant idea. That's what happens. Where does he get the brilliant idea? Well necessity is the mother of invention, as we all know. Let's say the gypsy chorus croons the brilliant idea into his eager and receptive ear.

"And here is the brilliant idea: What about that deadly dull tape of judge Piggott's, with nothing on it except juridical word play and forensic futilities—when we last heard it, that is—what about it? Perhaps if I went back to it now, in my hour of need, who knows, it might even have grown a whole new track where Piggott, very conveniently, names his murderer and Singer himself comes out with his hands up, shouting, 'Guilty, Guilty, I done it, I done it!'

"Ladies and gentlemen of the jury, if you believe that, you would believe anything!"

"For God's sake, Ben, that is downright racist—all that stuff about gypsies and tinkers" cried Denis.

"It is. Price would rebuke him a few times. He'd back off momentarily, and return to the attack, worse than ever. Obviously, he wouldn't be as crass as I am doing it but, in effect, he would be saying the same things. The jury would buy it. We live in a pretty bigoted society—I know something about that."

"Surely no judge would let him get away with that stuff, even wrapped in tissue paper."

"A man with the noose around his neck gets away with murder," said Ben.

"Literally, in this case."

"Literally."

WEDNESDAY, NOVEMBER 25

S T. CILLIAN'S PRIORY IS A MONASTERY OF THE STRICT observance, built on the slopes of some pleasantly wooded hills, fifteen miles east of Wexford town. The community numbers some fifty monks, who spend their lives in prayer, silent work, and austerity. There is a guesthouse attached to the monastery that can accommodate up to thirty retreatants, men and women from all walks of life, who come for a few days, perhaps a week, to recharge their spiritual batteries in an atmosphere of recollection and peace.

It was half past eight o'clock in the evening. Compline, the monastic night prayer, had just concluded with the singing of the beautiful *Salve Regina* in Latin at the shrine of the Blessed Virgin. A serene quiet pervaded the darkened priory church. The long hours of choral prayer completed for yet another day, gray-cowled monks glided noiselessly about their private devotions. Some knelt in adoration at the Blessed Sacrament altar. Others followed the Way of the Cross, depicted in the fourteen stations on the church walls. A few of the older men, faithful to traditional monastic piety, moved slowly from one side chapel to the next, invoking the tender patronage of lifelong friends, the saints of God, commemorated at the various altars. The guests, too, wrapped in the soft mantle of prayer and peace, breathed in the healing myrrh of pure devotion.

Old Father Aelred, from his place in the choir stalls, cast a solicitous eye upon two guests in particular. For both, this was their first visit to St. Cillian's. They had been here for two days now, and would be returning to "the world" tomorrow, spiritually fortified for further combat against the flesh and the devil. Father Aelred had been most impressed by their uninhibitedly demonstrative religious fervor. What were their names, now? Ah yes, Frank Keogh and Barny Coughlin. That was it. Barny was a retired garda officer. He did not have much to say for himself—just got on with his prayers. A salt-of-the-earth type, obviously. Where would we be without them? People like Barny Coughlin, Father Aelred reflected, had a great reward awaiting them in heaven, no doubt about it.

The other one, Frank Keogh, was a bit of a mystery He had let slip some secrets of his prayer life to Father Aelred. Extraordinary, really. According to himself, he was not conscious of having said even a single prayer in over thirty years. Only the great saints experienced such extreme states of desolation. Frank was either a very holy man, or else—well, we must be charitable. Father Aelred was not quite clear about what Frank did for his living. He had described himself as a "problem-solver." Apparently, people brought their problems to him, and he solved them. Rather like the monks, really.

Discernment of spirits, counseling, prayer, the sacraments of the Church: These were the monkish therapies, with occasionally a little amateur psychology and herbal medicine thrown in as well. Frank had been rather evasive about his own approach to problem-solving. It was nothing newfangled, anyhow. "Good old-fashioned methods," he had declared almost defiantly, adding that those he treated never came back to complain. An interesting person.

It was bedtime now, for the short sleep of monks. They would reassemble in their chilly choir at 3:00 A.M. for the Great Vigil office of psalmody and sacred reading. Frank and Barny would be there. Indeed, Father Aelred suspected that they would not sleep very much between times. A man of prolonged vigils himself, he had encountered the two of them in the cloisters toward midnight on both previous nights. They had been walking up and down together, no doubt reciting the fifteen decades of the Rosary and other favorite prayers. He shook his head in admiration. No doubt about it: The laity were the backbone of the Church!

"I'll get it, Mr. Singer. Who could it possibly be at this hour of the night?"

It was nearly eleven o'clock. Alf, Singer's latest acquisition, shuffled toward the hall door in his bare feet. He had been watching television in the den. Albert was in the kitchen, doing something clever about a broken percolator.

Alf barely saw the thickset block of a man, with his pig's eyes and dirty green balaclava, nor the brutal snout of the firearm clutched in his butcher's hand. No word was exchanged. A crude iron knuckleduster exploded in his face. Flung backward, Alf struck his head hard against the wall and slid softly to the ground.

He heard vaguely, as if from a distant planet, a shout, Singer shouting, then glass shattering: He had thrown something, the percolator perhaps. Good man! Singer was a tiger. He would leave this idiot for dead, whoever he was, or even dead. He was ruthless; he had killed Piggott. Singer could do anything, and he would . . .

The roar of a frenzied animal, once, again, and a third time. He knew confusedly that these were shots.

Then somebody was stepping over him roughly, out the hall door. He could hear the adenoidal engine of a motorbike, skulking and snotting, ready for the sudden surge up its hobbledehoy scale of rasping gear changes. And off it sped, whinnying the cowardly victory of its pillion rider into the stunned silence of the night.

Alf clawed to his knees, retching, head swirling, scarcely seeing, his face a spaghetti junction of converging pains. The kitchen—which way the kitchen? Why could he not stand? Crawl, grovel, drag. Where was the door? Did it open out or in? Which way was out . . . and which . . . ?

"Sir, Mr. Singer, sir!" He had . . . Jesus, oh Jesus! Where was his face? Sweet Jesus, where had his face gone?

> *O Lord, open my lips!*
> *And my tongue shall proclaim your praise!*
> *O Lord, open my lips!*
> *And my tongue shall proclaim your praise!*
> *O Lord, open my lips!*
> *And my tongue shall proclaim your praise!*

The thrice-repeated invocation to begin the Great Vigil office. Frank Keogh etched the sign of the cross on his lips with the tip of his right thumb, just as he saw the monks doing it. His hooked trigger finger unconsciously aped the sacred sign on his pock-marked chin below.

Barny Coughlin stood beside him, dumpy, ugly, hideously aware of the awful blasphemy. "Peace be with you," he said sacrilegiously, like Judas suggesting a kiss.

"And also up yours," Keogh replied, fully in touch with his own deep feelings.

———

They knew it was Keogh. Of course, they knew. Keogh was Dublin's surest and most ruthless hired gun. Everything bore his trademark: attention to detail, time, transport, dress, brutality, even the weapon. The three bullets, prized from wherever they had splattered gobbets of Singer, matched the ballistics of four previous killings, all known to be Keogh's handiwork, not one of them provable.

If nothing else, the obscene impertinence of the alibi screamed Keogh's authorship. He enjoyed giving the reverse big five to the police.

Keogh and Coughlin stuck to their story. Three days of prayer, fasting, and vigils at St. Cillian's Priory, a hundred miles away from Singer's home in Ballsbridge. Compline, over by 8:30 P.M. on the night of the murder, had been followed by pious loitering among the sacred shrines of the priory church. Vigils began at 3:00 A.M. Frank Keogh was there, once again, present, contrite, and correct, in full view of the angels, the saints, and an abundance of unimpeachable witnesses.

Six and a half hours in the interval between Compline and the Night Vigil. More than enough to get to Dublin in Frank's powerful red Mercedes, change to butcher's clothing, get carried to the slaughterhouse, blast Singer to eternity, then do it all in reverse and appear demurely in the small hours to sing divine praises.

"No way!" said Keogh.

"No way!" said Coughlin.

"Not possible!" they both said. Between 11:00 P.M. and midnight, Frank Keogh and Barny Coughlin, the retired policeman of unblemished reputation, had been marching up and down the priory cloisters, reciting the fifteen decades of the Rosary, the Litany of the Saints, and other vintage pieces from *Faith of Our Fathers.*

————

Father Aelred had been a monk for close on seventy years. For the things of this world, as befitted one who had so long abandoned it, he lived in a time loop. Loving all men sincerely—and even Protestants and women since the Second Vatican Council—he was still, as in his youth, pro-Dev, anti–Free State, and allergic to both the army and the police force.

This man of God was shocked and saddened to hear that Frank Keogh and his companion had not got even halfway on their journey back to Dublin when the Free-Staters had dragged them from their car and accused them of murder. He thought of the simple piety of those two good men, of their devotion and zeal over the last three days. He was utterly appalled. It was the devil's work. He did not doubt it.

Lennon interviewed him. Father Aelred found him courteous, even likable, which surprised him—in an RIC man, and one who, on his own admission, came straight from the castle, that hated stronghold of British rule.

The vital period, apparently, was between the end of Compline and the beginning of Vigils on the night of the murder. Had Father Aelred seen both men, during that exact period, on precisely that night?

The old man closed his eyes and thought anxiously. He must tell the truth. He must get it right. He was sure that he had seen the two of them together in the cloisters, toward midnight, at least twice. Had he seen them every night? Had he seen them on *that* night? He was sure that he had, well . . . almost sure.

Was he sure that Keogh was one of the two men he had seen? How near had he been to them? Were his eyes good? How good? Did he use spectacles? Didn't he have a little problem with cataracts?

Father Aelred felt miserable. He was old, he told himself, and stupid. All these questions were confusing him. "Inspector, I am not certain, not like I would be certain if the pope said it, or if it was in the Bible. But I think, I really think that I saw Mr. Keogh and Mr. Coughlin here in the cloister, on the very night when that poor man was murdered—God rest his soul."

"Thank you, Father. That is very fair."

"It is the best I can do."

And not worth tuppence, Lennon thought sourly as he politely took his leave.

Coughlin could have led anyone roughly the same build as Keogh down the cloister and past the old gentleman. In the semi-darkness, he would be easily deceived.

Lennon's chat with Barny Coughlin was neither cordial nor cozy, and there was no liquid lunch this time. Barny was not bothered. A man of low expectations, he did not mind the inspector disbelieving the St. Cillian's story, so long as he could not disprove it.

Lennon shook him only once, for a split second, but long enough to be sure that Coughlin was lying.

"Keogh obviously forgot to tell you he was pulled for speeding on the way back from Dublin after the murder. Now, that's kind of awkward for you, Barny. Imagine, doing nearly a hundred as he was, coming into Wicklow. Didn't want to miss his vigils, I suppose."

Coughlin's mouth twitched a semiquaver. Snake eyes slid rapidly over Lennon's face. He recovered instantly. A crooked smile. "Really, Denis, you shouldn't tell lies. You haven't the talent."

"I can't return the compliment."

"I don't understand you, Denis. Last time we talked, you were gunning for Singer, you hated his guts. Now somebody takes him out—and suddenly you're his long-lost best friend.

Barny, will you cut the bullshit? You are right out of your depth this time, do you understand? This is murder. You are as guilty as if you pulled the trigger yourself."

"Denis, Denis! Don't be so melodramatic. My guess is half the country is happy that Singer got his comeuppance."

Lennon and Quilligan sucked their pints morosely.

"Singer used to remind me of what one French politician said about another one: 'He has only one defect: he is absolutely unbearable. Apart from that he is a grand fellow!'"

Quilligan laughed. "Denis, if Molly had killed Singer, it would be for being unbearable. But if Keogh killed him—and we know that he did—he did it for money, a lot of money. Ten grand, they say, is his going rate."

"Well, who gave him ten grand to take out Singer?"

"You tell me. Strange, isn't it? Lots of people loathed him, even in his own profession. But those people don't take each other out, not that way, anyhow. Now, if he was a tinker, he would have got his face broken long ago."

"Well, thank God, I am not on the case anymore. Neither is Molly."

"No?"

"No. I was for forty-eight hours, but the chief still thinks we made a mess of Piggott's case, so we are being punished—and rewarded, too, perhaps. Nobody can ever accuse our dear chief of consistency. I have an idea he also thinks that Singer got what he deserved."

"A dangerous idea for a police chief."

"Yes, well, he has a lazy fellow called Brennan on the job."

"The guy they call 'Athlete's Flatfoot'? I wouldn't put him in charge of a hen run."

"That's the one. The crooks can smell him a mile away. I think the idea is that, sooner or later, we'll get our hands on Keogh's gun. Then the ballistics guys will nail him for half a dozen jobs, including Singer."

"Meanwhile we do feck-all?"

"That's about it."

"One other thing, Denis. I don't know how to say this, but we were wrong about Isa Roundstone, weren't we?"

"We were right about the picture, right that she had the motive, right about everything except—she didn't do it, and she didn't get it done, and she did not use her son in the shameful way I suggested. About that I was one hundred percent wrong. I am sorry."

TUESDAY, DECEMBER 22

IT WAS THREE DAYS BEFORE CHRISTMAS. MOLLY POWER had wangled a whole week off. After an early lunch in her Harcourt Street flat, she and Jan-Hein were heading for Fethard-on-Sea in his fourth-hand VW beetle. Test drillings with her family had proved positive on the occasion of previous visits, so the major question of nuptials was to be broached with the ancestors over plum pudding and porter.

Cutting across the South Circular Road, they got to Portabello Bridge and turned right, along the canal. Jan-Hein was telling a story about something that had happened in the conservation workshops at the gallery that morning. Suddenly Molly grabbed his arm.

"Jan-Hein!"

"Yes, sweetheart," he answered, startled.

"Stop!"

He did so, hastily, pulling in awkwardly behind a roadworks corral.

"What is wrong, Molly?"

"Say nothing, Jan-Hein, say absolutely nothing."

They sat in solemn silence for thirty seconds—a long time for someone in Jan-Hein's situation. Molly sat bolt upright, her eyes closed tightly in deep concentration.

"That's it," she exclaimed equally suddenly. "That's it. Quick, Jan-Hein, go on, straight on, take a left at the next bridge."

He slid into gear and moved off. "Left? No, darling, it is straight on, out to the Mad Cow Roundabout. I want to take the M50. It is the way I know."

"Left, Jan-Hein. It has just come to me . . . I'll explain. Here, here, Jan-Hein, left at the lights. Now go on, about a hundred yards. Yes, in here on the right."

"In there?"

"Yes, yes."

"What is this place?"

"The Hospice for the Dying."

"Good Lord, what a way to start Christmas!"

Jan-Hein drove obediently up the short avenue, circled the flower beds, and halted in the landscaped parking lot. He took Molly's hand.

"So what is it, my love? You feel a sudden attack of old age coming on?"

She laughed. "Not quite. Sorry, Jan-Hein. The thing is, I have just thought of someone who might know who killed Albert Singer, or rather, who paid for it."

"Oh?"

"Yes. We have been asking the wrong question all the time: Who hated Singer enough to want to kill him? The real question is: Who loved Piggott enough to want to avenge him? The candidate list for that is super-short. I know only one name."

"He lives in here?"

"He may do. Driving into Harold's Cross today—it just clicked in my head. I may be barking up a wrong tree, but it's worth a try."

"Do I come?"

"Of course. I'll swear you in as a deputy sheriff."

Sister Margaret received them smilingly in her office near the entrance hall. Happy Christmas was par for the course. They had already passed two Christmas trees and a pretty crib. Here there was another Christmas tree, a small silver one, topped by an androgynous angel, twee, even as angels go, but clearly well intentioned.

They sat on comfortable divan seats in the embrace of a wraparound window, a professedly nonconfrontational conference space, designed with equal input of architectural acumen and psychological innocence.

Would they like a cup of coffee? No, thank you, they had just had lunch.

Of course, Sister remembered Tony Macklin. "A character. A tough nut in his young days, I should think, but a simple poor man. He made a good end, God rest him."

"Ah, he is dead. When did he die?"

"I remember that very well, because he died on December eighth, the feast of the Immaculate Conception, a lovely day to die."

Jan-Hein looked unconvinced.

"The eighth of December," Molly said. "Just two weeks after Albert Singer, even less."

"Albert Singer. You mean the lawyer who was murdered, just around the corner from here, in Ballsbridge?"

"Yes."

"It is funny you should mention that poor man. Tony was very upset about him."

"Upset by his death?" Molly asked.

"No, not that. Indeed, if he died only a week or two before Tony did, I doubt if Tony even knew about it. He was more or less comatose himself for the last two weeks of his life."

"So what was he upset about?"

"That they let Mr. Singer out of prison. I was actually watching the six o'clock news with him the night the court released him. It was just a few weeks before he died. When he heard that Mr. Singer was found not guilty, I thought he was going to keel over and die himself, there and then on the spot. He nearly had a seizure, I mean literally. We had to send for the doctor and have him sedated."

"Really? What did he think should have happened?"

"'He should be hung,' he kept saying. He was very angry about it. He also claimed that he had been a great friend of Judge Piggott himself."

"Did you believe him?"

"To be honest, I didn't pay much attention to him. With what he had, if you know what I mean, his complaint, the poor head sometimes gives out near the end—though, mind you, he was sharp enough about everything else. He was deadly serious about Mr. Singer. The next morning he was in here to me at eight o'clock. He wanted to see his envelope."

"Envelope?"

"He had a big brown envelope with all his money. I used to keep it for him here, in the safe. Some of them are like that, you know. Quite large sums. They won't put it in a bank, and they don't want their families to know that they have it. Tony had the best part of twelve thousand euro in his envelope. Earlier on, when he was stronger, he might take a few euro now and again and go out for a couple of drinks. Once or twice, he gave money to various charities. But he didn't spend much, the creature. It was all to be kept for his funeral. He used to say, 'I have lived like

a tramp, I'll be buried like a gentleman.' Well, he took the envelope that morning and counted it all, there on the very seat where
you are sitting. There was every sort in it, fifty euro notes, coins,
even some English pounds. I never saw it again, because he took
the envelope away with him. He gave it to the police, to help
prove that that poor Singer man was guilty."

"He gave it to the police?"

"Yes, he asked me to ring them."

"And did they come?"

"His friend Superintendent Coughlin came. That was who he
asked me to ring. He had the number."

"Coughlin? I don't know any Superintendent Cough . . . You
don't mean Barny Coughlin?"

"That's the man, Barny Coughlin. A dumpy little fellow. He
had already called to see Tony a few months before that. They
were great pals. Well, I rang him and he came, the same day, I
think. They talked for ages."

"Let me get this clear. Barny Coughlin came. They talked for
ages, and Barny left with twelve thousand euro in his pocket."

"Well, it wouldn't have fitted in his pocket, the way it was. But
yes, Tony gave the money to Superintendent Coughlin."

"How did you let him do such a thing?"

Sister Margaret looked uncomfortable. "It was his money,
Sergeant. Dying people can be very sensitive about whatever
poor little things they have about them. We have no right to take
them over, so to speak. They are free people, right to the very
end—even if what they do seems foolish to us."

Jan-Hein broke his good-mannered silence. "I agree, Sister. It
is very important." He blushed slightly.

"To tell the truth, I was going to ask him about it that night.
But when I went to see him, he was so happy, I felt that whatever
he had done, it was what he really wanted."

"He was happy that evening, after talking with Barny Coughlin?"

"He was. He said to me, 'Sister, today, for the first time in my life, I have done something good.' Or no, 'I have done something just,' that was the word he used, 'just.' 'I have done something just.' I said, 'That is wonderful, Tony. What did you do?'"

"And what did he say?"

"He smiled—and he winked at me. "She blushed." That was all. We never had a chance to talk about it again. I am nearly sure it was the next day or the day after that he started to slip into a coma. I must admit that I was a bit worried about the money, because the receipt was not on official garda notepaper. It was just signed by Superintendent Coughlin."

"There is a receipt?" Molly asked excitedly.

"Oh yes. For our own protection, I had to insist on that much. Families can sometimes be awkward, you understand, after a person dies. We need to be able to account."

"We may need that receipt eventually. Keep it safe. Perhaps in the meantime you could give me a photocopy."

"No problem."

As they were leaving the room, Jan-Hein asked, "What about Tony's fine funeral?"

Sister Margaret smiled sadly and shook her head. "Poor Tony. We did what we could. I know we gave him any flowers left in the garden. But I think you would have to say—it was a pauper's funeral."

They walked to the car, hand in hand.

"Does that make him a saint?" Jan-Hein asked.

"Does what make who a saint?"

"Tony Macklin. He gave up his own funeral—and obviously, it meant a lot to him. He gave it up in the cause of justice. In a sense, it was all he had. I guess that makes him a saint."

"Well, that's a new one on me: Somebody gets canonized for bankrolling an assassination. I don't see the pope doing that one!"

"I'd do it flying, if I was pope."

"That is why you are not pope."

"No, there is a better reason."

"Yes, what?"

"You!"

"That's very nice!"

They kissed.

"Poor old pope!" Jan-Hein said.

"This stuff will keep until after Christmas," Molly said. "Drive south, young man!"

THURSDAY, DECEMBER 24

CHRISTMAS EVE IN THE EARLY AFTERNOON. COLD AND crisp. Red faces exhale white steam. Body contact the whole way from Stephen's Green to the Parnell Monument. Strangers smile at each other. Children seem like a good idea. Tinsel and fairy lights, enough to gift wrap the Grand Canyon. Santa Clauses ring bells and go *hohoho* at every street corner. Carol singers, good, bad, and awful, sing carols. Even the churches are doing business. Henry Street traders are in full cry:

"Last of the Jumpin' Jacks!"

"Five for a *yew-row* the juicy oranges!"

"Take yer dirty hands offa that, young fellah!"

"Fresh in from the Congo, missus, picked only yesterday by the Ba-lubas!"

"Jesus, Mary, and Joseph, I'm putrified with the cold!"

"Christmas toilet rolls, three for a *yew-row*. Look at the lovely holly, mister. Feel that on yer arse! *Ha-ha!*"

Philosophy and intonations unchanged since the age of Swift. Ulysses here is mere Johnny-come-lately.

"Joyce? Is it Lord Haw Haw you're talkin' about?"

Rip van Winkle, he wandered up Grafton Street, alone, marveling at so many changes during his long incarceration in the clinic. Shops he had known were gone. There were new malls and nosheries, shoehorned into every space and corner. And why had Brown Thomas crossed to the other side of the street? He found that disconcerting. Shops shouldn't cross the road. His mother, he knew, would not approve. So neither did he. They were getting to agree about more things these days.

Turning into Duke Street:

"Hey, you are David Roundstone, aren't you?"

He shuddered. While the police were chasing him, nobody saw him; since his release he was recognized everywhere. He could sense people looking and telling each other. Sometimes he heard their comments. Total strangers gave him curt nods in the street, which he had absolutely no idea how to acknowledge. One day a girl asked for his autograph. He stammered something and turned in to the nearest shop, which sold only ladies' underwear.

Two nice faces. A boy and a girl, about his own age. Chestnut curly hair, brown eyes, freckles, black shirt and jeans, navy reefers—both of them. Can there be boy/girl identical twins?

"Dave, I'm Rick Moore. Remember? This is Rose."

Rick Moore. He had not seen him since his precipitate departure from boarding school ten years earlier. They had been good pals. He remembered now something small that had meant a lot to him at the time. The Christmas after his expulsion, Rick Moore had sent him a Christmas card—the only one of his former companions for whom he still existed. He had cried, but he did not answer.

Rick had not changed. Bigger, of course, but the same honest, good-humored face, still obviously believing that everybody else was as nice as himself.

They went for coffee.

"No, Rose is not my twin, not my sister even. She is my wife—well, more or less. You know how it is, everything except the paperwork."

Rose blushed and smiled at David. He made friendly eyes in return.

Rick and Rose had met in Cathal Brugha Street, the Hotel and Catering College. Love at first sight, and ever since. They had done their stint in hotels and hostelries. Now, not interested in the residential side of the trade, they dreamed of a little restaurant of their own. They had even got a place . . .

"So why not?" David asked.

"Money, David."

"Also," Rick added, "we need somebody with us, somebody who doesn't mind working crazy hours, and perhaps not always getting paid absolutely every week."

"Rick, Rose, I would love to work with you." He blurted it out, then stopped, amazed at himself. They both smiled. He continued. "The only thing I have done since I left school, that I really liked, is restaurant work, cooking, and, like, houseboy stuff. No real training, but I know a few things . . . and I am, like, at a crossroads now—well, you know that, I guess."

Rick and Rose looked at each other. His fists were lying on the table between them, clenched so tight the knuckles shone white. Rose put her small hands down, one on each.

"David, will you come with us . . . for richer, for poorer, for better or for worse?"

"Rose, there is truly nothing I would love better."

Another hour. They parted. At the entrance to Clarendon Street Church, a Little Sister of the Poor stood with her begging box. Her thin black cloak seemed like a bad joke in this Siberian winter. Her calloused feet in open sandals were blue and red with the cold. He hunted in his pockets. Twenty euro remained, in a single note. He pushed it into her box.

She curtsied and said in a pale voice, "Thank you, sir. May God bless you."

He smiled into her patient eyes. "Thank you, Sister. I think He just has."

He walked home to Donnybrook because he had no money left for the bus. By Herbert Park soft snowflakes were falling.

"A white Christmas," he whispered in wonder, "a white Christmas, the first white Christmas ever!"